neshuipress

Published by Neshui Press
St. Louis, Missouri

ISBN 9780965252812

# BENCH WOMAN

a novel

Howard Sterinbach

# Chapter 1

Pigeons are all over the place. Kids throwing bread have brought about this mob of pigeons. But no pigeons are going to move me from my place on this bench. It is too nice a day for me to spend my lunch indoors. No threat of pigeon snow on this glorious day will deter me from sitting on this bench this hour. If a pigeon blizzard is to fall on my jacket, my hair, or all over me, let it fall. This lunch hour is mine to enjoy on this bench.

That woman walking towards this bench is beautiful. I mean really beautiful. She's sitting down on this bench. Nothing is between us. Why did she choose this bench? Could it be me? It must be the prime location here. She should talk to me. No. I should talk to her. But what should I say? How should I say it? Forget it. She probably just wants to relax here during lunch and enjoy the view. But maybe I am part of the view she sat down to enjoy. Right, and the Pope is Catholic. Wait a minute, the Pope is Catholic. She doesn't want me, a perfect stranger, to start talking to her. Besides, I don't know what to say. I'll just spend my remaining lunch hour getting some sun.

But who knows? She may have sat here on the chance that I would start talking to her. It is within the realm of possibilities, however slight, that she has observed me sit on this bench every once in a while during lunch hour over the course of the past few months and made the bold move to sit on this bench today after weeks of preparation. She even may have bought a new outfit, been to the beauty parlor, and spent all morning preparing her make-up just for this moment. If it took her weeks to build up the courage to sit here, it will take her a few more weeks to get up the courage to speak to me. She's gone this far, and tried so hard, it's only fair if I break the ice. No way. Why would anyone so beautiful need to build up courage to talk to me? No more dreaming. All she wants to do is sit here and relax.

However, if her sitting here had to do with me, I shouldn't let her down. On the one in a million chance that I am the cause of her sitting here, it is my duty to talk to her. But what should I say? How should I say it?

When she looks this way, I should give her a sly wink or a soft yet strong smile. That would make me more exciting to her than words alone. She may get so excited by a sly wink, or a soft yet strong smile, that she would become deranged. She'd have to jump into the Hudson River to control herself. Maybe I'll skip the sly wink or soft yet strong smile approach and simply say,

"Hello, how are you?"

She may respond with,

"I've been dying to be with you for months. I have been worshipping you from afar."

No way. There's no way she'll say that. I should just say to her,

"Hello, how are you?"

It would be great if she responded by saying,

"Hello, how are you? It is such a beautiful day to be here."

That would be nice.

It would be great if we exchanged pleasantries and then walked to the water and listened to the small waves beat against the dock. After that, we would watch white fluffy clouds dance across the sky. The water, the skyscrapers in the distance, and the playful atmosphere in the park would make us feel wonderful.

"I'm hungry," she would say.

"Chinatown is only a short distance away," I would reply.

"I'm hungry for you," she would answer.

My mind sees us rush toward the subway when, out of the blue, a limousine arrives to meet us. We would wear excited yet embarrassed smiles as Claude, our limousine driver, stops the Lincoln Town Car limousine in front of my apartment building. I would lead the way to my apartment door, then open it, then quickly shut it behind us. I would enter my apartment, with this woman whose name I do not yet know. The passion would last for hours.

In the life I envision for us, we would stroll through the park every day, accompanied by two violinists playing Beethoven. Night after night we would go to romantic restaurants, and after every meal we would go to the beach to eat chocolate and drink wine under the moon and stars. After the last bite of chocolate and sip of wine we would make love as the ocean waves crash violently upon the sand. We would buy a house by the water and plant vegetables in our garden. We would first get an Old English Sheepdog and then have a child.

Something lands on my jacket. A fresh green

and white blob sits prominently on the right shoulder of my dark blue suit. I look to the sky and watch the culprit pigeon fly away. It is ten minutes after the hour, time for me to get back to the office. To my left sits the beautiful woman, oblivious to the life we just shared.

# Chapter 2

"Hi Ellen."

"Hello Matt honey. How have you been? You haven't been around in a few days."

"I'm all right."

"What would you like?"

"I'll have a cup of chicken and rice soup and an order of the baked chicken special."

"Italian as usual on the salad?"

"Sure. I'll also have a double order of mashed potatoes, instead of one potato and one vegetable."

"No problem, honey."

"Also an iced tea."

"Ok sweetie."

"Wait, forget the baked chicken special. I'll just have the cup of soup and a London broil sandwich."

Ellen, my waitress here at the Pasture Diner, is a few years older than I am. I'd guess that she's around thirty-five, but she has this rugged look that makes her seem older. It is not that she doesn't look good or healthy. In fact, she looks both good and healthy, but she looks older than her years in a motherly, comforting, soothing kind of way. For two years I've been coming here to the Pasture, a few times a week, yet I know nothing about her. She has what looks like nice long dirty-blondish hair, but unfortunately she keeps it tied up. When she lets her hair down it must be wonderful.

"Sweetie, here's your iced tea and soup."

How many people has Ellen called "honey" or "sweetie" in her life? In only the past few minutes

I've heard her say it to the guy a few booths away and to the kid at the other table. To many, if not to all of her customers, she uses such terms of endearment. Does she address customers that she does not like with those terms? Although I know she says it to mostly everyone, I can't help but believe that when she calls me honey, she means it, at least a little bit, but that she is faking it when she says it to others.

"Did you finish your soup, honey?"

The soup was like lead. By the end of the day, after sitting in the pot all day, the soup at the Pasture is really thick. Despite its thickness, it isn't bad.

"Here's your sandwich, baby."

From my vantage point I can see the heavily sweating male cooks behind the grill. I know it must be hot by the grill, but to see them sweating so much by the food is unpleasant. The soup is probably so salty because of their sweat dripping into the pot.

"You all finished dear?"

"Yeah, I'll have the check."

This was not a bad meal. It's tough to go home and cook for one. Not a bad meal tonight at the Pasture.

"Have a good night sugar."

# Chapter 3

Despite the good meal at the Pasture, I wish I had something sweet to eat here at home now. I should have stopped at the grocery store on the way home from the Pasture.

Tomorrow I've got to bring this suit to the dry cleaner to get rid of the gift that the pigeon deposited on the right shoulder of the jacket, although the stain does not look so bad now that it's dried into the material.

Should I get onto my usual position on the couch or is it too early? Once I'm on the couch I'm doomed for the night. It just sucks me in. I bought the couch used at an outdoor market in Brooklyn. Who knows where it has been and what it has seen in its many days? But it is comfortable, although not comfortable in the traditional sense. It is comfortable only in that it makes a person tired. The couch saps the energy right out of a person. You start out feeling strong and fresh, but after a few minutes on the couch, it is impossible to move.

I had my chance with that woman sitting next to me on the bench in the park today at lunch. Would it have been so bad if I said something to her, anything? Instead I sat mute. I said not a word. Nothing. I did not even smile at her. At least I have her memory every time I look at the pigeon dropping that has dried on my jacket. Maybe I should not clean the jacket. That way whenever I look at the stain I can think of her. I wonder what her name is. Lola, no. Patricia, no. Priscilla, no. Candice, Candy, Alexandra. No, no, no. I'll just refer to her as Bench

Woman. Yes, Bench Woman. What is Bench Woman doing now? Is she thinking about me? Yeah right. Really, where is Bench Woman right now? What did Bench Woman eat for dinner? Who did Bench Woman eat with? Tomorrow at lunch I will go back to that same park bench. If Bench Woman reappears, nothing will stop me from talking to her. I will become Bench Man.

# Chapter 4

This morning's shower feels good. There is nothing to eat for breakfast, though I have no one to blame but myself for that sad state of affairs.

What suit should I wear today? It is important for me to look good today at lunch when I sit on the park bench. If I am to be Bench Man and attract Bench Woman, everything needs to be perfect. I'll wear my dark gray suit. Can't go wrong with that. Or can I? Is it too conservative, or not conservative enough? No. It's a good choice. But it is the tie that I choose to go along with the suit that will be the key to Bench Woman's heart. I believe that Bench Woman will fall for me if I wear the maroon paisley tie.

"Buddy, what can I get for you, the usual?"

"Yeah."

"Here's your very, very dark coffee with two sugars and a bagel with a little cream cheese. Have a nice day."

"You too," I say to the bagel man, who maintains an outdoor bagel cart one block from my office.

It looks like rain. I hope it doesn't rain because not only have I lost my umbrella, but rain could spoil my potential meeting in the park with Bench Woman. The radio news said that it would be overcast in the morning, but would gradually clear up as the day goes on. It should, therefore, be perfect for my paisley tie and I to charm Bench Woman.

"Hello Matt."

"Hi Betty. How was your daughter's school

play last night?"

"She was great. She was the star, you know. Snow White. She looked so pretty and, I must admit, she was by far the best. Some of the other kids were cute, but my Tammy, oh, she was an actress. She was gorgeous, beautiful, and talented. Her teacher, Mrs. Fletcha, came over to me after the play and told me what a joy Tammy is and blah blah blah..."

"That's great. Sounds like you have quite a talent on your hands, and if she's as pretty as her mother. . . ."

"Stop it. Oh, but her teacher did say that with Tammy's obvious talent that maybe one day blah blah blah..."

"Sounds fantastic."

Betty, the receptionist, is very nice, but she does tend to talk, especially when it comes to her nine-year-old daughter Tammy. I can't blame her though, she just adores her daughter.

I sell insurance plans to small to midsize businesses for Total Cover Insurance Company, which we call Total Cover for short. It is a good job. The day moves quickly. I sometimes leave the office to meet prospective clients for lunch, sometimes dinner. I'm not leaving the office today. I will meet with Robert and Michael, the two new salesmen I supervise. I'm twenty-eight years old and already have been here five years, so I'm now in charge of my own little group.

Both Robert and Michael are meeting new clients this afternoon. I need to talk with them before they go, just to make sure they know what they are doing.

10

"Hi Claire. Who made the coffee?"

"I believe Karen made it. Matthew, I'd like to talk to you about something. I'm going to be busy this morning, so let's talk later if you're free."

"Sure."

"Ok, see you later."

I wonder what Claire wants to talk about. Claire is Mary Pinnyon's secretary. Mary Pinnyon is one of the vice presidents here. Claire is a very nice girl, but she is not happy here. She hates Mary and I can't blame her. Although Mary has done nothing to me personally to make me hate her, I still don't like her. Mary treats the secretarial staff as if they are her slaves.

Claire is friendly to me and sometimes comes into my office to make small talk. Except for "hello" and "good-bye," it seems to me that Claire doesn't talk to many people in the office. She's not unfriendly. She's just quiet. She probably wants to talk with me about a problem that she's having with Mary. Unfortunately, there's nothing I'll be able to do about it. I can't stand it when Karen makes the coffee. It is too weak.

"Yeah, come in."

"Hey Matt, what are you doing for lunch?" It is Ken, another sales representative.

"I'm planning on buying a sandwich and going to the park," I say.

"Are you kidding? Look what's going on outside. It's pouring."

I look outside and, to my disappointment, I see what looks like a monsoon.

"I didn't even notice the rain. I suppose I won't

be going to the park today. Where are you going to eat?"

"Mark and I are going to the Starlight. You want to join us?"

"Yeah all right, when are you going?"

"In about fifteen minutes."

"Ok, I'll come by your office."

It's disheartening to eat lunch with Ken and Mark today instead of possibly meeting Bench Woman in the park. But it is raining like crazy, so there is no way Bench Woman will go and sit in the park. It is quite a disappointment to waste my maroon paisley tie on a lunch with Ken and Mark.

# Chapter 5

That lunch was good. Things sometimes get a little greasy at the Starlight, but today my cheeseburger deluxe was good. Of course, I wouldn't have worn my best tie for lunch at the Starlight, unless I were at the Starlight with the beautiful Bench Woman. If I were with Bench Woman, however, I wouldn't want to eat at the Starlight.

"Who is it?"

"Claire."

"Come in."

"Matthew, why do you always keep the door to your office closed? You're the only one on the floor who keeps the door closed. What do you do in here anyway?"

"I have wild secret parties. I can't tell you about it."

"Yes. Okay Matthew."

Claire is standing in front of my desk looking a little anxious. I can't imagine why she feels that way.

"You said that you wanted to talk to me about something. What's up?"

"My friend Debra is getting married a week from Saturday night."

"Yeah, that's nice. Do I know her?"

"No, you don't know her. Matthew, I'd like to go with someone to her wedding. Would you come with me? It wouldn't be a date. We'd just go together as friends. You can think about it and tell me later."

This is certainly not what I thought Claire was going to talk to me about, although I didn't have any

13

idea what she was going to talk to me about.

"Sure, I'd love to go with you," I tell Claire.

"That is great, Matthew. I was feeling a little nervous asking you. You don't have to say yes just to be nice. You really would like to go?"

"I'd be very happy to go with you to the wedding."

"If you feel uncomfortable, we don't have to tell anyone in the office."

"I'm happy to be going with you. I don't feel uncomfortable about it at all."

"Thanks Matthew. I need to get back to work. We'll talk more about this later. Remember, it's not this Saturday night, but next Saturday night.

That's interesting. I'm going with Claire to a wedding. We've been friendly in the office, but we've never done anything remotely social together. I know that Claire said that she only asked me as a friend. While it may simply be that she doesn't have anyone else to ask, it may mean that Claire, even subconsciously, thinks that the potential exists for more than friendship with me. I like Claire as a person, but never have I contemplated spending time with her romantically. That's not completely true. I've thought about it maybe once or twice. Claire has never given me any indication that she likes me as more than a friend.

Claire is pretty. She's also tall, not that tall, but she's probably 5'6". That must be about right. I'd estimate that I'm three inches taller than she is. She's skinny, sort of like a board. Not so skinny that she looks emaciated, but she's just a flat all over kind of skinny. Her face is pretty. It's simple, but nice. It

14

is hard to believe Claire doesn't have a boyfriend to go with to this wedding. She is very nice.

## Chapter 6

Chow mein or pizza?  Actually, I wish I had such a choice for dinner, but unfortunately, my favorite Chinese restaurant in this neighborhood doesn't even serve chow mein.  Chow mein is not real authentic Chinese food, so they say, so they don't serve it.  I would love some good old-fashioned chicken chow mein with an egg roll.  But here at Wong Fat Tok, my favorite Chinese restaurant, chicken chow mein is not available.

"Hello.  I'll give you my order in a minute."

I could get pepper steak or sauteed chicken and shrimp combination, but I think I'd prefer something hot and spicy, something in red on the menu.  General Chang's chicken could be good, but I should get something with vegetables, considering that Chinese food is my main source of vegetables for the week.  I do, however, eat fruit on a regular basis.  The chicken with broccoli is a possibility, a little bland, but at least it's healthy.

"Are you ready to order?"

"I'll have an order of chicken with garlic sauce to go."

It's spicy and I think that it comes with some vegetables, but I'm not sure.  Of course it comes with rice.  They give the choice of white or brown rice.  I know that brown rice is supposedly healthier, in that it is filled with fiber, and it is definitely trendier, but I'd rather get white rice.  There's nothing like good sticky white rice from a Chinese restaurant.

"That will be $8.75."

I have to remember to pick up the pigeon

16

stained suit at the dry cleaner later this week. It was sad that the rain this afternoon left me with no opportunity to go back to the park to see Bench Woman.

Imagine if Bench Woman went to the park even though it was raining at lunch time. Imagine if she then took off all of her clothes and ran around naked in the park in the pouring rain. Her very dark and long hair would get flattened out by the rain and look even darker and longer and flatter as it would stick tight to her pale skin--reaching almost all the way down her back. The water would just keep dripping down her smooth skin, each water droplet resting momentarily on her breasts, as if stopping to notice the beauty of its surroundings. Yet the droplets would make her cold and she would shiver, goosebumps multiplying all over her. In the distance she would see me. I would come to her carrying a blanket for comfort. I would wrap the blanket around both of our bodies. First my heat would remove all of her chill and then our touches would make us hot and the water would steam off her body.

"Who are you?" she would ask.

"I am Matt, but you can call me Bench Man."

"I love you Matt, Bench Man," she would scream.

I'm very sure that Bench Woman is not sitting down at this moment eating take-out Chinese food in an apartment with a barely working air-conditioner thinking about the time she spent yesterday on a park bench with someone who didn't say a word to her. This chicken with garlic sauce is not bad. It's pretty good.

I need something sweet for dessert. I should have bought something at the grocery store while I waited for the take-out at the Chinese restaurant. I'll go back outside and buy something.

With my stomach craving a sweet dessert, I think to myself that when Bench Woman and I are finally together, I'll tell her all about the pigeon, the dove of love, who relieved himself on my shoulder as I sat beside her. Perhaps the pigeon and Bench Woman are connected and I will see Bench Woman only after this same pigeon relieves himself on her. No, how can I even think of such a thing happening to someone as beautiful as Bench Woman. Am I mad?

# Chapter 7

I lost the lottery again. It's depressing that I lost. It's actually pathetic because when I buy my ticket I truly believe that I'm going to win. But do I win? Never.

It would be a very good thing if I won, let's say $20 million--$1 million every year for the next twenty years. Actually, it would only come to about a-half million dollars a year after taxes. I'd accept that. I'd give a lot of it away to family, friends, and charity. I'm so wonderful. Then I'd buy a car, an apartment, and a house with a big front porch and a bigger backyard. But most importantly, Bench Woman would be mine.

Bench Woman, and all women, would flock to me in my black convertible purchased with the lotto money. I'd say,

"Bench Woman, come to me, we are going to spend the week together in Paris."

After Bench Woman packs for Paris, I would tell her that we are going to spend the week in Cleveland instead of Paris, at which time she would say,

"Can't we go to Paris?"

"No," I would say.

Then she would say to me,

"With you, my love, I'd even spend a week in Cleveland."

When she would be all set to go to Cleveland, I'd take her to Paris. At that point she would adore me so much that she would be unable to control herself on the plane. I'd have to get her drunk and sleepy to keep her from making a scene. After dinner and an evening in Paris, we'd go to Belgium for a breakfast of Belgian waffles.

It would be in Belgium with Bench Woman where I would discover the joy of eating Belgian waffles in Belgium.  I would then use my lotto winnings to start a chain of restaurants in Europe called American Matt's Very Delicious Belgian Waffle Cafe.  The dishes would range from your standard plain Belgian waffle to the ultimate Bench Woman Belgian Waffle, which would be a Belgian waffle with ice cream, fruit, and whipped cream on top.  After making American Matt's Very Delicious Belgian Waffle Cafe a household name in Europe, I'd start the chain back home in the United States.  In only a short time, the financial magazines would be raving about the man who won the lottery and turned his millions into billions.  All this would happen with Bench Woman at my side.

Unfortunately, what would probably happen if I won the lottery would be that I would quit my job and sit on my couch all day to watch television.  The couch would sap every ounce of my energy, and I would eat cookies, mostly Mallomars, Yankee Doodles, and Yodels, all day long.  I'd get very fat and depressed and I'd stop taking showers.  What reason would I have to be clean?  I'd become easy prey for some illegitimate cult leader who would mold my mind and, without any reluctance, I would endorse the yearly lottery check to his name.  One day I would go to the cult's headquarters to discover that Bench Woman is the cult's goddess.  Bench Woman would have her servants chain me up against the wall and I'd be forced to watch her and the cult leader, Darmooot, a grotesque giant, make love right in front of me. They would keep me drugged and locked up in a small cell, but would let me out once a year to endorse my yearly lotto check to them.

I must buy another lottery ticket tomorrow.

## Chapter 8

The morning sunlight streams through the window. It feels like only a moment ago when I went to bed at 11:00 p.m., but now my alarm is ringing at 6:45 a.m.

Maybe this morning, instead of getting my usual bagel and coffee from the street vendor, I'll eat the cereal that I keep in the office. I could, however, treat myself to a real breakfast at the Pasture, where I can sit down with the newspaper and have a full breakfast before getting to the subway. Many times I go to the Pasture for breakfast on the weekend or during vacation or holidays when I don't go to work, but rarely do I sit down and have a full breakfast on a work day. I should go there today. Life is short.

It feels different at the Pasture in the morning than at night. At night, Ellen is here calling me "honey" and "sweetie." I miss her, although this weekday morning crew appears friendly.

"I'll have the Belgian waffle special, with orange juice and coffee," I tell the waitress.

My newspaper and I await the waffle, which I will smother with syrup. I don't believe in adding butter on top of the waffle. I don't believe that the added butter makes the waffle taste any better. I eat the waffle straight up with syrup. No added butter is necessary.

The waffle placed in front of me looks good. It is a light golden brown. More importantly, it is nice and fluffy. Some people like their waffles crispy, but I like them fluffy. It can't get much better than a fluffy waffle, syrup, and a newspaper. I need to put

22

enough syrup in each hole of the waffle. Most restaurants, the Pasture included, do not actually serve real maple syrup. Instead they serve a sweetened corn syrup that tastes and looks like real maple syrup. It tastes pretty good, even if it's not the real thing.

This waffle is as fluffy as it looks. It's wonderful. It's amazing how the Pasture, and how a lot of diners, have so many different items on the menu and make most of them taste pretty good. For dinner, a customer can come here and eat red meat, chicken, fish, Italian food, all kinds of sandwiches, salads, soups, and vegetables. Even in the middle of the night, or at any time, the Pasture will serve eggs or waffles. And of course they always serve ice cream and a large selection of cakes and pies. Yet not everything is good at the Pasture. I've had my share of disappointing meals. But usually they do a good job.

"I'll have more coffee. Thanks."

This morning's waitress gives good service. What does Ellen, my usual evening waitress, do during the day before she comes to the Pasture? Is she sleeping now? If yes, is she alone or with someone? I envision Ellen sleeping with a man named Hans, or possibly Mario. It is rejuvenating to sit here savoring each bite of this sweet, fluffy breakfast. It gives me the urge not to go to work at all today. I rarely call in sick. I should do it today. There's nothing at work today that I can't put off until tomorrow. I will call the office and tell them that I am too sick to come to work. I'm going to sit here with this newspaper and savor every bite of this waffle knowing that I am not going to work.

"Hello Claire, how are you? This is Matt. I'm not coming to work today. I don't feel well. I just thought I'd let you know. Please just let the others know."

"Sure Matthew. I hope you're not staying away from work as an excuse so that you do not have to go with me to the wedding. If you don't want to go to the wedding, just tell me so. Please don't think that you have to call in sick for the next week and a half."

"I want to go the wedding. I am just not feeling well today. I'm sure I'll be in tomorrow. Can you transfer me to either Robert or Michael? I have to tell them a few things. Thanks."

"Ok, good-bye. Hope you feel better."

Now that I've called in sick, I turn on the television and lay on the couch.

What would it be like if I got the chance to sit on this couch with Bench Woman? Unfortunately, I'll probably never know. If Bench Woman were to come to my apartment, she probably would land on my couch. If the couch would have the same effect on her that it has on me, it would make her sleepy. I would hope that such a feeling would make her think about the wonderful man next to her on the couch.

"I love this couch and I love you," she would say. "Please," she would continue, "take off my clothes here and now on this couch."

While Bench Woman will most likely never sit on this couch, it is very possible that, in only a week and a half, I could be sitting on this very couch with Claire after her friend's wedding. It would be very late at night if Claire comes back to my apartment after the wedding. That could be strange. Claire on the couch, after a few drinks, very late on a Saturday night after her friend's wedding. What would happen?

What should I do now that I'm not going to work today? I could go to the park and wait on the bench to see if Bench Woman arrives. I cannot do that because the park is too close to work and I do not want to be seen by anyone at work since I just called in sick. It would be enjoyable to go to Atlantic City. But I don't want to go alone on the bus from the Port Authority Bus Terminal to Atlantic City. On days like this, I wish I had a car. But cars are difficult to park in Manhattan. Also, I don't have a lot of spare money to lose in Atlantic City today. Maybe I should just relax today. Why would I want to take a three hour bus ride, alone, just to go play blackjack and probably lose, and then be short on money until next paycheck?

"I'll have a roundtrip ticket to Atlantic City."

There is an interesting assortment of people taking this bus to Atlantic City on this weekday morning. Some people waiting for the bus look retired, but what about the rest? Are they all on vacation? That cannot be. Does it mean that these people are unemployed, in which case they shouldn't be going to Atlantic City. Could these people be so rich that they don't have to go to work? That is impossible. Rich people do not take the bus from the Port Authority Bus Terminal to Atlantic City. Could it be that all of these people called in sick today from their jobs and are dreaming of winning millions of dollars?  Does that mean that every day, when I go to work, there is an entire universe of people who decide not to go to work but go to Atlantic City instead?  There also must be other people who decide not to go to work for the day, but who then go to places besides Atlantic City.  Usually when I call in sick I just want a day off, but I don't go to Atlantic City.  I like being a part of this underworld of people who call in sick and gamble the day away.

I show my ticket to the bus driver and take a window seat.  I hope that no one sits next to me on this bus ride.  I want to spread out comfortably on this bus.  As I sit on my seat, people walk by and there are still entire pairs of seats available.  I am, therefore, confident that nobody will sit next to me.  It does not look like it will be a full bus.  But the bus keeps filling up, so now one of the two seats out of every pair of seats is taken.  It is now quite possible that someone will sit down next to me.  Yet it probably wouldn't be so bad if someone sat down next to me.  A miracle could happen and Bench Woman could sit down next to me.  If that were the case, I would hope that I would say something to her during the three hour bus ride.  Lightning should strike me if I were to sit next to Bench Woman for a three hour trip and remain silent.  What are the chances that a woman as beautiful as Bench Woman would take the bus alone to Atlantic City?

How come all these people are walking by the empty seat next to me and are instead sitting next to other people?  Is something wrong with me that causes these people to pass by me, but gladly sit next to others?  Do I look funny or do I look like I have some kind of communicable disease?

"Is this seat taken?"

"No."

This person sitting next to me is no Bench Woman, but he looks pleasant enough. What is he avoiding today by going to Atlantic City?

He has magazines in his bag. I should have bought a magazine myself at the bus station. I see the two magazines that are in his bag on the floor in front of his seat, but I can't make out the names of the magazines without staring. The man is closing his eyes, so now I can take a better look. One magazine is Guns and Ammunition. What does the other say? I think it says Hustler. I am sitting on a bus with a guy sleeping next to me who has two magazines: Guns and Ammunition and Hustler.

Two hours into the trip and sleeping beauty next to me has yet to open an eye. He begins to move and now he's awake. He leans towards his bag and pulls out a magazine. Which one will he choose? He chooses to read Guns and Ammunition. When will this ride end?

# Chapter 9

My goal at this casino is to double my money every half hour until my life is changed forever. To do so, however, I need to pick the perfect blackjack table from which I can win a lot of money.

It is vital that I do not sit at a table with a very good looking woman dealer. That is far too distracting. There would be too much pressure both to impress her with my skillful but daring play, and to be charming at the same time. For example, if Bench Woman were the dealer, I would lose all my powers of concentration and my money would vanish in no time at all. She'd look at me and laugh inside, knowing full well that her beauty caused me to lose everything.

Of course, there is the small possibility that I would be able to summon all my courage with Bench Woman as the dealer. Then I would win money in front of her and become her hero. She would swoon over my blackjack mastery and gladly hand me chip after chip with every blackjack. In only a short time she'd realize that I was the man, her man, and that we were meant to be together. As my pile of chips would grow to the sky, she would slip me a piece of paper reading "Room 20L, be there at midnight." After winning $100,000 in only one hour, I would depart from the blackjack table and throw Bench Woman one final glance, both of us anxiously awaiting our midnight rendezvous. I would purchase a tuxedo for myself and a diamond necklace for Bench Woman. I would come to her room at 12:15 a.m., fifteen minutes late, and the door would be ajar. I would walk in and enter the most lavish suite in the hotel. Bench Woman would appear wearing a small white negligee, displaying her beautiful shape. She would take my hand, embrace me, and then take off my jacket, tie, shirt and pants, leaving me with only my socks. I would start to take them off myself, but then Bench Woman would pull them off with her teeth. She would lie down on the huge heart-shaped bed and beckon me to join her. As I would move towards her, I would hear a noise and see two men, one of whom would slam a glass bottle to my head. I would try to get up, but fists would fly all over my face. Lying on the floor, bloodied and nearly unconscious, I would see Bench Woman and her two thug friends pillage my wallet and take the money that I had won earlier in the day.

Fortunately for me, that scenario is not likely. Bench Woman is probably not a blackjack dealer here in Atlantic City.

This table looks fine. The dealer is a Chinese man. His name-tag says Mao Chin, from Philadelphia, Pennsylvania. He looks to be around twenty-five years old. He has a pleasant looking face with very short dark hair. There are two open seats available at the table. I take the seat that is the second from the last. There are two Japanese men at the table who each are placing very large bets, much more than the $10 minimum bet allowed. There are two young women playing, neither of whom appear to know what they are doing. Yet they are wearing a lot of jewelry and possess many chips, so they must be getting a lot of money from somewhere. I suppose, then, that they do know what they are doing. There is one older man at the table who inhales his drink with the vigor of a pack of hyenas at their kill.

"Good luck," Mao Chin says to me as he takes my $100 and hands me five $10 chips and ten $5 chips.

"Thank you," I reply.

Astonishingly, after thirty minutes I am up $150. I've more than doubled my money. I put my original $100, which is now in chips, into my pocket. I will cash in those chips at a later time. I will not play with those chips. No matter what happens to my winnings, I will leave here with at least the same amount of money that I started with. I have another blackjack. Suddenly Mao Chin leaves the table and is replaced by a dealer whose name-tag says Jan, from Wilmington, Delaware. She is beautiful. She smiles at the whole table, but I know her smile is meant to taunt me. Even though I normally don't play at a table where the dealer is so beautiful, I stay here because my luck has been so good at this table. Why should it change just because Mao Chin is replaced by Jan from Wilmington, Delaware?

Jan deals me a 20. Things are not so bad.

"Dealer has 21."

She got lucky that time.

"Dealer has blackjack."

This is incredible. The dealer's luck will have to run out soon. I am dealt nineteen. Jan has a six showing so I should win this hand.

"Dealer has six, sixteen, twenty."

This Jan is lovely, even though I am losing money fast with her as the dealer. Only the two Japanese men and I remain at the table after ten minutes with Jan. I think Jan just smiled at me. I can't leave this table now, especially since I know that in her heart Jan wants me to win money from the casino. I get blackjack. Jan smiles at me again. I believe she is happy to pay me.

I've now won three hands in a row. I knew it was only a matter of time before Jan would deal me winning hands. We have a special bond that is palpable. The two Japanese men and Jan exchange a very knowing glance. What does it mean? The two men leave the table.

Jan continues smiling and dealing me winning hands. Other people come to the table. My winnings are now up to $250, but Jan suddenly leaves the table, says "good luck," and the reliable first dealer, Mao Chin, comes back to deal.

I leave the table with my winnings and, for some reason, discreetly follow Jan. She is oblivious to my presence even when I enter the crowded elevator with her. I exit the elevator on the same floor as Jan. It is floor ten of the hotel-casino. She walks to a room, knocks on the door, and is let inside. From my vantage point in the hallway I cannot see who opened the door. Like a spy, I stand in front of the closed door and listen. I hear the familiar voices of the two Japanese men from the blackjack table. I listen for a few more minutes until I sit myself down on the hallway floor by the door. A maid from the hotel walks by. She does not ask me anything, but I volunteer to her that I am waiting for a friend inside that hotel room. The maid, who obviously could not care less what I am doing on the floor, says nothing to me and proceeds down the hallway. The floors in a

31

big hotel casino like this must be videotaped for security purposes. Yet I remain seated on the floor. After a few minutes I hear no voices and I forget why I am even sitting there. I become sleepy.

I wake up abruptly when I hear the door open, and then close, and see Jan leave the room alone. I do not believe that she even notices me on the hallway floor near the door. My mind tells me to follow her, but my body remains on the hotel hallway floor. Jan leaves my sight and enters an elevator. I hear the elevator door close, taking with it Jan from Wilmington, Delaware, the beautiful blackjack dealer. I look at my watch and cannot believe that I have been on the hallway floor for over an hour.

I should just go back home. However, I have won $250. While that is a success, it will not change my life. But I can take this money and try to make some real money with it at the casino.

I swell with confidence as I roam the casino floor. My successes with both Mao Chin and Jan from Wilmington, Delaware, demonstrate that I can win with any dealer.

I ask for $200 in chips at a table headed by Rick, a relaxed and easy-going type of dealer. Scanning the table I see two young guys who look as if they are down to their last chips. I also see a man and woman who appear to be a couple, but who play separately. Both of them have a high pile of chips. I should do well at this table.

I'm sitting pretty here with a twenty.

"Dealer has eighteen."

I win again. This is easy. I may win millions today.

32

"Blackjack for the gentleman," announces Rick, referring to me.

I win $250 more at this table. I have now won $500. It's already 6:30 at night. What should I eat for dinner? Should I take a bus home now, or should I have a quick dinner while here in Atlantic City, and then go home with my winnings. I'll treat myself to a good dinner here, a really good dinner. That is the best idea. I might as well spend some of the winnings.

I enter a restaurant in the hotel. It is overpriced, but since I've taken this casino for so much money, I don't mind spending some of it. It's interesting sitting here alone. It is not like sitting alone at the Pasture being served by Ellen. Here comes my waiter.

"How are you, sir?"

"I am fine. Thank you."

"Would you care for a drink before ordering?"

"No thanks. I'll have the porterhouse steak, medium well. You know what, make it medium. You only live once, right?"

I can't cloud up my head with drinks just in case I play more blackjack. I need to stay alert. In a quick change of heart I call the waiter back.

"Waiter, I'll have a vodka and pineapple juice."

This steak is good, really good. I look at the steak. It is hard to believe that it was once part of a living, breathing cow. I wonder what part of the cow? I am eating another animal. I know that animals eat other animals. The whole system is crazy. I am nothing but an animal. I'm making myself sick thinking about the poor cow. What did it do to deserve this fate? I can't eat it anymore. This steak is delicious though, especially with this steak sauce. I'll eat it. The steak is doing neither me nor the cow any good just sitting on the plate. Hopefully, I'll use some of those aggressive, animalistic instincts back at the blackjack table. Does a cow have aggressive, animalistic instincts?

"I'll have $400 in chips," I tell a different dealer.

"Good luck."

"Dealer has seventeen."

I win with eighteen. I haven't been counting my pile of chips, but it has gotten high. I have another blackjack. A man working for the casino leans towards me and speaks.

"Would you like to be rated?"

"Sure," I say to the man.

I don't exactly know what they mean by being rated, but it cannot hurt. This winning streak has never happened to me before. The casino people are interested in me now that I have a lot of chips on the table. After two more hours playing at this table, I am offered a hotel room on the house for the evening.

I have over $1,000 in chips in front of me at this time, along with the offer of a free room. What about work tomorrow? Maybe I should call in sick at work again. There is nothing so important at work that cannot wait at least one more day. How many times in my life am I going to have a lucky streak like this? I was once advised that it is always better to call in sick for at least two days in a row, instead of calling in sick for only one day. In that way everyone thinks that you are very sick and not just pretending to be sick for the day. That makes sense to me. It's already 11:00 at night. There is no way in the world that I'm going to drag myself up on the bus for the three hour ride back home tonight. I'm just going to enjoy and savor my free room and my winnings. According to this card given to me by the casino man, I am entitled not only to a free room, but also to a buffet breakfast tomorrow morning.

I am given room 1002. It is, coincidentally, on the same floor, and only a few doors from, the room where I earlier saw Jan from Wilmington, Delaware enter, and then exit. The size of this bathroom is unbelievable. The jacuzzi is big and there is a telephone right next to it. I go into the jacuzzi and toss some bubble bath into it. I call room service.

"This is room 1002. I'd like a bottle of red wine and an ice cream sundae with chocolate ice cream, with lots of chocolate syrup, no nuts. Please, no nuts. Thanks."

There is a resounding thud in the hallway, as if someone has been thrown against the wall. I get out of the steaming bubble bath jacuzzi to see what happened. I place a towel around me before I crack the door open just enough to see into the hallway. I see Jan, my former blackjack dealer, and she sees me. She is crying quietly.

"Come in," I say.

# Chapter 10

"Jan, are you ok?" I ask.

"How do you know my name?"

"You were my dealer at a blackjack table earlier today."

"Yes, I remember," Jan says faintly.

The bubble bath that I prepared for myself foams in the jacuzzi within our sight. I suggest to Jan that she go into the very warm bubbly water and relax. A small smile comes to her face and right in front of me, without shyness or embarrassment, Jan's clothes come off her as if they were on her body no more tightly than a leaf on a tree in late autumn. She slides into the bubble bath and closes her eyes. She says nothing. There is a knock on the door.

"Room service."

Dressed with only a towel around my waist, I go to the door and take the chocolate ice cream sundae and the overpriced bottle of wine from the waiter. I see the exorbitant bill for the wine and ice cream, and pay for those items and also give a big tip. With Jan from Wilmington, Delaware in the jacuzzi, I have no time to ask for change.

With the ice cream and wine in hand, I go to the bathroom and see Jan sleeping among the steaming white bubble bath bubbles. I sit on the bathroom floor right beside her. Only her head outside of the water can be seen. Her body is beneath the white bubbles. I am too much like a Peeping Tom when I try to look through the bubbles. I therefore turn away.

The ice cream sundae is sweet, chocolaty, and

cold. This is perhaps the best chocolate ice cream that I've ever had. Maybe it's that Jan is in the jacuzzi next to me that makes it taste so good. I wonder if I can buy this brand of ice cream in the supermarket. It's so good I should offer some of it to Jan, but I don't want to wake her up for it.

What was Jan doing in the hallway and why was she thrown against the wall and what was she doing with the two men from earlier today? Why was she crying? I want to ask her, but it's none of my business. I want to drink the wine, but it doesn't seem right to do so with such a sad, but beautiful woman in the jacuzzi. I'm not going to wake her. I pour a glass of wine for myself.

The wine is tart. I drink a glass of it quickly. I am envious of Jan as she sleeps in the jacuzzi filled with the warm bubbles, while I sit on the bathroom floor wearing a towel. Yet I am enjoying this cold ice cream and slightly chilled wine. While I don't want to disturb her, and I don't know if she'd welcome me in the jacuzzi, there is plenty of room for me to go inside the jacuzzi without bothering her. I feel the effects of the wine as I stand up. I take off the towel and enter the water. Jan's eyes open when I enter the warm wonderful water on the opposite side from her. She says nothing and neither do I. We sit across from each other in the hot water. Between us is an endless ocean of bubbles. I feel Jan's feet and toes next to my legs. Through the bubbles Jan looks in my direction. I pour her a glass of wine. However, she takes the wine bottle and drinks directly from it. "I am so sleepy," she says, and she closes her eyes once more.

Jan falls asleep. I am very comfortable also. I am more at ease than I remember being in quite a long time. I fall asleep, but awaken after a short time. Our bodies are going to shrivel up from the jacuzzi. I struggle to lift the wet, and sleeping, Jan from Wilmington, Delaware, out of the jacuzzi and place her down on the large bed in the room. I lay my wet body down next to the beautiful, but mysterious blackjack dealer, who looks serene as she sleeps.

Light streams in through the window and wakes me. It is the morning already. Jan is not in the bed. I did not see or feel her leave the bed. There is a piece of paper on the table.

> I never found out your name, but thank you for taking care of me last night. Yesterday was my last day at the casino. I am leaving Atlantic City today to start my acting career out West.
>
> Thank you again.
> Jan English

Jan English. That is a nice name. I need to wash up. It is with happiness and sadness that I look down upon the jacuzzi, where Jan and I shared wine last night. During my shower I suddenly remember that I need to call the office to tell them that I'm not coming in to work again today because of my sickness.

"Hello Betty, let me speak to Claire. This is Matt."

"Matthew, this is Claire. Are you not coming in again?"

"I'm not feeling well. After one more day off I should feel better."

"Please tell me if you are pretending to be sick just to avoid going with me to the wedding next weekend."

"Don't be crazy. I can't wait to go with you to your friend's wedding. Please, that is ridiculous. Just tell Robert and Michael that I'm sure I'll be in tomorrow. If they have any problems with anything, I'll speak with them then. I'll see you tomorrow."

I go to the casino's buffet breakfast, where I ravenously consume orange juice, scrambled eggs, rye toast, a bagel with lox, a cranberry scone, and coffee. Last evening's events have heightened my hunger this morning. I can get accustomed to this life. I enter the casino after breakfast.

It is now noon on Thursday. The casino is quiet. Despite her note saying that she is no longer a blackjack dealer, I look for Jan English. She is nowhere in sight. I play a little blackjack. I have $1200 with me and I came with only $100. I see Mao Chin dealing at a nearby table.

"I'll have $300 in chips please."

"Good luck."

This is a good start. I have a 20.

"Dealer has 21."

Oh well, you can't win them all.

"Dealer has blackjack."

This is pathetic. I lose $300 in one half hour. I must leave this table. I go to play at an adjacent table because there looks to be a dealer who will give me good fortune.

"Give me $500 in chips."

I place large bets so that I will be able to win big money. Unfortunately, I lose $500 in a short time. I should leave. Yet I still have $400 with me. If I quit now, I'm still up $300 total, plus the free room, food, and of course my time spent with Jan English. I'll quit now, while I'm ahead. I've got to stop playing. The blackjack table over there looks very inviting though. No, I'll just take the bus home.

I make a quick $100 bet on black at the roulette wheel. The roulette wheel lands upon red. I must leave this casino.

Finally I step on the bus going home. I still have $200 more in my wallet than I had when I arrived. I suppose I'll never see Jan English from Wilmington, Delaware again. That makes me unhappy. This bus is not crowded. It looks like no one will sit next to me on the trip back. I just want to sleep.

I hunger for food when the bus arrives in New York. I take the subway uptown and enter the Pasture for dinner. It is comforting to see Ellen, the evening waitress.

"Hi sweetie, how have you been?"

"I'm ok. I'll have a London broil sandwich and an iced tea. No, make it a coke. You know, instead of the London broil sandwich, I'll have the chicken cutlet sandwich, with a side order of mashed potatoes."

"Ok honey."

Did Jan English actually go out West to become an actress?

40

"Here's your chicken cutlet sandwich, sweetie."
This is good. I'm tired. At least tomorrow is
Friday and then there is the weekend. The whole
idea of calling in sick worked out quite well.

"Thanks a lot. The food always tastes
especially good when you serve it."

"Good night, sugar."

# Chapter 11

It is difficult to get out of bed this morning, but knowing that today is Friday makes it easier. I walk quickly past the Pasture this morning because, if I decide to treat myself to another good breakfast of waffles with syrup, I might be tempted to call in sick again. That would not be so bad. I would then have a long weekend. No one would believe that I'd call in sick three days straight without actually being sick. I avoid the temptation of the Pasture.

The subway arrives. My subway ride to work is twenty minutes, but I never get a seat. I don't hate the subway. Many days I do my relaxing and best thinking on the subway. I would not take a subway ride for pleasure, but for the most part I prefer a subway ride to a taxi cab ride. I get crazy in the back of a cab with all the starting and stopping in city driving.

Pleasantly, the train is not unbearably crowded today. There is some room between people, enough room so that I'm not breathing directly on someone or having someone breathe on me. What's going on? The train has just stopped here in the dark of the subway tunnel, somewhere between 72nd and 42nd Streets.

"Blah blah blah..."

I cannot understand a single word that is being said over the train's loudspeakers. Why have we stopped?

As we stand here in an underground subway car that isn't moving, we are also standing on a planet that is rotating around itself and revolving around the sun. I'm dizzy just thinking about it. Also, the whole galaxy is moving away from all the other galaxies. As all this movement is going on, this subway can't make it from 72nd to 42nd Street.

A woman stands about ten feet from me. She looks queasy, as if she is about to faint. A man gets up and gives his seat to the queasy lady. That was nice.

"There is a disturbance in the train in front of us at the 42nd Street station. We will proceed as soon as the situation clears up. We will be moving shortly. We apologize for the inconvenience."

That message was understandable.

Is there life on other planets? Is there anything comparable to a subway stuck in a tunnel on another planet? It is hard to believe that there is no life on any other planet in the universe except earth. Although who knows, maybe there is no other life on any other planet and earth is a test planet. Maybe there is no intelligent life on other planets, whatever intelligent means. If we discover a bear on a distant planet, will we say that there is intelligent life there? I think so. Bears are pretty smart.

There is a large fish bowl in the front of my take-out Chinese restaurant where live lobsters are kept. A customer can come in and select one of the living lobsters for dinner. The claws of the lobsters are tied shut by rubber bands. The bowl is so crowded with lobsters that they walk all over each other. They wait to be picked out as somebody's dinner. That looks to me to be the most horrible existence imaginable. I assume that the reason the lobsters are kept like that is because we believe that they are not as intelligent as we are, and thus, they are entitled to no better. How do we know how smart they are? Even if lobsters are stupid, what right do we have to keep them like that? What if some super intelligent creature from outer space picked us out one by one for dinner? Actually this subway car is not so different from the bowl where the lobsters are kept, except that there is no water. I look overhead to make sure that something is not going to grab me and cook me for dinner.

Do dogs have souls? A minister's son once told me that dogs do not have souls, but only people do. He seemed confident of that. He believed that people have souls, but that no other animals have them. If I have a soul that can live on after I'm dead, why can't a chimpanzee have one? What about a dolphin? They're very smart. Why can't they have souls? Yet if dolphins and chimps have souls, why not dogs? But if dogs have souls, I have to believe that all animals, at least all mammals, must have souls. But could it really be that only mammals have souls, but not amphibians, reptiles or birds? That cannot be. What about spiders and ants? Does a mouse have a soul, but not a worm or a butterfly? Is that fair? Is there some point at which an animal is so low that it simply does not have a soul? Maybe no animals have souls, people included, although I hope we all have souls. I once read that, immediately after a person dies, the body weighs slightly less than it did when it was alive. The writer speculated that the difference in weight could be the soul leaving the body. That is a mystery. Another great mystery is whether this subway will ever make it downtown.

At least the subway is air conditioned. I don't mind that the train is not moving. I will just get into work a little late. Once I get into work everyone will ask me how I'm feeling. I'll have to tell them that I had a terrible cold for the past two days, but that I decided to come to work today for the good of the company. Do people get colds in the summer? I suppose they do. I will probably tell Claire about going to Atlantic City. I will, however, avoid any reference to being in the jacuzzi with Jan English. Not that she would be jealous or upset, but I'll keep that to myself.

The train moves forward.

"Forty-second street, Times Square. Transfer here for the blah blah blah..."

Things seem to be moving well now. I should arrive downtown to work in ten minutes.

## Chapter 12

Before going into the office, I get my usual breakfast from the street bagel cart.

"Hi. I'll have the usual."

"Here you go. Have a nice day."

"You too. Have a nice weekend."

I enter the office with a bagel and coffee.

"Hey Matt, how are you feeling?"

"Pretty good, thanks."

"Matt, how are you?"

"Much better today, thanks."

It's enjoyable, but awkward, when people ask me how I'm feeling, especially because I was feeling fine both of the days that I was not here at work. In fact, I probably felt better both of those days than I have in a long time. I wonder how or where Jan English is, and if she really left Atlantic City to go to some unspecified location out West.

"Hi Claire."

"Matthew, how are you? I've been worried about you."

"Well, don't tell anyone, but when I called in sick on Wednesday, I just took the day off because I wanted a day off. But I really did not feel well yesterday."

I know that I just lied to Claire about being sick yesterday, but I'm hesitant to tell her the truth about Atlantic City. If I start to tell her about my time there, I might tell her all about my time with Jan English. I don't want to do that.

"Are you feeling better now? You look a little pale," Claire says to me.

46

"What do you mean I look pale? I feel fine. For the next week I'm going to take extra good care of myself to look good for your friend's wedding."

"What are you doing for lunch today? It's going to be beautiful this afternoon. Would you like to get sandwiches and go to the park?"

"Sure. That would be fine," I tell Claire.

"I'll be able to tell you all about what the wedding should be like. Is 12:30 a good time for you to go to lunch?"

"That's great. I need to get some more coffee. Who made the coffee? Wow, this coffee is so strong. It's like mud. It's undrinkable.

"Matthew, I made the coffee. It's not that strong, you're exaggerating."

"This is the strongest coffee I've ever had. If this coffee kills me, you can have my plant by the window and my autographed baseball from the 1986 Mets."

"Maybe the coffee is a little strong. I'll see you later for lunch."

It looks as though Michael and Robert did a good job with the work when I was out. I was hoping that this place would fall apart without me. Unfortunately, things have gone on as normal. That's too bad. I thought this place couldn't get along without me. But why should I care? If the President of the United States decides to quit, in no time at all there would be a new President and, after a few days, the country would go on as if nothing happened. People would still go to the bathroom, take the subway, and make terrible coffee. Does anything actually matter? That's a bad attitude. Perhaps it

47

was in the stars for me to go to Atlantic City and meet Jan English. So what if this insurance office didn't miss me. Maybe Jan English will become a star out West. She'll make a movie and the hero will be based on me, the man who let her into his hotel room bubble bath. Who will play me? Or was my meeting Jan English a meaningless occurrence?

Today's newspaper reports that there was a small earthquake somewhere out West last night. No one was killed, but three people were hurt when a tree fell on their car. The earthquake may have been a welcome sign for Jan English as she arrived out West for her new life. She will write in her autobiography that the "earth moved when I landed in the West." That's exciting.

"Come in."

Claire comes into my office.

"It's 12:30. Are you ready to go to lunch?"

"I can't believe that it is 12:30 already. I've done no work so far today. I might as well take a break for lunch."

Claire tells me that she will probably get a tuna salad on pita bread. Tuna doesn't sound appetizing to me. I don't hate tuna fish, but it is neither exciting nor invigorating. What should I get? The sandwiches here at Frank's Sandwich Take-out are pretty good as far as these take-out sandwich shops go. Every once in a while, however, the person behind the counter makes a super sandwich. I don't come to this sandwich place often, but if my memory serves me, this guy behind the counter today makes good sandwiches. It is the Frank of Frank's Sandwich Take-out who is behind the counter today.

Even though the different sandwich-makers use the same ingredients, some of them make good sandwiches and some do not. There is an art to it. Frank is a master. He even makes Claire's tuna salad sandwich look delicious. What should I order?

"I'll have roast beef with tomatoes and a little Swiss cheese. Also some salt and pepper. No mayonnaise. On a hero bread."

"Would you like some oil and vinegar on the bread?"

"Ok."

The roast beef looks great. It is not too rare, but just a little rare in the middle. The bread looks nice and crusty on the outside, yet fresh on the inside.

"Here's your sandwich."

"Thanks a lot."

It is nice being with Claire. It is, however, conceivable that Bench Woman might be back at the park today. Imagine if Claire and I are on a bench and Bench Woman sits down next to me. What are the odds of that happening?

"Why don't we sit down here, Matthew?"

"That sounds good to me."

"I hope you have a nice time at the wedding next week. Debra is an old friend of mine. We met as campers as little girls and later we were counselors. Her fiancé is named Richard and he is originally from California but he lives here now. They met at church. She is a paralegal and he is a doctor. Debra and I used to be very close, but we have not seen much of each other the past two years. I've only met Richard twice, but I like him. I hope that you don't mind going to the wedding."

"I look forward to going. I'll wear a solid blue suit, with a white shirt and floral tie. The tie is dressy, but not as boring as what I usually wear to work. Does that sound ok?"

"I remember that you wore a floral tie at the office Christmas party. Is that the floral tie that you are talking about?"

"Yes, it is."

"I like that tie very much."

I'm surprised that Claire remembers my tie. Has she been thinking about me? After complimenting my tie, Claire tells me that the wedding ceremony will be held at a church on the east side of Manhattan, and the reception will be at the Nottingham Hotel, a few blocks from the church.

"How's your tuna fish?" I ask.

"It's very good. How is your sandwich?"

"This is a delicious hero. The cheese is melted and the meat is very tasty and not dry, yet not too rare. Even the bread is good. I'm very happy eating this. It's nice outside today, you know."

There is something nice about Claire. Eating on the park bench, with the sunshine splashing on her, makes her look much happier than she does in the office. She has a pretty smile. Even her voice sounds lighter and happier than it does in the office. There is a sadness to Claire in the office that has been lifted away by the sunlight. I feel like holding her hand. I know she doesn't like work, and seeing how much better she looks here in the park, out of the office, makes me realize how much she must hate being there. Claire, who has transformed into a happier person right before my eyes just during this lunch, must hate Mary Pinnyon, her boss, more than I thought. It is as if here, outside, a cloud of unhappiness has been lifted from her.

"You really hate work, don't you?" I ask Claire.

"It pays the rent, but I do hate it. I am thinking of going back to school to become a nurse. I have started preparing applications for schools."

"You should do it. You'd be a wonderful nurse."

If I were sick, I'd like Claire to take care of me. In fact, my throat is feeling a little scratchy.

"When you were a kid, what did you want to be when you grew up?" Claire asks me.

"I wanted to be a professional baseball player. I only dropped that fly ball at the company picnic last year because I lost the ball in the sun."

Pigeons swirl overhead. Claire seems oblivious to them.

"I still want to become a baseball player. In fact, I often think about making a game saving catch or hitting a home run in the World Series."

"You lead a busy fantasy life."

I am unable to focus on my conversation with Claire because, out of the corner of my eye, Bench Woman has come into view. She is coming closer. Is she going to sit on the next bench? She looks fabulous today. Could she have followed me? Is she jealous because I'm sitting here with Claire? I don't think so. She does not sit down. She just walks by. Has Bench Woman come into the park the past few days and left disappointed because I was not there? No way. She must work in this neighborhood. Did I

51

just see her wink at me while standing at that tree over there? Maybe she did. I can't know for sure. She's too far away. She most likely had a bug fly near her eye.

"Are you ok, Matthew? You look like you just saw a ghost."

"Huh? Yes, I'm fine. I'd love to walk away from this bench and buy a chocolate ice cream cone. I'll even treat you to one."

"That's very nice of you. Why are you getting a chocolate cone? The ice cream shop has so many interesting flavors."

"I like chocolate. I don't think that I should have to succumb to peer pressure to get some elaborate flavor just because people mistakenly believe that good old-fashioned chocolate is dull."

As Claire and I leave the park and walk towards the Many Flavored Ice Cream Parlor on Fulton Street, where they have over 50 flavors of ice cream, I see Bench Woman standing partially under a tree. Half of her is in sunlight and half of her is in shade.

## Chapter 13

Not only was my sandwich meaty and tasty, but the chocolate ice cream was rich and creamy. I see nothing wrong with eating chocolate ice cream if that's the flavor that I enjoy. Why should I eat a flavor that has nuts or other things added if I just want ice cream? If I want nuts, I'll buy nuts, and if I want ice cream, I'll buy ice cream. Who would ever believe that the world would become so crazy that it is frowned upon for someone to eat chocolate ice cream? Everyone at the ice cream shop, even the person behind the counter, looked at me funny because I ordered chocolate ice cream. If you order banana coffee cream nut fudge swirl they think that you are normal, but if you order chocolate they are ready to send you away to an insane asylum.

Claire thought my desire to be a professional baseball player was strange. She asked me what I wanted to be. Why shouldn't I tell her the truth? I know that I'm not good enough to be a professional baseball player. I might not even make it on a good little league team. I'd probably make it on some little league team, a bad one at least. I've always had a nice level swing. But I certainly couldn't handle a major league fastball, let alone a curveball or slider. What is a slider anyway? Baseball players often pull their muscles and go on the disabled list. I'm going to tell my boss that I pulled a hamstring on my way from lunch and that I have to go home. Actually, I may have pulled a groin muscle when Bench Woman walked into the park as Claire and I ate during lunch. A groin pull can be worth a month on the disabled list for a baseball player. But no one at my job would care if I pulled a muscle. If I pulled a groin muscle, my boss would say, "Son, you can still sell insurance."

There is a knock on my office door.

"Come in."

"Matthew, you do love keeping your door closed," Claire says.

"Didn't we talk about the door issue a few days ago," I say with a smile.

"What's up?" I then ask Claire.

"During lunch you mentioned that you weren't doing anything this weekend. I am thinking about buying a car and you must know more about cars than I do. The auto show is in town this weekend. Would you like to go with me to the auto show on Sunday?"

I would like to go to the auto show. But I had planned on going alone, so that I'd be able to wander around at my own pace. However, it would be a good idea to go to the auto show with Claire this weekend. This way we can get comfortable spending time with each other outside of the office before the Saturday night wedding next week.

"I'd like to go with you," I tell Claire. "It will be fun. I didn't know that you wanted a car. Let's meet for breakfast Sunday morning at about 11:00 and then we can go to the show. Does that sound good?"

"Yes Matthew, it does. I'll take the subway into the city from Queens, which lets me off at 59th Street. We can meet in front of the Plaza Hotel."

"That sounds good to me. It's a date," I say to

Claire.

"I'll see you Sunday. I'm leaving the office a little early today because I have a dentist appointment. Good night. I'll close your door."

The last words that left my mouth were "it's a date." But is it a date? Should I have called it a date?

I return some business calls, then look at my watch. It is after 5:00 p.m. I can't believe it. Today went fast. What am I going to do tonight? I hear everyone lingering in the hallway. The one bad thing about keeping my door closed is that I can't see into the hallway. They all talk loudly on Friday afternoons, like caged animals, although caged animals do not talk. I walk out of my office to see what's going on.

"Hey Ken. What's up?"

"Some of us are going out for drinks at the Peacock Pub. Coming?"

"Why the Peacock? It's always too hot in there. Why don't we go to the Forest Tavern? At least they serve food."

"But the Peacock has pool tables. Besides, I told your lackeys, Robert and Michael, who already left the office, that I'd meet them there. Also, the Peacock has started to brew its own beer and I want to try it. Mark is also already there with a friend of his."

"So it will be me, you, Michael, Robert, Mark, and Mark's friend at the Peacock."

"Let's go. It will be up to you to find us some women," Ken says to me.

Ken and I enter the elevator with Mary

Pinnyon, who is also leaving for the weekend. Now that I know how much Claire dislikes Mary, I like her less than I used too, which wasn't too much to begin with. Ken, on the other hand, worships Mary's ascent in the company and brown-noses her to death.

"Hi Mary," I say.

"Hello Matt, I haven't seen you at all today. Are you feeling better? When you are out, I worry about your accounts."

Mary smiles, whereupon Ken starts his brown-nosing barrage.

"Mary, blah blah blah..."

"You look great blah blah blah..."

"Are you guys doing anything particularly exciting this weekend?" Mary asks.

Ken quickly jumps in and tells Mary that we are going to the Peacock for a few drinks.

"Would you like to join us?" Ken asks Mary.

"I'll have a drink," Mary says.

There is a loud noise and the elevator suddenly stops. The elevator is stuck between floors with only the three of us in it. We apparently are stuck somewhere between the 15th and 16th floors. Ken and I look at each other as Mary takes lipstick out of her purse and puts some on her lips.

"I'm very claustrophobic," Mary announces.

Fortunately, in about six seconds the elevator returns to working order and we continue our descent to street level.

"To the Peacock," Ken declares, as we triumphantly leave 100 Broad Street for the weekend.

<u>Chapter 14</u>

There is something about the Peacock that I don't like. It is always too hot and too dark. But it is never dark in the way that a good bar should be--the kind of dark where there is a feeling of excitement in the air. Instead, inside the Peacock it is just too dark to see, but without any excitement. But I haven't been to the Peacock in a few months. As we step inside now, it is lighter looking than I remember. While it is still dark, it is bright enough so that I can actually see around me. Also, the walls are now lined with bright electric peacocks that were not there before. The peacocks are not beautiful, but they are big and colorful. Everywhere I look on the wall I see colored peacocks looking back at me.

Upon entering the Peacock we see Robert, Michael, Mark, who is a lawyer in the company, and another guy who must be Mark's friend. They are sitting at a table near the back. There is room at the adjacent table for us to sit next to them. Mark sees us and lifts up an empty pitcher of beer. This is his way of telling us that he needs more beer. I stop at the bar.

"I'd like a pitcher of beer."

"Do you want to try the beer brewed right here? It is a dark, rich brew that we call Peacock Brew," the bartender says.

"Sure, give me a pitcher of the Peacock Brew," I respond.

To my amazement, the bartender pours the Peacock Brew into a pitcher shaped like a peacock. I watch the beer from the draft flow into the legs of the peacock-shaped pitcher. Ken and Mary are already seated at the table with the others. I ask for three mugs to go with the pitcher. The three mugs given to me are also shaped like little peacocks. The bartender informs me that he only gave me the peacock-shaped mugs because I ordered the new Peacock Brew. People who order regular beer just get plain mugs.

"Enjoy our new Peacock Brew."

"Thanks."

Like a victorious hunter carrying his prey, I proudly, but cautiously, carry the peacock pitcher full of Peacock Brew and the three peacock mugs over to the table.

I am greeted heartily at the table because of the Peacock Brew that I carry. To my surprise, I see that the others at the table are drinking plain old regular beer out of a plain pitcher and mugs. How boring. I feel superior as I place the peacock pitcher on the table and give the peacock mugs to Ken and Mary.

"What's that?" Ken asks as he stares at the peacock pitcher and pours some of the beer into his peacock mug.

"Those peacocks are cute," Mary Pinnyon notes approvingly.

"This is pretty good," Ken says immediately after gulping down his first mouthful of the Peacock Brew.

Mark and his friend, a corporate lawyer named David, start making fun of our peacock mugs. It is, of course, easy to see that they are jealous of our peacock mugs and how our beer flows up and down the peacock's elaborate glass feathers and legs, while their beer goes straight up and down their plain mugs. David and Mark are not funny as they make fun of the peacock mugs, which I defend like a mother peacock defending her baby peacock. Are female peacocks called "peacocks"? For that matter, are baby peacocks called peacocks? I'll have to look this up when I get home. However, Mary hangs onto every word said by David, the corporate lawyer, who is wearing what is obviously the most expensive suit at the table. In fact, after drinking one mug full of Peacock brew, Mary tells David that he is wearing a beautiful suit.

In only a few minutes, there are three distinct conversations going on at the table. Robert and Michael talk together. They are happy being out with their superiors. Then Ken and I talk to each other, although we hardly say anything. We are just watching the others. Mark, David, and Mary are having their own private conversation.

Ken flags down a waitress and asks for another pitcher of beer. "Peacock Brew," he specifies. The waitress comes back in about two minutes. It is an enjoyable and gratifying sight to see her bring the peacock pitcher filled with the dark golden liquid.

There is something about Mark's friend David that I don't like. By looking at his suit, I believe that he makes tons of money. My jealousy is not a pretty thing. Am I that shallow? I suppose that I am. All of a sudden, this David, the corporate lawyer, gets up and says,

"It was nice meeting you Mary. Unfortunately, I have to meet a client for a dinner uptown. I'll speak to you later Mark. Good night."

With that, David and his expensive suit are gone. David's sudden departure from the table leaves Mary visibly upset. Mary calls David a snob, even though Mark, David's close friend, is at the table. Mark says nothing to Mary in response. Would I have had the moral courage to say something back to Mary if she had just called a close friend of mine a snob? Who knows? Ken and I simultaneously stand up and walk to the bathroom. The Peacock is crowded as we walk there. Inside the bathroom, I notice how few people wash their hands. There is laughter when we get back to the table.

"We will have another pitcher of Peacock Brew," Mark says to a passing waitress.

The waitress arrives quickly with a glistening peacock pitcher.

## Chapter 15

The peacock pitchers keep rolling along and, in no time, David, the corporate lawyer, is out of our collective memory. At 8:00 p.m., Robert and Michael leave for the night, and Mark leaves shortly thereafter. Ken, Mary, and I remain at the Peacock together. Our peacock mugs are now only half full. The three of us do not normally socialize together, except at office parties.

"I had a strange dream last night," I say.

"What was it about?" Ken asks.

"I had a dream about some bread."

"You dreamed that you were bread?" Mary asks.

"No. I dreamed about some bread. One night last week I went to a grocery store. It was a store I rarely go to. I wanted bread and I bought a loaf of bread that they make there."

I continue,

"I brought the bread home and started eating it. It was good. I mean really good. It was slightly sweet because it was flavored with honey. It was so good that I ate the entire loaf. Last night that bread was all over my dream. I don't even know what my dream was about, but everywhere I was, so was this bread."

"What an interesting dream," Mary says sarcastically.

Ken chimes in,

"Now this bread, was it good looking? Did you sleep with the bread? Did you take the bread dancing?"

Mary continues,

"What happened to the bread? What was its name? What was the bread wearing?"

"Or was it naked?" Ken interrupts.

In defense of my dream, I continue,

"I know it is unusual to dream about bread. But you have to understand how delicious and addictive the bread was the night I ate it. I don't know what happened to the bread in my dream. It just floated around. Wherever I went, the bread was close by. That's it. That was my dream."

"Did you at least get to eat the bread in your dream?" Mary asks.

She sounds sincere in her question.

"I don't think I ate the bread. I just saw the whole uneaten bread floating around."

Ken asks,

"Was it a good bread or a bad bread? Was it the devil disguised as an innocent bread?"

I don't know why I told them about my bread dream. It is not an adventurous-type of dream that a person brags about. It was embarrassing telling them about it. Who cares? I'm craving the bread just thinking about it. Maybe the bread really is evil and it will taunt me for the rest of my life. I can just imagine that the night Bench Woman calls me on the telephone to see her, I would tell her, "No, I'm happy just watching television here with my bread." Perhaps there will come a time when Bench Woman and I will be stranded on a deserted tropical island. Instead of having any desire for me, all she would want to do is cook bread. Bench Woman would say to me, "I have no time for you Matt, I must bake bread."

"We'll have another peacock pitcher," Ken barks.

Mary suggests that after we finish the upcoming pitcher we go out for dinner.

Ken and I concur. While the Peacock has undeniably become an improved place with the addition of the electric peacocks on the wall, the peacock-shaped pitchers and mugs, and the Peacock Brew, the place would be better still if it served food. Perhaps they should serve up some peacocks? No. Peacocks might be on the endangered species list. Is that fair? Even though a chicken may be a member of a species that is not endangered, the slaughter of an individual chicken must hurt the chicken. Simply because there are many chickens does not mean that an individual chicken wants to get killed any more than an individual peacock.

"Will you be all right if we find a place to eat that serves bread, or will that be too painful for you? I don't want you to have any more bad dreams," Ken says to me.

I ignore Ken, who doesn't understand that my bread dream was not a bad dream. To the contrary, to see the bread floating in space was soothing. The bread was benevolent as it floated around. The three of us leave the Peacock for dinner in Chinatown.

"What should we eat? We should get a few different things and split them."

"Let's get dumplings."

"I hate dumplings."

"Let's get a shrimp dish."

"I think I see a mouse on the floor," Ken says in a calm voice.

63

"Really?" Mary asks.

"I think I saw a mouse behind the radiator, but I don't see it anymore."

At most other restaurants, the sighting of a mouse would cause quite a commotion. Yet here, at the Fat Chin Wing Restaurant in Chinatown, if a mouse is out of sight it is out of mind. I suppose that is because we all assume that there will be mice, rats, and other assorted creatures here in this small restaurant in this very old building. After conferring with each other, Mary tells the waiter,

"We'll have two won ton soups and one egg drop soup. Also, a large order of spare ribs, one order of beef chow fun, and one order of General Chang's chicken. And we'll each have a beer."

Mary ordered the beers for us, without asking, although it is fine with me and I'm sure it is fine with Ken. We all feel the influence of the Peacock Brew we drank earlier. The soup arrives with the beer. While this Chinese beer is good, it is no match for the thrill we felt when drinking the Peacock Brew in little peacock mugs.

Out of the blue, Mary tells us about her past relationship with a man named Adam. I met this Adam at the office Christmas party last year. I don't particularly remember him, except that I recall he was very skinny. Apparently, Mary and Adam were close to getting engaged when, three months ago, Adam, without consulting Mary, accepted a new job in South Carolina and just walked out of her life. Two weeks ago she saw Adam, who was back in New York. Adam told her that he was not suited for South Carolina life. Adam also told Mary that he had fallen in love with a divorced older woman in his new building since coming back to New York one month ago.

"Adam told me that this woman is fifteen years older than he is. What could be going through his idiotic mind?"

"What about you Matt?" Mary asks. "Are you seeing anyone?"

"No," I say.

Without listening, she continues, "You and that skinny secretary Claire seem pretty friendly. Is anything going on between the two of you? I saw her speaking with you in your office with your door closed."

It was nasty the way Mary referred to Claire as the "skinny secretary." Mary must hate all skinny people because her former boyfriend Adam was so skinny.

Do I like skinny people or fat people better? I don't think that I care about a person's weight. It may depend on how fat or how skinny the person is that we are talking about. But why should that matter? If someone is so emaciated that all their bones show, would I like that person less? Or would I like that person more? What about fat people? Do I like them? If someone weighs 600 pounds, am I more likely to become a friend or do I avoid that person? There is more of that person to like. What about myself? I am becoming chubby. Bench Woman is the perfect weight though. But what if I married Bench Woman and she became incredibly fat or incredibly skinny during our marriage? Would I still love a too fat or too skinny Bench Woman?

"Claire and I are just friendly at work," I say in response to Mary's inquiry. I think to myself that my relationship with Claire may change after we go to the auto show this Sunday and then to the wedding next Saturday night.

Mary then asks Ken if he has a girlfriend.

## Chapter 16

After Ken, in numbing detail, tells us--mostly he tells Mary--about his most recent unsuccessful relationship with someone named Joan and his quest for a suitable woman, the conversation turns to the usual work-related subjects. The spare ribs are especially juicy, and they taste spicier than typical Chinese spare ribs. They taste especially good with the beer. I am hungry and see that Ken and Mary must be hungry too. We devour the food with the enthusiasm of lions after a deer kill. Ken is by far the biggest and heaviest of the three of us, but he does not seem to eat any more than I do. Ken is 6'1" or 6'2" and must weigh over 200 pounds.

"Ken, how much do you weigh?" I ask.

"Why?"

"Just curious."

"About 230."

Ken's big all over. He's much bigger than I am at 165 pounds and huge compared to Mary who is no taller than 5'2" and thin. I think that I am eating more than Ken is eating.

We sit contentedly after eating every speck of food. The conversation comes to a halt as we begin digestion. Upon paying the bill, Mary announces that she is going to hail a cab to take her home to Brooklyn Heights. Mary says good-bye, leaving Ken and me in the middle of Chinatown.

Ken asks me if I have any plans for the weekend. I hesitate, but then I tell him that I am going to the auto show with Claire on Sunday. I stress to him that we are only going together because

Claire wants to look at the new model cars to help her make a decision for her upcoming new car purchase. Ken does not know that Claire and I are going to a wedding together next Saturday. Ken tells me that he has no definite plans for the weekend.

We are in no mood to drink more tonight. We buy a newspaper to look at the movie listings. As we sift through the newspaper at the corner of Canal and Mulberry Streets, an airplane flies directly overhead. It seems abnormally low and loud.

"You have nothing to do, right?"

"Yeah," Ken replies.

"I'm not meeting Claire until Sunday morning and don't have anything to do until then. Let's go to an airport and take a flight somewhere, anywhere. We'll get there late tonight and come back tomorrow night. We'll take the cheapest flight available to anywhere."

With that plan in mind, we withdraw money from a bank cash machine. I take $150 in spending money. I will pay for my airplane ticket with my credit card. This is crazy, but we don't care. We head by cab to Newark Airport, which Ken believes is closer to us than either LaGuardia or Kennedy Airports.

We book a 10:45 p.m. flight to Las Vegas that will arrive in Las Vegas at around 1:00 in the morning, Las Vegas time. We book a return flight leaving at 9:00 p.m. tomorrow night that arrives back at Newark at 5:00 Sunday morning, eastern time. This schedule gives us nineteen hours to spend in Las Vegas. It will also give me enough time on Sunday morning to go back to my apartment for a shave and shower before meeting Claire for breakfast and then the auto show.

The large plane is crowded. I am sitting in a middle seat. I'd rather be sitting next to a window. Ken is seated at an aisle. I'm next to Ken, and there is a man, I'd guess he's in his early 60s, seated next to me. He looks pleasant and we say hello to each other. I like take-off. It is an amazing miracle. Are there any other kinds of miracles? This plane is just a piece of metal, yet when it hits a certain speed, its wings move just a little and it goes into the air. It actually flies. A heavy hunk of metal, filled with fuel, people, luggage, equipment and a lot of other things that I don't know about, and it manages to fly through the air without anything holding it up. No strings, nothing. Why doesn't it just fall down? Actually, I think this plane is falling down. No. There is just some turbulence. We are moving at hundreds of miles per hour, yet it feels as if we are hardly moving at all. The flight attendants are nice, but Loretta, our flight attendant, is especially nice as she hands us our chicken breast dinner. I could get a better dinner at the Pasture, but I'm not hungry anyway. It was not too long ago that we had the Chinese food. Loretta gives us a very nice smile as she hands Ken a soda and me an orange juice, which Ken and I use to toast our unexpected cross-country flight.

The man to my right, Sam, is visiting his recently married son and daughter-in-law who moved to Las Vegas a few months ago. This is his first time out there. He is not too talkative. He looks tired. Indeed, he informs me that he is very tired and only took this late flight because of a last minute change of plans. Sam, I notice, although not speaking much, has a wonderful speaking voice. It is not too deep, not too high, but it is remarkably soothing. He should work in radio. Actually, maybe he shouldn't work in radio because his soothing voice would make drivers drowsy, creating chaos on the roadways.

Ken and I are on an airplane going almost the entire length of the country and we don't even have the smallest of suitcases. Nothing. We are going to arrive in Las Vegas with just the money in our pockets and the clothes on our backs. It is like we are pioneers, except that we are wearing the suits that we wore to work and I imagine that most of the pioneers were not wearing suits and ties. Although I would be more comfortable in casual clothes, I believe that I have a better chance of winning money at a blackjack table in a suit. It gives the impression to everyone that I came to play and win, and that I am not just some guy with lousy clothes. The mental attitude is half the battle with blackjack. In fact, it is more than half the battle.

We fly over the Great Lakes. The captain announces that if we look out of the window on one side of the plane we can see the pockets of light that comprise Chicago and Detroit, and if we look out the other side we can see Milwaukee. Or did he say one side is Chicago and Milwaukee and the other side is Detroit? And we recently passed Buffalo, Pittsburgh, and Cleveland. Millions of people live their lives in these places, but from up here, each city is just a small cluster of lights surrounded by darkness. From up here, we can see that so much of the country is

70

fields or countryside, without any light at night. I wish I were sitting next to a window. I do, however, get a glimpse of one Midwestern city when I walk down the aisle of the plane to go to the bathroom. Where does everything go after it is flushed down an airplane's toilet? That is the age old question, or at least the age old question as long as there have been airplanes. The waste must get put in some sort of storage. Maybe it falls out of the plane, but because of the plane's altitude and speed, the waste must somehow disintegrate before hitting land. That cannot be correct. All the human waste from the people of this flight must be stored somewhere in the plane. What do they do with it when the plane lands? It must be treated with chemicals.

I fall asleep for a short time, and awake disoriented. Ken is awake and we look at each other.

"This is a little crazy," I say.

Ken nods in agreement. He informs me that he is not much of a gambler. He went to Atlantic City only once in his life and played the slot machines for a few minutes.

"Maybe we should go to prostitutes while we are there. It is legal, isn't it?" Ken half asks, half states.

"I don't know. On the one hand I'd like to go, but on the other hand I don't want to go."

"We can think about it when we get there."

I can just imagine us going to a bordello in the middle of the Nevada desert called the Desert House. An older woman would put me in a small red room with a small bed. A voice over a loud speaker would tell me to take off all of my clothes. The lights would be dimmed so that I'd barely be able to see anything. Someone would enter the room and would start to take her clothes off. Then a bright light would shine on her and I would see that it is Bench Woman. I would quiver in disbelief that the beautiful Bench Woman is selling her body at the Desert House. Bench Woman would say, "I have followed you all night, Matt, from the Peacock Pub to Chinatown and now here. I just got a job with the Desert House tonight so that I could be with you." That is not likely to happen.

The plane, thankfully, lands uneventfully at 4:15 a.m. on my watch, which is 1:15 a.m. Las Vegas time. Ken and I hail a cab at the airport. I ask the driver to take us to the Coyote Hotel and Casino. Why did I say the Coyote? I've never been to Las Vegas, but I've heard of that hotel before. I have seen pictures of the Coyote Hotel in brochures. It has bright electric coyotes outside, reminiscent of the electric peacocks adorning the walls of the Peacock Pub, except on a much larger scale.

The streets are packed with people on the famous Las Vegas strip, even though it is now after 1:30 in the morning. The hotels are incredibly bright and glitzy.

"Here you are guys. We have arrived at the Coyote Hotel and Casino. By the way, do you have luggage?"

We get out of the cab and give the driver a big tip. Ken tells the driver that we have no luggage as we are only in town until our flight tomorrow night, nineteen hours from now.

"Good luck," our driver says.

We look in front of us and see the bright hotel lights shining down the strip.  The otherwise dark desert night sky in the distance is lit with a sliver of a crescent moon overhead.  We enter the Coyote Hotel and Casino.

## Chapter 17

The Coyote buzzes with activity, even at 2:00 in the morning. Ken and I are both exhilarated to be in Las Vegas and exhausted. It is 5:00 in the morning New York time. We enter the casino and I lose two quarters in a slot machine. Ken puts one quarter in a machine and wins five.

"This is easy," Ken declares confidently.

Ken puts another two quarters in the slot machines and loses. He puts in another quarter and wins ten in return.

"Watch this," Ken says with a laugh. He puts a quarter in the slot machine. The quarters that he just won disappear into the slot machine in the next minute.

"I hate gambling," Ken says.

After Ken's gambling glory and defeat come and go, we sit down at the hotel's coffee shop to map out a plan for our stay. After very hot, but tasteless coffees, and some filling blueberry muffins, we get a room. Our plan is to sleep for a few hours, wake up early, and then win money--a lot of it. If we get up at 8:00 in the morning, we will have had almost five hours of sleep, which will leave us with 12 hours to conquer the casinos before taking our return flight.

We get room 1108 in the Coyote for $130 for the night. It is a good sized room with two double beds and a big television. I wish that I had a toothbrush or toothpaste because I have a peculiar taste in my mouth. We are both very tired. Ken intelligently calls the front desk to give us a wake-up call at 8:00 a.m. It would be stupid to sleep all day tomorrow, our only day in Las Vegas. Once on the bed, I fall asleep in one minute.

The wake-up call comes at exactly 8:00 a.m. To my surprise I had slept the night in my suit pants, with my shirt and tie still on. Although I want to take a shower, I don't want to wear this same suit afterwards. I also desperately want to brush my teeth now. My breath is vile. When I was a kid I never woke up with such a bad taste in my mouth. What is changing in my body that now I need to brush my teeth immediately upon waking up? Ken, who was smart enough to take off his suit, does not wake up from the wake-up call.

I leave the room with Ken still in bed. I go to the hotel lobby to see if there is a store to buy toothpaste, a toothbrush, and a comb. There is a small drugstore in the lobby. I buy two toothbrushes, a blue one for me, a green one for Ken, a mint gel toothpaste, and a comb.

"What's the weather going to be like today?" I ask the 50ish year-old woman behind the counter.

She is amused by my question. She reminds me that it is July in Las Vegas.

"It's going to be sunny and hot. It will be over 100 degrees today. But you're from the East aren't you? Are you from New York?"

I answer yes.

This woman, who tells me her name is Maggie, says,

"It's hot here. But for someone like you from the East Coast, you won't feel so hot. It's dry heat, not humid. But that suit you're wearing won't keep you cool, no matter how dry it is."

I pay for the items and say good-bye to Maggie, who in turn wishes me luck. She convinces me to go to the hotel's gift and clothes store right across the lobby to buy some clothes, so that I don't have to wear the suit all day. Unfortunately, the store, called the Dressed Coyote, opens at 9:00 a.m. When I get back to the room Ken is still in bed, but he is awake. We decide that we will eat breakfast, buy some lighter clothes to wear, and then shower. Then we will win money. I feel like a new man after brushing my teeth vigorously.

Wearing our suits, Ken and I sit in a booth at the busy Coyote Coffee Shop. Ken's American cheese and ham omelette, and my Swiss cheese and onion omelette, are mediocre. The orange juice is good though. It is 9:15 a.m. and already the coffee shop is busy. Our waitress is wearing a name-tag that says Martha. Martha looks suspiciously like Maggie, the woman who sold me the toothpaste this morning.

"Martha," I ask, "do you know Maggie, the woman in the drugstore?"

"Why yes, I do. We are first cousins. We have lived here in Las Vegas since our families moved together from Texas when we were small children. Both Maggie and I got married and stayed here."

"You and Maggie look similar," I tell Martha.

Martha and Maggie do not look exactly alike, but their family resemblance is evident. They are both big-boned and graying, but Martha, our waitress, is taller than Maggie. They look attractive and healthy. They were probably gorgeous brides.

"Would you like more coffee?"

Ken and I nod affirmatively. Martha pours in

piping hot coffee and places the bill on the table.

"If you need anything more, let me know. Enjoy your stay," she adds smiling.

After I finish my fourth and Ken finishes his third refill of coffee, we say good-bye to Martha for the third time, leave the coffee shop, and enter the Dressed Coyote. With credit card in hand, I buy one pair of sneakers, one pair of khaki pants, two T-shirts, and two pairs of shorts. One of the T-shirts shows the desert and says "Nevada" on it and the other one has a scene of the Las Vegas strip at night.

We leave the store and walk past the pool, which is crowded despite it being only 10:00 a.m. Ken suggests that we sit outside by the pool for a bit, take showers, and then devote the afternoon to winning money. That is a good strategy. We go upstairs to change our clothes.

It is hot out. However, as Maggie said, it is a dry heat. I proudly wear my desert scene T-shirt and new shorts and Ken wears the "Hoover Dam" shorts that he just purchased at the Dressed Coyote. Some early swimmers are getting drinks at the pool's bar. I take off my shirt as I lay on the lounge chair. I am a little embarrassed at how pale I am. Ken, on the other hand, while not exactly tan, is not as blindingly white as I am. People need to use sunglasses just to look in my direction. If it weren't so hot, people sitting here by the pool would think that I am a mound of snow. My dark chest hair keeps me from looking totally white. In reality, I am not so white, but the people who are sitting in lounge chairs in my general vicinity are quite tan, making me look lighter by comparison.

It is incredibly warm for so early in the morning. To my right sits a girl, between sixteen and eighteen years old, with a woman who must be her mother. Listening to them speak, they sound as if they are from the South. I think I hear one of them say the word Macon. Or are they talking about bacon? Both mother and daughter are quite tan. The mother's skin looks like leather. The daughter's skin still looks like skin, but it is so tanned that one day it will likely look just as leathery as her mother's skin. I'm suddenly feeling a healthy pride about my pale skin. I take a deep breath expanding my chest and triumphantly look at my skin that looks like snow, but not like leather.

The mother and daughter look this way. I believe they are talking about Ken. I think the mother likes Ken. The mother is probably about forty years old, but in a peculiar way, looks both older and younger because of her skin. Ken is thirty-two years old. The difference in their ages is not enormous. Ken, who is big and healthy looking, does not notice their stares.

I ask Ken if he wants a drink from the bar. He tells me that he is going to go for a dip in the pool and that he would like a beer. Ken asks me if I can hold onto his wallet while he goes into the pool.

A beer this early in the morning is not appetizing to me. Yet for some reason, when I get to the bar I say "two beers please." The bartender is a tall attractive blondish woman in her twenties. She looks to be quite athletic and solid all over. She is not too thin, not too heavy. She smiles and hands me the two beers with her long strong pale arm. It is

78

surprising to see that her skin is the same light color as mine. She wears a name-tag that says "Michelle." There is something familiar about her, but I cannot place it. I sheepishly rationalize to her about having a beer so early in the morning. She tells me to enjoy myself while I am on vacation. She suggests that I take side trips to The Hoover Dam or the Grand Canyon. I respond by telling her that I am leaving tonight and will not have time to take those trips. She smiles and tells me to win a lot of money.

"I'll take those trips on my next visit."

"Good luck," she says.

Walking away from her I realize that she reminds me of Maggie, the drugstore lady, and Martha, our waitress. She is much younger. I go back to the bar.

"Michelle, can I ask you something?"

"Sure."

"I met two women here, Maggie and Martha. You are much younger than they are, but you remind me of them. Do you know them?"

Michelle smiles, "Maggie is my mother and Martha is my aunt."

When I arrive back at our chairs, I see Ken standing in the shallow end of the pool talking with the daughter from the leathery mother daughter pair. The mother is sitting in her chair sipping what appears to be orange juice. I feel like an alcoholic as I sip this beer so early in the morning. Most of the other people sitting by the pool are drinking either juice or coffee. But the beer tastes good in the early morning hot desert sun of Las Vegas. Ken comes out of the pool and so does the daughter, who, Ken tells me, is named Pam. Pam and Ken say good-bye to each other as Ken sits in his chair and Pam goes to sit with her mother.

"Thanks for the drink," Ken says to me.

Pam and her mother get up and leave. Pam waves good-bye to Ken. Ken tells me that Pam's mother and father were recently divorced and that Pam is going into her senior year of high school in North Carolina.

"Pam's a nice girl," Ken begins. "I'm thirty-two and she's seventeen. We are in Las Vegas. I'm going to go to a Las Vegas chapel and elope with her. I need a change in my life. What do you think of that?"

Ken continues,

"She told me that she never liked her mother or her father. Since their divorce she hates them more than ever. In the few minutes we spent together in the pool I think that she wanted me as both a husband and a father. She has a cute body too. She would probably do anything for me just so that she wouldn't have to be with her mother. Don't worry, Matt, I'm not serious. I'm not going to elope or even see her anymore."

Ken didn't need to tell me to relax. I did not believe for a second that Ken was going to elope with Pam after a five minute conversation in a pool. And it would be none of my business anyway, although I probably would try to talk him out of it. If Ken eloped with Pam, this seventeen year old from North Carolina, it might be a good thing, who knows? When he'd be forty, she'd be twenty-five. What's age anyway? Bench Woman will look just as wonderful at sixty as she does now. How old is Bench Woman?

80

Does Bench Woman's timeless beauty really have an age?

I step slowly into the pool's water, which cools my skin that has been heated by the strong Nevada sun. The world is wonderful with the blue sky, the heat all around, and the cool water. The water's temperature is just right. It is slightly cool and it mixes perfectly with the hot air. I like the dry heat.

## Chapter 18

When I get back to the room, after sitting in the hot but dry morning desert air, the cool water of the shower invigorates me as it hits my skin. I could stay under this water all day, but obviously I will not do so. Ken still has to take a shower and there is money to be won, and perhaps other things to be done while in Las Vegas. We haven't again mentioned going to prostitutes, but in the hotel lobby we picked up a local paper and saw advertisements for various "ranches" outside of the city in the desert. Maybe after we gamble for a few hours we will think about whether we should go or not.

This shower water is wonderful. There is tremendous water pressure. Where is the water coming from? This city is in the middle of the desert. I suppose the water is irrigated from somewhere, but where? It looks as if there is only desert surrounding this city for hundreds of miles. Are there underground pipes running hundreds of miles? It rarely rains here, yet this entire city is able to shower, swim, and of course drink water as if it rains everyday. The water faucets flow as freely here in Las Vegas as they do at home. People are mostly water. I am mostly water. Bench Woman is mostly water, although she is of course made from the best bottled water that exists. Dogs, cats, and cows are mostly water. As I towel myself dry and look at myself through the steam of the bathroom mirror, I see that I got sunburned from sitting poolside for the hour and a half.

I'm not going to shave. That is good because I

don't have a razor blade or shaving cream with me. I like the pair of pants that I bought downstairs. But because of the heat I put on one of the new shorts that I purchased at the Dressed Coyote. I also put on my other new shirt that I bought there, along with my new sneakers. The colorful shirt looks good with the shorts. I look good with my sunburned unshaven face, and my new shirt, shorts, and sneakers. Since I only have the dress socks that I wore to work, I will not wear any socks. Socks are not necessary with this outfit anyway.

Ken is taking a very long shower. Just because he's a big guy, does that mean his shower should take longer? I suppose it does because there is more of him to clean. Is how long a person showers related to a person's height and weight? It cannot be. Although, if a person is only four feet tall and weighs eighty pounds, then there is much less to clean as compared with a seven foot tall person weighing three hundred pounds. But within the range of average sized people, which both Ken and I fall into, I don't believe height and weight are related to time of shower. I can't blame Ken for taking such a long shower because the shower in this hotel room is fantastic. My shower was longer than my usual pre-work morning shower.

Ken and I, both now wearing our recently purchased clothes from the Dressed Coyote, enter the casino floor. The place resounds with activity at 12:30 in the afternoon. Ken wanders to the sports betting area of the casino floor. I go to the blackjack tables. To my surprise, although there are crowds everywhere, there are some available seats.

I want to stick with my theory of avoiding tables with beautiful dealers. That theory may not be valid any longer since I did win money in Atlantic City with the beautiful Jan English as the dealer. But still, in Atlantic City I started my play with Mao Chin as the dealer. Jan English came later. If I began play with Jan at the table I may have lost all my money very quickly. Why tempt fate?

I hear a familiar sounding voice nearby but I cannot place it. I know that it is not Ken's voice. Who else do I know in Las Vegas? I must not know the voice very well. If I did, I'm sure I'd recognize it right away. It's a pleasurable voice. It's soothing and deep, but not too deep. This is mystifying. I feel a tap on my left shoulder.

"Matt."

I turn around and see Sam, who sat next to me on the airplane. It was his soothing voice that I have been hearing for the past few seconds. Sam is with a man and woman. They must be his son and daughter-in-law.

"What are you doing here in this casino?" I ask him.

"As I told you, I'm visiting my children. Instead of cooking me a warm breakfast at home, they took me to this hotel's breakfast buffet. Now I'm going to watch my son, the gambler, play craps. This is my son Paul and my daughter-in-law Stacy."

Sam introduces me to Paul and Stacy and tells me that he likes what he has seen of Las Vegas. Sam's son and daughter-in-law live a few miles from "The Strip" in a quiet residential neighborhood. Sam tells me about his first morning in Las Vegas, but I barely hear his words. Instead I just listen to how he says things. His voice and unhurried manner of speaking are hypnotic.

"Good luck Matt. Go back to New York rich."

"I'll try. Nice seeing you."

Sam, Paul, and Stacy walk away. I again stake out the blackjack tables, looking for the perfect table. Before selecting a table, Ken joins me.

"I'll play blackjack with you," Ken tells me.

We sit down at a table with two sisters who are from Detroit, Jane and Irene, and their friend, also named Irene. The dealer is named Mark, originally from Baltimore. He is nice enough. Obviously he is not like the beautiful dealer Jan English. I will be able to concentrate fully with him as the dealer. There is a $5 minimum bet requirement at this table. We are allowed to place larger bets. The maximum bet at this table is $100. I will not be placing such a large bet. Ken gets blackjack. I lose my first four hands.

A crowd gathers about halfway down the casino floor, near the crap tables. After I lose a hand with 17 and Ken wins with a 20, Ken and I leave the table to get a closer look at the commotion. Something has happened to someone at another table. Casino personnel and an emergency medical team swarm the area. A person is on the floor, but we can't see who it is because of all the people gathered. I don't want to get in the way by getting too close. It's good to see the emergency crew spring into action so quickly. Two people standing next to me say that the person apparently had a heart attack.

At exactly the same instant, Ken and I see Sam, my airplane neighbor, on the ground suffering the heart attack. Except for the medical people, I can clearly see Paul and Stacy. The two of them are holding each other. In a minute, Sam is taken away, with his son and daughter-in-law following behind.

Ken and I say nothing. I feel terrible for Sam. I barely know him, but he was a good man to sit next to on the airplane ride. Is it fair that Sam goes to Las Vegas to visit his family and then suffers a heart attack while gambling? I just spoke with him. He looked fine.

I am in no mood to play blackjack at this moment. There is nothing I can do to help Sam, and that knowledge makes me feel worse. What good am I if I can't help my airplane friend Sam, a man with such a wonderful speaking voice? I got a look at Sam's son Paul, and Paul's wife Stacy, as Sam was being tended to by the emergency crew. They looked so frightened, but more than that, they were helpless. That is what made it most painful. Even looking at them for a quick second, you could see in their faces how helpless they knew they were. If I, practically a stranger to Sam, feel useless during this emergency, I imagine how worthless Paul must feel watching his father suffer a heart attack before his very eyes as an emergency crew is needed to give his father a chance at life.

Ken and I leave the Coyote and walk down the famed Las Vegas Strip. We enter the Lucky Wheel Hotel and Casino. This casino, though smaller, is also busy. There is a loud constant ringing from the slot machines. Ken goes into a candy store in the hotel lobby to look at newspaper headlines and I go to the men's room. There is a washroom attendant handing out washcloths. This way after one does his business and then presumably, or hopefully, washes his hands, a dry cloth is available. Upon entering the large bathroom, I hear two men talking. They are unfamiliar to me, but one of them, a man dressed in casual but neat attire, has a voice very similar to Sam's deep, soothing voice. This man's voice, which is speaking about his bad luck at the roulette wheel, is not as soothing as Sam's voice, but it is similar.

I want to try and find Sam in the hospital and see how he is doing. But Sam, having just had a heart attack, does not want or care about a visit from me, a virtual stranger from his airplane ride. Sam may not survive the heart attack. If he dies, what happens to his wonderful voice? Is it gone from the music of the world, lost forever? Perhaps parts of his voice would spread out to people that remain in the living world.

Ken and I are hungry, so we go into a small restaurant in the Lucky Wheel. A young waiter named Mitch, no more than twenty years old, greets us and places down menus. I order a grilled American cheese sandwich and an iced tea. Ken orders a turkey breast sandwich and a soda. As Mitch takes down our order, I can't help but notice his physical resemblance to Martha, Maggie, and Michelle, the three related employees from the Coyote. I ask Mitch if he is related to them. As I speak, he coughs. He then replies, in what I can't help but notice is a remarkably tranquil and pleasant voice,

"Excuse me. I just had a funny feeling in my throat. Now, what did you ask?"

"Do you have any relatives that work at the Coyote?"

"Not that I know of," Mitch replies. "Why do you ask?"

"No reason."

With that, Mitch takes our orders. Ken and I relax in our chairs inside the busy restaurant filled with gamblers, and we wait for our food.

# Chapter 19

We leave the Lucky Wheel Hotel and Casino after the rather bland sandwiches. The afternoon Nevada sun beats down on us with all its power when we step outside. There is not one cloud in the deep blue sky. It is hot, as evidenced by the temperature sign at the Las Vegas Savings Bank, which reads 104 degrees. However, as Maggie the shopkeeper reminded me, it is a dry heat, not a humid one. If it were 104 degrees at home it would be unbearable, but here, in this desert city, 104 degrees does not feel that bad. Granted, I don't know how I'd feel if I played a set of tennis in this heat, but I feel comfortable walking outside on the Las Vegas strip in my new clothes. I do not feel the need to go right inside and seek air conditioned comfort. In fact, I like this heat. It's hot, but dry. As I stroll in the 104 degree Nevada summer air, I am hot, but I feel good.

It is already 2:30 in the afternoon. What happened to Sam has dampened my spirit. The hours until our flight home dwindle rapidly. Ken and I stand in front of the next casino on the strip called "The Fortune Maker." Before we go inside, we look at the local newspaper and see an advertisement for the Rocking Horse Lounge, which is a strip bar. I want to do something mindless. Ken says that he needs a drink more than he needs to hear the sound of slot machines. He says that he would welcome the opportunity to be served by scantily-clad women at the Rocking Horse. Ken hails a cab.

"To the Rocking Horse Lounge."

The driver nods. We head to the Rocking

Horse. The driver tells us that the Rocking Horse is across town and is a favorite with out-of-towners. Out of the cab's window, we catch glimpses of the gray desert expanse beyond the city of Las Vegas. Ken asks me if I'd like to have this cab take us out into the desert to see some scenery instead of going straight to the Rocking Horse. That sounds like a fine idea. I have never been in the desert. We ask the cabbie, named Andy, to drive us one half hour into the desert and then take us back to the city. We agree to pay him $70 for the one hour of driving. It is well worth $35 each for us to see the desert. We will still have the chance afterwards to see the women who dance at the Rocking Horse.

Only minutes out of the city, it is as though we are on a different planet. We drive into the desert towards Death Valley. It is flat and a grayish light brown for as far as I can see. It is really flat, like a table, except for the mountains in the distance, and there is less color than I have ever seen. It is beautiful, ugly, boring, and enchanting all at once. Except for the small cactus plants and other small grass-like plants, this looks, I imagine, like the Moon or Mars. Compared to the greenness of the East, this is not pretty. But it is dramatic in a way that I will not soon forget. It is even somewhat frightening. We sit in a nice air conditioned cab, yet it is over 100 degrees outside in what looks like a lifeless gray pancake. To get stuck out in the middle of this desert would mean almost certain death if no one were around to save you. After 20 minutes of driving into the desert, I ask Andy to pull over so that we can experience the flatness, the heat, and the color of the desert while outside of the car.

Andy obliges, and Ken and I walk outside. How wonderful it would be to be here with Bench Woman. Bench Woman's light skin surrounded by her very long black hair would stand in dramatic contrast to the gray desert floor. If I were here with Bench Woman, the desert floor beneath our feet, hot enough to fry eggs, would require us to take off all our clothes. We would walk hand in hand. Bench Woman and I would, of course, keep on our footwear, since the heat of the ground would be too hot for our bare feet.

"Want to keep going, or should we head back to town?" Andy asks us.

Ken and I confer, and tell Andy that while we have enjoyed seeing the desert and wish we could see more, we need to get back to town. We decide not to go to the Rocking Horse, but rather, we ask Andy to take us back to The Strip, where we will go to a casino and gamble.

Andy takes us back to the Coyote. Despite the bad memory of Sam having his heart attack at this casino, and the fact that we already checked out of our room here since checkout time was noon, the Coyote feels to us as if it is our home base. It is 3:30 p.m. and we have hardly gambled. The drive in the desert has made us hungry, so we go to the Coyote Coffee Shop for a light snack. There we will plan the remaining hours of our stay in Las Vegas.

We sit down and are greeted by Martha, our breakfast waitress. She warmly asks us how our day has been. Not wanting to discuss it in detail, we tell her, briefly but pleasantly, that our day has been enjoyable.

"I'll have a blueberry muffin and coffee," I say. Ken orders the same.

"Matt," Ken starts, "we left the room with our suits and other new clothes up there. I totally forgot about the clothes when we gave back the hotel key."

Ken is right. After taking wonderful showers, we simply returned the room key, checked out, and completely forgot about our suits and the other new clothes we bought earlier this morning at the Dressed Coyote.

"Here are your muffins and coffee," Martha says cheerily, totally unaware that her customers' clothes may be missing.

"Let's just eat these muffins and then we'll see if our clothes are still in the room or if they are somewhere else or lost," Ken wisely says.

Just like when we first arrived to Las Vegas in the middle of the night and went to the Coyote Coffee Shop and had muffins, these muffins are quite filling. However, they are not fresh. Also, some of the excitement that accompanied our first visit to the Coyote Coffee Shop is now absent. We leave the coffee shop and Ken sees the tanned and leathery mother daughter pair from the pool this morning enter the Dressed Coyote. Ken, who spoke to the daughter at the pool this morning, wants to say hello to them. I tell him that at 4:30 p.m., which is half an hour from now, I'll meet him in the casino, right next to the coyote statue. I go to the front desk to try and track down our clothes.

"May I help you?"

"Yes. My friend and I were in Room 1108 last

92

night and we checked out this morning. We forgot to take our clothes with us when we checked out. We only have the clothes, no luggage."

"Let me see."

The woman behind the desk is about forty years old and named Marie. She is blondish and big boned. I assume that she is related to Martha, Maggie, and Michelle.

"No one has yet checked into that room today. The room has either been cleaned or is now being cleaned. You can go upstairs. If the room is open, you can check if your clothes are there. If the clothes are not there, I will have someone find where they were put. You have no luggage, but you have clothes. Let me guess. You came here last night on the spur of the moment with just the clothes on your back, and you bought some clothes here. Am I right?"

"You are exactly right," I reply. I am in awe of Marie's accuracy. Is she a psychic?

"You know," Marie continues, "the man who is now my husband came to Las Vegas from Delaware for just one night with a friend. That was sixteen years ago."

I go up to Room 1108 to see if the clothes are still there. The door to the room is closed. But I turn the door knob and feel that the door is not locked. I push open the door, hoping to see our clothes there. I walk in and see something different than our clothes. Two naked women are on one of the beds together caressing. They are hotel maids. Their cleaning wagons with their cleaning products are inside the room. In reality, one of them is not totally without clothes. Around her neck, she is wearing my tie that

93

I wore to work on Friday. She tied it well, much better than I tied it on me. There are awkward smiles all around as the one wearing my tie asks me, with what sounds to me like a Mexican accent, what I am doing here.

"I was in this room last night and left the clothes here by mistake."

Smiling, the woman wearing my tie tells me that she cleaned the room and folded all the clothes, suits and all, in a neat pile. She says she was going to bring them down to the hotel desk when she and her friend were done "cleaning." I thank her sincerely. The clothes are, in fact, folded in a very neat pile.

"Is this your tie?" she asks, referring to the tie she is wearing.

Before allowing me to answer, she tells me that after she was finished "cleaning" with her friend, she was going to put the tie with the other clothes.

"You keep the tie," I say. "It looks better on you than it ever did on me."

The tie, which is the one I bought at Macy's last year, looks excellent flowing down her medium dark colored skin. It would be a shame to have her take it off.

"Please," she says, "you didn't see us here like this."

"See what? Good-bye."

"Good-bye," the two of them say in unison in a friendly manner. It was the first sound I heard from the other woman.

"Good-bye," I say again. As I close the door I take one final look at them. The woman wearing what used to be my tie is kissing the other one all over. Once outside the door, I realize that I forgot all of the clothes on the top of the dresser. I open the door again and enter slowly.

"I forgot these. Maybe you should lock the door after I leave," I suggest.

They nod. I smile and leave Room 1108, shutting the door behind me.

## Chapter 20

I tell the woman behind the front desk, Marie, that the maid was very considerate and folded the clothes neatly. Since Ken and I came to Las Vegas with no luggage, I am now in the position of having to hold the pile of clothes, which includes our suits, dress shoes, and the new clothes we bought in Las Vegas, until our flight leaves tonight. Seeing my dilemma, Marie suggests that she put the clothes in a large plastic bag and keep them behind the front desk until I am ready to leave. I thank her and go into the casino to find Ken.

The casino is packed with people and noise. I don't see Ken by any of the blackjack or roulette tables. He is nowhere to be found at the slot machines.

There is a nightclub-type area with bar stools on one side of the casino floor. There is also waitress service and tables with deep burgundy chairs facing a stage. The area is called the Coyote Lounge. A jazz band stops playing and someone announces that in a few short minutes another band will begin to play. In the interim, there is mellow music playing softly from a sound system. I see Ken sitting in one of the comfortable burgundy chairs. The leathery mother from this morning is seated in the chair next to him. They are drinking colorful drinks in tall glasses. Ken sees me but discreetly waves me off, so I don't come over to him. I don't want to spy on him, but I would like to get a drink. I sit at a bar stool on the other side of the Coyote Lounge. Where is the leathery mother's less leathery daughter while her mother sits drinking tall colorful drinks with Ken?

"I'd like a vodka and pineapple juice," I tell the bartender, who introduces himself as Neville.

I give Neville money for the drink and realize that, if I were sitting at a blackjack table at this very moment, I could get a free drink. To my right is the chaos of the casino floor and to my far left is Ken with the leathery mother and others whom I do not know, and whom I will probably never meet. Neville makes a strong drink. I drink it quickly and feel it rush to my head. This is the most potent vodka and pineapple juice I've ever had. Yet it tastes good. The vodka does not overwhelm the pineapple juice. There is just the right mix of ingredients.

"Neville, what did you put in this drink?"

"What did you have again?" Neville asks.

"I had a vodka and pineapple juice."

"Then," Neville replies, "I put in vodka and pineapple juice."

"I'll have another one of the same."

"Was that was a vodka and grapefruit juice?" he asks quizzically.

"No. I'd like a vodka and pineapple juice."

"Ok, here's a vodka and pineapple juice. Enjoy."

"Thanks."

Maybe they deliberately make the drinks strong in the casino. This way, after having a few drinks, or after even only one, the customers get just giddy enough so that they squander all their money in the casino making foolish bets. That will not happen to me. I guarantee it. Perhaps it is the desert air mixing with the drinks that gives the drinks extra potency. That probably doesn't make sense because I am breathing cooled air conditioned air, not the hot air outside. But still, the air in here is cooled desert air, not cooled humid air of the East, and maybe there is a difference in the way that the desert air, even air conditioned desert air, mixes with alcohol. These two drinks have given me enough of a buzz so that I should not play blackjack right now.

I leave the Coyote Lounge while Ken and the leathery pool mother continue to sit and sip drinks. I walk into the hotel lobby. I am slightly wobbly and disoriented from the quickly consumed two vodka and pineapple juices. I am not drunk, but I do feel the drinks in my head. Why is it that there are times when I can drink a lot of alcohol and feel nothing, yet other times, like now, after only a small amount of alcohol, I feel quite loopy? It must have to do with how my mind feels each different time.

What is the mind anyway? Is the mind the brain or is it something else? It seems that the brain is the actual physical thing inside the head between the ears. The brain actually can be touched, examined, and operated upon. Someone can become a brain surgeon and fix a broken brain. But where is the mind? Is the mind the soul? Does a horse have a mind? A horse definitely has a brain though. Without a brain a person could not live since part of the brain regulates heartbeats and breathing. But does a person need a mind to live? Maybe there is no mind but only a brain inside a person's head. No one ever gets a mind tumor. Whether people have minds or not, these two vodka and pineapple juices have affected something in my head, whatever that thing may be.

I walk to the enormous pool area. I now notice that the pool is shaped like a large coyote. I see the leathery mother's daughter from this morning sitting alone. I walk over to the chair next to her. If I remember correctly, her name is Pam.

"Is anyone sitting here?" I ask.

Pam looks up, says hello, and we each smile. I wonder if she knows that Ken is having drinks with her mother at the Coyote Lounge. I sit down on the lounge chair and immediately feel the bright sun heating my clothes and exposed skin. I take off my sneakers to allow the Nevada sun to warm my feet. I take off my shirt and relax in my new shorts purchased at the Dressed Coyote. Pam's eyes are closed, but I don't think that she is asleep. She is facing the sun and I can see how dark her stomach is compared with mine. Is it good to be so tan?

"Is your friend still with my mother?" Pam asks in a cold tone with her eyes closed.

"Yes. They are having drinks in the Coyote Lounge."

Pam and I speak to each other only once every few minutes. The sun is very strong. My shoulders and face are getting quite sunburned.

"Would you rub some suntan lotion on my back?" Pam asks.

I take some of Pam's extremely oily lotion and place it onto my hands. I get out of the lounge chair, move right next to her, and rub it into her very tanned high school age shoulders. She is wearing a colorful yellow and blue bikini. I am actually the one who needs to have suntan lotion since I am so pale and will get terribly burned. Therefore, I ask Pam to put some lotion on my snow colored shoulders. She agrees to do so.

As Pam starts to put the lotion on me, I hear a new band begin to perform inside the Coyote Lounge. A female is singing, rather well, a popular song. The singer's voice sounds vaguely familiar. I can't exactly place it. It sounds like a typical nightclub singer's voice. I am strangely drawn to it, and must go inside. I thank Pam for putting suntan lotion on my shoulders, but I abruptly put on my shirt and sneakers and tell her that there is something I must do inside. She tells me that I should visit her in Room 715 in one hour. I tell her that I cannot do so. I am sure that she has no real interest in me in particular. I believe that she would like me to come to her room as a way of somehow getting back at her mother. I am old enough to be her substantially older brother. I say good-bye to her and walk towards the casino. For some reason, I stop at the pool's bar and buy a soda for Pam.

"Thank you," she says.

"You're welcome," I reply.

I enter the casino and head straight for the vaguely familiar voice that sings in the Coyote Lounge. I feel summoned to the voice. I look to the stage and am shocked by what I see. The singer is Jan English, my Atlantic City blackjack dealer who left Atlantic City for the West.

## Chapter 21

Jan English's voice powerfully fills the Coyote Lounge with song. When she was in my hotel room in Atlantic City she hardly spoke at all, and what she did say was barely above a whisper. Yet here, in the Coyote Lounge, her voice is strong. She is wearing a deep green dress with silver sequins on her shoulders. The sequins reflect all the colors of the casino and give her face a greenish glow. She is not exactly dancing on the stage, but she is swaying back and forth with the music. I am looking right at her, but I don't think she notices me. Although the Coyote Lounge is not jammed with people, there is enough of a crowd so that when she finishes this song there should be a nice round of applause.

"Thank you everyone," Jan English says after the audience finishes applauding.

She begins singing again. I do not recognize the song, but it is quite beautiful. The words of this slow song tell the story of a young man wearing blue who saves a woman from a band of evil bandits. As she sings this song, could Jan be thinking about me as her hero saving her from harm in Atlantic City? Listening carefully to the words, it seems that the rescuer, this man in blue, gets killed by the evil group after saving the woman. The disturbing words to this strange but beautiful song resound through the Coyote Lounge.

"Why did my hero have to perish?"

That last question, sung by Jan English in a particularly delicate yet also vibrant tone of voice, ends the song. The sadness of the song leaves the

Coyote Lounge silent for a moment, but the applause soon begins. The applause for this beautiful but sad song is much louder than it was for the previously sung pop tune.

Jan English thanks the patrons of the Coyote Lounge for the applause. I sit at the bar where I am once again greeted by Neville.

"What would you like?" Neville asks with a smile.

"I'll have a vodka and pineapple juice."

In a few seconds Neville comes back with my drink.

"Thanks."

Jan tells the lounge audience that she wrote that last song herself. It was both beautiful and sad.

Jan starts singing again, but this time it is a popular hit. I take a sip of my drink, which is very sour. This is not a vodka and pineapple juice. It is a vodka and grapefruit juice.

"What did you get for me?" I ask Neville.

"Didn't you ask for a vodka and grapefruit juice?"

"No. I ordered vodka and pineapple juice. It's ok. I'll keep this. The sour taste is good for a change."

It is a welcome change to drink this sour drink, as compared with the sweet vodka and pineapple juice. Although Neville and I have been friendly at the bar in terms of our bartender-customer relationship, it seems that he is somewhat distressed that he did not serve me the drink I ordered. My intuition is correct as within a few seconds Neville gives me another drink.

"Here's a vodka and pineapple juice to go along with the vodka and grapefruit juice. It is on the house."

"Thanks."

I am getting drunk because these drinks are strong. Perhaps Neville gave me the wrong drink first, followed by this free drink, as part of a casino conspiracy to get me drunk so that I gamble foolishly. That cannot be true. Good friendly Neville would not be a part of such a devious plan. Or would he?

Jan sings another very pretty ballad. Her voice, which has an unusual, even disquieting, quality to it, is especially satisfying during the slow songs. Her voice has the ability to sound as if it is personally reaching out to everyone who is within hearing distance. I finish my vodka and pineapple juice and see Ken and the leathery mother walk out of the Coyote Lounge. How can they walk out while Jan is singing? I wish I could go on stage and be with Jan. She looks in this direction. Our eyes meet, at least I think they meet. I am not sure. When Jan was at a pause during the last song, I think her gaze stayed in this direction for more than a fleeting moment. But she is now looking in a different direction. It must be difficult for her to see clearly from the stage because of the glare from the stage lights. She now looks in a different direction. Does Jan English know that I am here? Would she care if she did?

Jan begins her next song. It is another song that she composed herself. Before starting, Jan says that she dedicates it to her special friend from Atlantic City, New Jersey. Could that be me?

It is another slow song. While it does not have the same haunting melody of the earlier song that she composed herself, it also has an eerie but seductive melody. The words of this song are similarly chilling. It is about three children trapped in a small building, but who are saved by a hero. I believe this hero is the same man wearing blue like in the earlier song. These songs are incredible. The songs tell stories and have a common character, the man wearing blue who saves the day. At the end of this song, the savior of the children, the man wearing blue, dies again, just as in the earlier song. Who is this man in blue? Does he exist? How can he die twice?

"The hero lies dead and bloodied, but the children are saved. Why did it have to end like this?" Jan ends the song with those words.

The music fades behind her. The audience needs a few seconds to recover from the sadness of the song before applauding.

"Thank you," Jan says to the crowd at the Coyote Lounge, which has grown larger so that now nearly all the tables and all the seats of the bar are filled. These people are undoubtedly drawn into the lounge area because of the haunting melodies sung by Jan English. Jan announces that she is going to take a ten minute break and that while she is gone, the band will play two instrumentals that were written by, and will feature, the band's saxophone player, Rex Bricker. The band starts to play and Jan exits the small stage through a rear door. The band starts with the piano player playing a jazzy tune joined in by the drummer. Rex Bricker starts playing his saxophone. I'd like to listen to the sweet sounds of Rex Bricker, and indeed, his saxophone playing is certainly worth listening to, but instead I say good-bye to Neville and try to find Jan English. How can I get to the back area where Jan must be spending her break? I can't go on stage while the musicians perform. I leave the Coyote Lounge in an attempt to find another entrance to the room behind the stage. It appears that the only way to go to the back room behind the Coyote Lounge is by going on stage. I go back to my bar stool.

"Neville, I'd like vodka and grapefruit juice."

Neville has converted me to the merits of vodka and grapefruit juice. I am enjoying the more sour and bitter vodka and grapefruit juice as compared with my usual sweet vodka and pineapple juice. There is something particularly satisfying about having a bitter drink as I sit here, listening to Rex Bricker on the saxophone, knowing that Jan English is literally only a few feet away from me behind the stage, but totally out of reach. I wish I could play the saxophone. The way Rex Bricker plays, it is as if the saxophone is an extension of him. The piano player, introduced by Rex as Fingers McKoo, is now playing a solo. He is fantastic. Focusing in on the very fast movement of his fingers against the keyboard, it looks as though the music is just pouring out of his hands and onto the piano. It is incredible that every time he plays a note, he is told by his brain where to put his fingers on the keyboard. Without his brain and with only his hands he could not play at all. It happens so fast. The fingers of Fingers McKoo appear to go directly to the correct keys without asking the brain where to go. The brain is miraculous. What is most miraculous is the way the brain, the hands, the fingers, and the piano work together to create the music. As much as I'm enjoying the music of Rex Bricker, Fingers McKoo, and the other band members, I long to see Jan English back on stage and hear her sad ballads.

The finishing notes of Rex Bricker's saxophone resound through the Coyote Lounge. After a good deal of applause for Rex Bricker, Fingers McKoo, and the rest of the band, Jan re-enters the stage. Without any introduction for her, the band begins to play and she starts to sing "Do You Know The Way To San Jose?" Although it was extremely moving listening to her sing her self-composed sad ballads, it is enjoyable to listen to her sing a pleasant upbeat song. As she sings, she smiles and her eyes look my way. I look back at her. I am sure that I detect a look of recognition in her eyes. Her eyes focus on me for a moment, then dart about the Coyote Lounge as she continues singing "Do You Know The Way To San Jose?"

It is 6:30 at night. So far in this set of songs she has only performed popular songs. She has not graced the audience with her sad ballads. After singing "What Do You Get When You Fall in Love?" Jan English tells the patrons in the Coyote Lounge that she is taking a short break. I am lightheaded from the drinks prepared by Neville. Jan English exits the stage during her break, but instead of walking behind the stage, she walks into the Coyote Lounge and to the bar, towards me.

"Matt from Atlantic City," Jan English says.

"Jan," I reply.

"What are you doing here?"

"I came with a friend last night. We're leaving in a few hours."

Jan stands next to me and we smile. We have nothing to say. I tell her how Ken and I ended up at the Coyote Lounge. I want to know her story. What happened to her at the Atlantic City hotel room that caused her to land in my hotel room and bubble bath? I don't ask her. I get the sense that she appreciated the comfort I gave her in Atlantic City, but she does not want to tell me personal things, which are none of my business. I tell her how much I enjoy her singing, especially her self-composed ballads. She tells me that she has to go back on stage.

"Good-bye," Jan says.

"Good-bye."

Jan English retakes the stage. She looks at me. I look back at her and smile. Then she begins singing another popular hit. I sit on the bar stool and enjoy her performance with the rest of the patrons at the Coyote Lounge.

"I'd like another vodka and grapefruit juice. No, make it a vodka and pineapple juice. Thanks."

Neville brings it very quickly.

"It is on the house."

## Chapter 22

I walk out of the Coyote Lounge. I proceed to the other side of the casino floor, as far away from the Coyote Lounge as possible. From my position now, next to the roulette tables, Jan English's voice in the Coyote Lounge is distant and fades completely away as the noise from the roulette tables, slot machines, and cheers from victorious craps players dominate. I have hardly gambled at all in Las Vegas and am not in the mood to do so now. However, almost out of obligation, I ask for a $10 chip at a roulette table. I get the chip and place it on black. The wheel comes up black. I leave the chips on the table and the wheel comes up black again. I now have $40. I again keep the chips on the table and again the wheel comes up black. I take my $80 in chips off the table and cash them in.

I see Ken enter the casino. I walk over to him and he tells me that we better get back to the airport. It is 7:15 p.m. and our plane leaves at 9:00 p.m. We go to the front desk to retrieve our bag of clothes, and we take a taxi cab to the airport. Our driver, named Monty, is broad shouldered and blondish gray. We learn that he is a cousin of both Martha, our waitress at the Coyote Coffee Shop, and Maggie, the salesperson at the drugstore. As we leave the cab and enter the airport terminal, Monty wishes us a safe trip home.

At the airport terminal, as we wait to board the plane, Ken tells me that he went back to the leathery mother's hotel room with the leathery mother, who is named Lisa. When he got there, Pam, the leathery mother's daughter, was wearing just the bottom of her bikini as she lay on the bed watching television. Lisa asked Pam if she could get dressed and leave so that she could be alone with Ken, but Pam refused. Then the mother and daughter started to fight. They were yelling and screaming right in front of Ken, who literally got between them so that they wouldn't hit each other. It was only when he determined that the situation was under control, and that they would not kill each other, that he excused himself and left the room.

"You are quite a gentleman," I tell Ken.

There is a bookstore at the airport terminal. In the front of the store is a table with old used books selling from 50 cents to $5. There is a dark blue tattered hardcopy book entitled "The Night Sky." It is a collection of short stories written in the 1940s. I buy it for the flight home.

Take-off is smooth. I take a last look at the lights of Las Vegas as our metal bird climbs into the darkness. Ken sits by the window to my left, and to my right is a young man, I would guess about twenty years old. Our flight attendant, Janine, bears a slight resemblance to the light-skinned Bench Woman, with her very long, dark hair. Janine is not as stunning as Bench Woman, but there is a similarity. What is Bench Woman doing now?

"What would you like to drink?" Janine asks.

"I'll have apple juice," I say.

After drinking the strong drinks prepared by Neville, I want no more alcohol tonight. My neighbor to the right, whose name is Joe, orders a Coke.

Ken bought financial and sports magazines at

the airport. He is reading about small business success stories. One day I would like to be an entrepreneur with my own business. I just need an idea. I open the tattered book that I bought at the airport. The first short story in "The Night Sky" is entitled "The Ice Man."

<u>The Ice Man</u>  by Kenneth Sniton

One of the most familiar figures in the neighborhood was Michael Savoni, the ice-man. Sturdy and robust, he was remarkably active despite his obesity. The stout rope which encircled his waist served two purposes--to hold up his belly, and to maintain his trousers in a state of respectability. Besides being an ice-man, he conducted a person-to-person loan agency, and was engaged in minor real estate manipulations. Although illiterate, he knew as much about the progress of the Italians in Ethiopia as Mussolini. His wife, forever a picture of dejection, was always pregnant, and therefore he supported about twelve children. Throughout the week, he smelled not of himself, but of his horse.

His unselfish devotion to his children made up for his many faults. In order not to spoil them with too much kindness, his alert mind thought of various schemes to teach them that this world was not entirely a bed of roses. Two of his sons, ages fifteen and sixteen, assisted him daily in the distribution of ice and coal. They arose at six o'clock in the morning to make the rounds with him, and by eight-thirty they were ready to go to school. Therefore, in class they often exhibited symptoms of sleeping sickness. However, Michael Savoni was unable to understand why they made such poor marks. But he finally decided that they must take after their mother.

He liked to visit the storekeepers in the neighborhood during his leisure hours. Occasionally he permitted one of his brood to accompany him. One time he was very much embarrassed by his little daughter whose nose was running in a very unladylike manner. He tore out the editorial page of the New York Times and vigorously rubbed her nose with this improvised handkerchief. As she had not been given a general anesthetic, she screamed lustily.

During the winter, when the sale of ice dwindled considerably, he balanced the budget by tending furnaces. In one of the cellars a large black cat became so much attached to him that she impeded his movements and hindered him in his work. One night he became so irritated that he cast the foolish feline into the furnace.

Michael Savoni was certain that the degenerative forces that were undermining modern youth were due directly to the lack of proper paternal guidance. All his children were zealously guarded under his protective wing. When one of his sons, Horace, wandered from the flock to visit a local dance hall, he was severely beaten. The second time the frivolous youth repeated his indiscretion, he was beaten again. The next morning, Horace was found hanging from a wooden beam in the cellar--dead. Michael Savoni was miserable for a few days, and was not his normal self for over a month.

The death in the family made Michael Savoni realize that his days on earth were also numbered, so proper provision was then made. He purchased a plot of ground large enough for four graves, each grave to contain three caskets, one on top of the other. When the deed to the land was drawn up, a peculiar clause was inserted, to the effect that, after Michael Savoni died, no member of his family should, in the future, be buried in the plot. He feared that a casket might be placed above him, and even in death Michael Savoni wanted to be on top.

### A Flower    by Michael Henerman

The fraternity dance was, as usual, a very messy affair. Crowds of people were huddled on the dance floor, trying to dance to the infernal pounding that is so popular these days. If you were to ask me, I think they were all mad. After all, the dense smoke that filled the room was enough to make anybody dizzy.

Suddenly I noticed a girl coming down the steps from the balcony that overlooked the floor. Immediately I saw that she was different from any girl there. She was small and very shy looking, with a kind of country-girl atmosphere about her. Her face was smooth and pretty. Her hair was honey brown and fluffy. But her eyes, light blue and very large, were truly distinctive. They just looked about with a mixed expression of fright and forlornness, a most sympathetic combination. At the bottom of the stairs she stopped and waited, as if expecting a catastrophe to befall her. I felt her misery, and hastened to her. I asked her whether she would care to dance. And then it was that her eyes smiled at me, a most happy smile.

The plane flies over the Rocky Mountains towards the great plains of America. I look out the window. But I am tired and so I close my eyes.

## Chapter 23

I wake up. We should land in less than one hour. Again, I open "The Night Sky."

The Party  by Kendall Finnie
The hostess of the party played bridge at our table, and very poorly, since from her place of vantage she was more interested in seeing that the proper respect was paid to the household furnishings than she was in the game. There were to be no ashtrays placed on the piano, no wet glasses on the varnished tables, and the like. Certainly she was having an unhappy time. So when my partner shuffled the new deck of cards too well, bending them into acute angles, a look of irritation appeared on her face, and the second time he repeated this feat, he won a sharp reprimand. All were embarrassed except Dr. Newell, who, in his usual philosophical manner, began to tell us one of those pointless stories about himself.

"Most of my childhood recollections, quite naturally, center around the several schoolhouses where, during our youth, we were imprisoned. I, for one, can recall many unhappy experiences which had caused varying degrees of mental anguish on my part. One of these minor tragedies is of particular significance to me as it had, strangely enough, a sequel later in life.

"This schoolteacher that I am going to tell you about was, to briefly sum up her character, very meticulous and fastidious, so much so in fact, that these qualities completely dominated her life. It was

114

the custom in those days to assign a definite room to each teacher in which she was often destined to be for the remainder of her years. Miss Stanton had been assigned to Room 201 when the school had first been opened and, as the years had passed, it became so much her property that I imagine she could have borrowed a mortgage, if she had so desired.

"This room, as I remember, was unlike any other in the building. It superficially resembled the others, with the blackboards in front, the windows at the side, and the wardrobe hung in the back. However, the other rooms were well worn with age, for it seemed as if they meekly surrendered to the uses and abuses that they were subject to daily. But Miss Stanton's room was remarkably new. The desks were still bright in their original varnish and the blackboards looked as if they were never humiliated by superfluities of the chalk sticks. It is needless to say that this remarkable state of preservation was accomplished through the dynamic fanaticism of Miss Stanton. So intense was she, that you imagined her to be in a constant state of warfare with time, refusing to concede an inch to this perennial antagonist.

"I often imagined a sudden thunderbolt striking the building with such violence as to completely disrupt the room so that it would become like all the others, with Miss Stanton vainly spending the rest of her days wandering through the corridors, hopelessly searching for her past glory.

"On a certain day when my mind was occupied with some such mental meanderings, I unknowingly spoiled one of her patterns. Unconsciously and without deliberate intent, I tipped the swollen ink-well off my desk, producing a vivid, deep, purple blotch on the floor below. As the ink soaked through the boards, it saturated her soul.

"The next day, before the session was to start, I caught a glimpse of her furiously attempting to scrape away the indelible stain with a sharp piece of broken glass. But the ink had penetrated so deeply that her efforts were futile."

Dr. Newell paused here for so long that everyone reminded him that there was to be a sequel to the story.

"Twenty years later when I was a young intern, I was assigned to work in this school as a part of the public health program which was being conducted at the time. As I walked through the building, the years turned backward. Automatically, I was drawn towards Room 201. Suddenly I was overcome by a vague fear and some impulse warned me not to enter. What it was that prompted this peculiar sensation I was unable to discern, except perhaps, that I might find this room just as I had left it years ago. I flung open the door and walked in. Time had taken its toll. The room was just as old and worn as the rest of the building. There was one thing more that I had to ascertain, and as I walked over to the desk that I had formerly occupied, I saw the deep ink stain on the floor just as if it had been made yesterday instead of fifteen years ago."

At the conclusion of his story someone asked if he had met Miss Stanton.

Yes, he had seen her. She was old, gray, serene, and reconciled.

Another said that he did not believe an ink stain could remain visible for twenty years unless, he added laughingly, it had been renewed.

Dr. Newell looked up.

"That is exactly what happened."

"But who renewed it?"

"She did. It was the only thing she continued to take care of."

The plane is now descending steadily. The wheels touch the ground. There is applause from some of the passengers. If a plane lands safely--not in a fiery mess--then the pilot did a good job. All of us passengers aboard the plane put our trust in a pilot that none of us know. I suppose it is better not to know who the pilot is because the passengers, me included, might panic if we knew the pilot. What if I discovered that the pilot is someone I knew in high school who was crazy then? Even if the person matured, I would not feel safe during the flight. It is better not to know the pilot. This pilot, whoever he or she is, did a good job.

It is 5:55 a.m. as Ken and I walk outside. We have no problem getting a cab.

"There will be two stops in Manhattan. The first is near Gramercy Park and the second is on the Upper West Side."

Our driver nods approvingly. There is little traffic on this very early Sunday morning. Ken is dropped off first.

"Take it easy," he says.

"See you Monday."

It is 6:30 a.m. when I get home. I am supposed

to meet Claire at 11:00 a.m., at which time we will first have breakfast and then go to the auto show. We are to meet in front of the Plaza Hotel. I go into bed and set my alarm for 9:00 a.m. I hope to get some sleep before I get ready for our breakfast and auto show outing. I'll need to shave and shower. Once in bed I think about Jan English and how we most likely won't ever see each other again. I wonder what happened to Sam. Did he die from his heart attack or is he recovering? And what was Bench Woman doing when I was in Las Vegas? And who was she doing it with? While it was enjoyable going to Las Vegas on the spur of the moment, I need a vacation.

Although I have had so little sleep recently, I can't fall asleep now. It is 7:10 a.m. when I devise a plan for this morning. I will get out of bed, put on some clothes, and go to the Pasture for a muffin and a wake-up cup of coffee. After this pre-breakfast snack, I will go back to my apartment to shave and shower. Then I will meet Claire at the Plaza Hotel and have a real breakfast as we planned. My hair is disheveled. Accordingly, I put on my baseball cap.

"Hi sweetie, how are you doing this morning?"

To my pleasant surprise, Ellen is working on this early Sunday morning. She tells me that she is working the weekend early morning shift to cover for another waitress. Sunday morning is probably a good time to work in a diner because people tend to eat breakfast out on Sundays. At least I think people do, although the Pasture is quiet now. But it is still early. I'm sure this place will become crowded in a couple of hours.

"What can I get for you, honey?"

"I'll have a toasted corn muffin, dry."

Without even having to ask, Ellen comes over with a tall glass of water filled with ice and a cup of coffee. She's fantastic.

"You just want a muffin for breakfast today?" Ellen asks.

"I'm meeting a friend at 11:00 for breakfast. This is just a pre-breakfast because I can't sleep."

"That's nice. I hope it's a special friend you're meeting," Ellen says with a smile.

I smile back at Ellen. Is my meeting with Claire a meeting with a regular friend or is it, as Ellen calls it, a meeting with a "special" friend? Next Saturday night, at Claire's friend's wedding, I will be Claire's date. But will I be her friend, or will I be a romantic date? Is there really such a difference? It's all in the mind. What is the mind?

The coffee is hot and the muffin is very fresh. While the blueberry muffins I ate in Las Vegas were large, they were not this fresh. This corn muffin is large and fresh. The muffin here at the Pasture is a great muffin. It is a muffin's muffin.

"Here's some more coffee, sweetie."

"Thanks."

After I devour three quarters of the muffin, Ellen fills up my coffee cup with one more cup of hot coffee. I am feeling wide awake despite having slept only for a few hours on the plane.

Ellen gives me the check.

"Have a good day," I say to Ellen.

"You too honey."

I walk outside feeling good after having that

119

pre-breakfast muffin and coffee. It is exactly 8:00 a.m. now and the streets are waking up with activity. It is warm outside. The sign on the bank says that it is 75 degrees. During my pre-breakfast at the Pasture, I heard someone say that today's high temperature will reach 85 degrees, but with very dry, low humidity air. Therefore, the weather should be perfect for going with Claire to breakfast and then the auto show.

# Chapter 24

This shower is refreshing. The hot shower water feels good as it hits my head and then rolls down my body. It was a truly wonderful shower in the hotel room in Las Vegas, but the shower in my apartment, while not as good, is not bad. In fact, the water pressure is getting stronger. I'd have to say that, at this moment, the shower right here in my apartment is performing almost as well as the shower in the Coyote Hotel. Considering that this building is nearly 100 years old, the shower is performing admirably.

What should I wear for my date with Claire, if, in fact, it is a date? What is appropriate summer wear for a breakfast and auto show rendezvous? It is warm enough to wear shorts and a T-shirt. Although shorts are appropriate, I'll look better if I wear a nicer shirt than just a T-shirt. I have a blue and maroon short sleeve shirt that will go perfectly with my khaki shorts. With my new sneakers purchased in Las Vegas, I will be dressed just right. The only time Claire has seen me out of a suit was when our office played softball last summer. Except for softball, we have never been together, just the two of us, when we were not wearing our work clothes. Will she like my legs?

My chest and shoulders got more sunburned in Las Vegas than I thought. It goes to show the strength of the Nevada desert sun. Just sitting by the hotel pool for a short time gave me a lot of color. Could I ever get as tan as the leathery mother and daughter? I doubt it. I would never get so tan even if

I sat outside everyday and applied the right amount of suntan lotion. I would turn red and burn to a crisp before I would get so tan.

It is 10:30 a.m. when I arrive in front of the Plaza Hotel. I have half an hour before Claire is supposed to arrive. Where should Claire and I go for breakfast? I think that there must be some place to eat near the auto show, but it would be wonderful to eat here at the Plaza Hotel's restaurant. Am I dressed nicely enough to have breakfast here? There is a beautiful restaurant in the hotel where they serve breakfast. It is a beautiful room with beautiful tables and chairs.

Looking at the menu, I see that breakfast costs a small fortune. I know Claire doesn't expect to eat at such a beautiful place. Yet it is a beautiful room with beautiful tables and chairs. Some of the breakfast eaters here are dressed quite formally, but others are dressed casually. After all, it is only breakfast. I think that eating here is too extravagant for our pre-auto show breakfast.

I go back outside to the front of the hotel. Claire walks towards The Plaza. She does not see me yet. She is wearing a light blue colored floral blouse with jeans. She may have felt uncomfortable wearing shorts with me, even though shorts are more logical than the jeans she is wearing on this warm summer day. With Claire wearing pants, I feel almost naked in my shorts. Perhaps naked is too strong a word. The shorts proclaim to the world either that I am vulnerable or that I am self-confident. I do not know which. I walk over to Claire, who does not see me because a group of tourists has gathered.

"Claire, over here," I call to her through the crowd.

"Hi, Matthew. I hope you weren't waiting long."

"Not at all. You're right on time."

"How did you get so sunburned when it rained most of yesterday? Do you go to tanning salons?"

I tell Claire how Ken and I went to Las Vegas Friday night on the spur of the moment, and how we just came back this morning. I do a quick editing job of the trip as I tell her about it, avoiding references to the leathery daughter, the two naked chambermaids, one of whom I saw wearing my tie, and Jan English.

"You must be exhausted. Are you sure you still want to go to the auto show? I would understand if you wanted to go home and sleep."

"No, I am not tired. I look forward to the auto show. I want to help you decide what type of car to buy. I'm hungry. Let's get breakfast."

Claire suggests that we find a coffee shop on our way to the auto show, but I ask her to come inside the Plaza Hotel to look at the breakfast menu.

"It's a beautiful place," I say. "It will be my treat. Let's go."

"We are not dressed for this place. I don't think they'll let us in."

"I'll ask."

"I'd rather go another time, when I'm dressed fancier," Claire says.

"Yes, I need to be dressed differently to eat there. We'll go another time."

We walk away from the Plaza Hotel. Two blocks into our walk in the direction of the auto show, we enter a place called the Woodsie Nook. Neither Claire nor I have ever eaten there before. It is a fairly large restaurant that displays a Sunday brunch menu in its front window. The restaurant's large size belies its quaint name. It is homey, however. Upon entering, Claire and I quickly refer to this place as the Woodsie. As its name implies, it is decorated with an abundance of wood. The Woodsie, at least by its dark wood endowed appearance, seems to be the perfect place to go to eat on a cold winter day. There is a fireplace in the corner. It is not burning now. Instead, it is filled with plants. But even on this summer morning the Woodsie looks to be a good place for brunch. A sign up front tells us to wait for the hostess to seat us. Within thirty seconds of our entrance, Karen, the restaurant's hostess, greets us and walks us to a table. It is bustling with brunch-eaters, but there are a number of tables available. Pleasantly, Karen sits us at a corner table, which provides us with a full view of all the activity going on at the Woodsie.

"Enjoy your brunch," Karen says as she leaves and places two menus on the table.

Claire smiles as she looks at the Sunday brunch menu, which consists of an appetizing array of omelettes, pancakes, waffles, sandwiches, and salads. Our waitress, named Sally, comes over to us. Sally places two glasses of water on the table and asks if we would like to start off with anything to drink. Both Claire and I say that we would like coffee. Sally walks away, allowing us time to examine the menu.

"I rarely go out for breakfast. This is nice,"

Claire says.

"I love going out for breakfast. It's my favorite meal to eat out."

Sally comes with our coffees and asks if we are ready to order.

"I need a few more minutes," I say.

"Take your time. The Woodsie Nook is a place to relax during brunch," Sally informs us quite formally.

"It is beautiful outside," Claire says. "I should have worn shorts like you."

Is Claire commenting on my bare legs? I have never seen her in shorts. I have, however, seen the lower parts of her legs when she has worn dresses and skirts to work. But that is different.

"I don't think I've ever seen you in shorts," I comment.

Claire smiles back slightly.

"What are you going to order?" Claire asks, changing the subject.

While I admire the Woodsie's pancake and waffle selection, I suspect that I will order eggs.

"The eggs look good. I'm going to order salami and eggs."

"Goodness," Claire says.

Claire orders blueberry pancakes. In addition to the coffees we ordered when we first sat down, we both order orange juice, which is freshly squeezed here at the Woodsie.

It is unusual sitting here at a restaurant on a Sunday morning with Claire. Only a handful of times have Claire and I eaten together during lunch at work. But this Sunday breakfast feels different. It feels different, but not bad. The conversation is enjoyable and we are, or at least I am, relaxed. Claire asks me about the trip to Las Vegas with Ken. She is amazed at the spontaneity of it all. Claire also wants to hear about the time with Mary Pinnyon at the Peacock Pub and in Chinatown before Ken and I decided to go to Las Vegas. I tell Claire that Mary was fairly pleasant. Given Claire's dislike for Mary, that bit of news dampens Claire's good mood. I quickly add that Mary wasn't actually pleasant, but just that she was not as annoying as she is in the office.

"So what did you do yesterday?"

Claire tells me that she went to the wedding shower for her friend Debbie, whose wedding we are going to next Saturday night. The shower was held at a restaurant on Long Island.

"Did a male stripper come out of a cake? Isn't that what goes on at those parties?" I ask.

"No," Claire says.

Sally then arrives with our food. Claire's blueberry pancakes look fantastic. The three individual pancakes are thick, yet light looking. There are a few fresh blueberries on top of the pancakes, in addition to the blueberries that are baked right into them. It is comical to see slender Claire take a big forkful of the blueberry pancakes into her mouth. It is unexplainably enjoyable to see Claire eat so robustly.

"These are delicious. Do you want to try them?"

The pancakes look so inviting that I cannot refuse her offer. As I put some of the pancakes in my

126

mouth I tell her, with my mouth full of the pancakes, that they are great.

"Do you want to try some of my salami and eggs? They are great also."

"No thank you. I'll never be able to finish these pancakes."

We settle down into a routine of eating, talking and smiling. I would heartily recommend the Woodsie to anyone on a date. Is this a date?

"So what kind of car do you think you want to buy?"

"I know nothing about cars. That's why I want to go to the auto show. I would like a small car, but I want it to have four doors."

"Ah ha," I say, "that narrows it down."

Claire says that she wants to concentrate on the Japanese cars because she has heard that they are the most reliable. I tell her that she should keep an open mind and that some of the domestic cars are good. While I don't own a car, I know much more about them than Claire does. She apparently knows nothing about them. I have, at times, thought about buying a new car and have even looked into it, only to determine that owning a car in Manhattan is too inconvenient. There is just nowhere to park.

"I'll have more coffee, please."

Sally obliges, and fills up both of our coffee cups.

"How is everything?" Sally asks.

"Wonderful," Claire says.

I have totally finished my excellent, and not greasy, salami and eggs. Claire has left over only a small amount of her pancakes. For such a thin person, it's hard to believe that she ate as much as she did.

"Come back again soon," Sally says to us as we leave the Woodsie.

# Chapter 25

It is a beautiful day as Claire and I begin our walk from the Woodsie to the Jacob Javits Center, which is all the way on the west side of Manhattan and where the auto show is being held. The walk should take about twenty minutes, the perfect amount of time for me to walk off the salami and eggs.

The strong sunshine glistens off of Claire's normally plain colored hair, making it look better than just plain. I have the incredible urge to touch her hair, or maybe hold her hand, but I do not do so. Then, because there are many cars as we start our way across Eighth Avenue, I take hold of her hand. I try to act as if the only reason that I am taking hold of it is because she will be safer if our hands are together. I mutter, "When we get hit, at least we will get hit together." But my true motivation is the simple desire to hold her hand. I believe she knows this. The moment of truth arrives after we finish crossing the street and we are on the safe sidewalk once again. Do I keep holding Claire's hand or do I release my grip? Claire did not flinch or object when I first held her hand under the guise of safety, so I do not let go now. We are both aware that we are holding hands, yet there is no safety reason for doing so. Our intertwined hands are sweaty. I want to dry my hand off, but I don't want to be the one to let go. She might interpret that as me not enjoying our hand holding.

We approach the Jacob Javits Convention Center. There are throngs of people outside and many vendors selling hot dogs, ice cream, and soda. We arrive at the entrance. Our hands separate so that we can go through different partitions of the revolving door. Perhaps one day, if we are ever truly a couple, Claire and I will walk through a single partition of a revolving door together. What am I thinking? I never even thought that I was interested in Claire or her in me. Yet why did I want to hold her hand? Claire is not the type of girl who would hold a guy's hand unless it meant something.

Letting go of Claire's hand gives me the opportunity to wipe my sweaty hand on my shorts. I am sure that Claire is also going to wipe her hand, but I have not seen her do so. She must have done so discreetly.

It costs $8 a person for admission to the auto show. When it is our turn to pay, Claire cuts in front of me and says to the person behind the counter that she wants two tickets. Claire tells me that I am doing her a favor by helping her look at the cars and so she wants to pay. My initial reaction is to protest her generosity, but she insists.

"Thanks," I say.

We enter the main floor of the auto show. It is huge. There are new cars on display for as far as the eye can see. It is also very crowded with people. Claire and I decide to look at all the cars, even the ones that she cannot afford.

The first exhibit we approach is from Buick. Although we both assume that the typical Buick is too big and expensive for Claire, we go there anyway. We are not holding hands as we head towards the show car future Buick, which is on a revolving platform.    It is a large, very futuristic looking prototype car. There is a spokesmodel standing next to this future Buick. The model has medium length blond hair, and eyes that are blue enough to be seen from fifteen to twenty feet away. She is telling those who surround the show car all about its structure. It is big and spacious, yet lightweight. It is made of a very strong but lightweight fiber, which is half the weight of steel, but stronger. Therefore, the Buick spokesmodel tells us, this future luxury car is not only comfortable, but will deliver better gas mileage than present luxury cars and it is safer. Unfortunately, at this time it is not feasible to mass market this car because the lightweight fiber is prohibitively expensive to produce.    But the spokesmodel announces, accompanied by a convincing smile, that in the not too distant future it will be possible to produce this car at a reasonable price. It is a beautiful car. Its dark green paint with tan interior is mesmerizing. The spokesmodel stops talking about this Buick of the future and walks off the revolving platform to take a sip of soda.  Claire and I walk over to Buick's present day luxury car.

Although it is a full-sized luxury car, and therefore, of no practical interest to Claire, I open the door to the maroon car and sit inside. The leather seating is comfortable. I ask Claire to join me inside and she enters the luxurious Buick through its front passenger door.

"This is very nice," Claire says.

It feels good sitting in this car with Claire.  I am in the driver's seat and Claire is next to me in the front passenger seat. It looks to me like Claire and I would look good together driving down a country road in a fine car like this. We smile at each other. The front seat of this car is a great place to observe the activity of the auto show. I feel as if Claire and I are alone, yet we are surrounded by many people. People standing outside of this Buick would like to sit inside of it. We exit after a few moments.

We examine the other Buicks. As we leave the Buick exhibit, we hear the Buick spokesmodel begin to speak again about the Buick prototype luxury car of the future. I glance back at the spokesmodel revolving on the platform and wonder what kind of car she drives. We walk over to the next exhibit, which is from Ford.

The Ford exhibit also includes a Ford prototype future car, which is Ford's sports car of the future. But there is no spokesmodel showing off the car. Perhaps the spokesmodel is taking a break in the bathroom. Why do I assume that there is a spokesmodel and that, if there is one, it must be female. Claire and I look at the Ford Focus, which is the Ford that Claire would most likely buy because of its size and price. We agree that the Focus looks good. But Claire has it in her mind to buy a Japanese car when she ultimately makes her purchase, whenever that will be in the future.

"Let's just sit in it," I say. "You sit behind the steering wheel."

I open the door to the driver's seat for Claire and then I close it and sit in the passenger seat. It is roomy for a small car.

"This fits me," Claire says. "My father always drove a Ford when I was growing up. My favorite car was our silver Ford Grenada with red interior. We had it for years."

"What does your father drive now?"

"He doesn't drive as much as he used to, but when he does drive, he drives his Toyota Camry."

We sit in the Focus. We are not rushed out of the car by others wanting to get inside of it. The Focus does not command a large crowd because it is not a glitzy model. We are able to sit in the car and even relax in it. We check out all the controls and move the seats back and forth. It would be nice to start up the car and hear the engine. But there are no keys in the cars at the auto show. Obviously you can't have people driving cars all over the convention center. Claire likes this car, but repeats her concern that a Ford may not be as reliable as a Japanese car. I get out of the car and then go back in, but this time I go to the rear seat with Claire. For a small car there is sufficient room.

Sitting in the rear seat of this red Ford Focus with Claire to my right is intoxicating. Perhaps it is the new car smell. But it is not only the new car smell making me giddy, although I do love new car smell. Claire has taken hold of my hand in the rear seat of this Ford Focus. Although we held hands outside on the street while on route to the auto show, holding hands while inside the Ford Focus is a bold move on her part. When I first held her hand outside, it was with the pretense that we should hold hands for the sake of safety when crossing the street. But for Claire to place her hand on top of mine here, in the rear seat of this red Ford Focus at the auto show, means that she is doing so just for its own sake. A family, consisting of a man, a woman, a girl, and a smaller boy walk over to the Ford Focus and apparently would like to get inside of it. However, they are too polite to ask us to leave. We leave the car. Because we each exit the car on different sides, our hands separate. Our hands reattach when we get back together outside of the car.

I lead us to a black Ford Mustang convertible. I sit in the driver's seat after two teenage males get out of it. I would like to have this car. It is sporty but it doesn't look like every other sports car, many of which look like rounded blobs. For the supposed sake of aerodynamics, most of the sports cars, and even most of the family cars, seem to be designed with totally rounded shapes. Yet this Mustang still has some actual edges and straight lines to it. Claire tells me that I look good sitting in it. I can't see myself of course. However, I know that I feel very good sitting here, and if I feel good, I probably look good.

A small crowd has gathered by the Ford prototype future sports car. We walk over and from our vantage point I see only the very long, very dark straight hair of the spokesmodel. She is wearing shorts and a blue shirt that says Ford on the back. I can't see her face because she is on a revolving platform. It seems that each manufacturer's special show car is on display on a revolving platform. I have not yet seen this spokesmodel's face, but I hear her begin to talk about the car's powerful engine and safety features. Claire and I walk, hand in hand, right up to the prototype. It is a beautiful silver car, although, unlike the Mustang, it is extremely smooth and aerodynamic looking. While I like the more angular lines of the Mustang, there is no denying that this Ford prototype future sports car is beautiful. The platform revolves towards us and, just as the spokesmodel begins describing the car's revolutionary suspension system, her face comes into view. I am shocked. The Ford spokesmodel is Bench Woman.

# Chapter 26

There stands Bench Woman revolving on a platform next to the future Ford sports car. She looks just the way one would imagine a Ford spokesmodel to look, but even better. For the first time I hear Bench Woman's voice. She is talking about the efficient but very strong powerplant under the hood of this future car. Bench Woman tells the crowd that this car, with its newly designed engine, is not quite ready for production, but that it will be soon. Bench Woman says that this car will deliver new levels of performance and economy for its owner. The words Bench Woman says are unimportant. It is the melodious way in which she says them that is captivating not only to me, but to everyone listening to her.

"Do you want to go to the next exhibit?"

I am shocked that Claire wants to walk away from this exhibit where Bench Woman is on a revolving platform speaking right in front of us. She can't be serious. Claire, of course, doesn't know that the spokesmodel is Bench Woman.

As Claire and I walk away from the Ford exhibit, Bench Woman's words about Ford's future sports car penetrate my ears. Although I walk further away from Bench Woman and am not facing her any longer, her voice becomes clearer and clearer to me, as if beckoning me to come on the revolving platform with her. I quicken my pace away from the Ford exhibit and take Claire's hand, but I believe I hear,

"Matt, Bench Man, why have you left the Ford

136

exhibit? Please, come back."

Upon hearing these words in my head, I want to race onto the revolving platform and enter the future Ford on the driver's side. In my daydream, I would see Bench Woman enter on the passenger side. With us together, I would turn on the ignition and the Ford future car would rumble with a roar like no other car. I would drive the car off of the platform and through the glass windows of the convention center with Bench Woman next to me to start our life of glamour.

"You are so daring, Matt, Bench Man, I worship you," she would say to me.

Claire notices my daydreaming.

"Are you ok, Matthew? You seem to be somewhere else."

"What makes you say that? Everything's fine."

Claire and I go to the Saab exhibit. The Saabs are nice cars, but also seem to be out of Claire's price range. But without hesitation, Claire and I head for the white Saab convertible. Right before we arrive there, two laughing young women enter the car. The one in the driver's seat motions to me.

"Can you take a picture of us?" she asks, handing me a Polaroid camera.

"Sure."

It is rare to see a Polaroid camera these days, but it is captivating to see a photograph develop right in front of your eyes. I take the photograph of the two smiling, Saab-sitting women.

Still smiling, the taller woman, who sees my fascination with the Polaroid camera, says that she will take a picture of Claire and me. That is very nice of the woman.

"That would be great," I say. Thinking quickly, I ask her to take the picture in front of the Ford future sports car. I tell her that the Ford future sports car is my favorite car at the show.

Claire, who was not listening to my conversation with the happy woman, is a little confused when I tell her that we are going back to the Ford exhibit to have our picture taken. I make sure that Claire and I are situated in a position from where Bench Woman, who is rotating on the platform talking about the Ford future sports car, can be seen in the photograph.

"Smile," the tall woman says.

She hands me the photograph. It seems like an eternity as it comes into focus before our eyes. Claire and I look pretty good with our arms around each other. The Ford future car is gleaming behind. Unfortunately, only Bench Woman's back can be seen because, when the picture was taken, the revolving platform revolved Bench Woman's face out of view. However, Bench Woman's long dark hair can be seen falling well below her shoulders. Who would have dreamed that today I would have a picture of Bench Woman's back and flowing hair.

Armed with the fully developed photo, wherein Bench Woman's back can be seen, I am fortified with renewed vigor. I take Claire's hand as we head back to the Saabs.

"We never got to sit in the white Saab convertible," I tell Claire, "let's go in it now, it's empty."

"Are you all right, Matthew? Your mind

138

seemed to have been lost for a few minutes, but now you seem wide awake again."

"I'm fine. It's a nice picture. Don't you think? You look great," I tell Claire.

Claire does, in fact, look good in the photo. But how is it possible to look at anything else in the picture but the back of Bench Woman and her hair? Of course I am feeling good. Claire is enjoyable company and Bench Woman is only about 60 feet away from me. I can even hear Bench Woman's voice. Yet it pains me to be so close to Bench Woman, but not to be with her. It is nice being here with Claire, but to be so close to Bench Woman and do nothing about it is difficult.

Claire opens the driver's side door of the Saab convertible.

"You sit in the driver's seat," Claire says to me.

I sit inside and open the passenger side door for Claire.

"These convertibles are nice, but here at the auto show with all of these people around, it's better to sit in a regular car so that when we close the doors, it becomes our own little world."

We exit the Saab convertible. I take a glance back at the Ford exhibit and see Bench Woman speaking with two men, both of whom also appear to be working at the Ford exhibit. The next exhibit is from Lincoln/Mercury. Here, too, many of the cars are too big and expensive for Claire, but as we go from one exhibit to the next, our focus has moved away from deciding what car Claire should buy. We are simply having a good time.

Claire and I see the smallest Lincoln at the

Lincoln/Mercury exhibit. It is a deep emerald green car with a black interior. It is very nice. I want to sit inside of it, but someone else is seated behind the steering wheel. The information sheet distributed by Lincoln/Mercury informs us about the car's powerful engine. Again, this car is too expensive for either Claire or me, but we like looking at it. Maybe one day I'll buy a car like this.

We enter the rear seat of the largest Lincoln. It is huge. There is a boy, perhaps eight or nine years old, sitting in the front seat behind the steering wheel. We sit in the rear seat and luxuriate in the car's spaciousness. The boy up front looks to be in his own world. He is happily moving his hands on the steering wheel and making car noises, such as those a car makes when it screeches to a sudden stop or rapidly accelerates. Claire and I look at each other and laugh. The boy turns around to us. Until Claire and I laughed, the boy apparently did not even know that we were in the car, even though when we entered the rear doors closed with a resounding thud. The chubby cheeked boy looks at us and smiles, but says nothing.

"He's cute," Claire says to me.

"What's your name?" she asks the boy.

"Michael Joshua," he tells us. With a smile on his face, he turns back around and continues his imaginary race behind the wheel of this deep blue Lincoln. In about another thirty seconds, he stops, glances back at us, says a soft but sincere "bye," and leaves.

"Take it easy, Michael Joshua," I say, but he is out of the car and back onto the floor of the auto show with his father before I even finish saying his name.

Claire and I sit alone in the back of the big Lincoln. I can hardly believe that I am sitting here calmly even though Bench Woman is so close. But Claire is even closer. In fact, she's very close--no more than one foot from me. Only a small area of the leather seating separates us. The leather seating in this car looks and feels good, yet I don't know how I feel about sitting on leather, which is from cow. I know I eat beef, but would I want to sit on a dead cow every time I enter my car? Would I be relaxed if every time I go for a leisurely drive I sit on a dead animal? Suppose the screams of the cows at slaughter could be heard every time someone sits on the leather. No one would want leather seats if that were the case. Do cows scream at slaughter? Even if they don't, it is still bad for the cows. Yet I've heard that leather is made from cows that have already been used for food. At least the cows are not killed specifically to make leather. On this theory, it would be wasteful not to use their skin for leather. Simply to eat the meat of the cow and then throw out the skin is worse than eating the meat and using the skin. Leather certainly makes fine car interior. All the nicer expensive cars have leather interior seating. If I ever have enough money to buy an expensive car, I'll probably have no choice but to have leather seats.

I move closer to Claire in the back of the Lincoln. Outside of the car, people mill about. In the cocoon that is this car, I realize what a good companion Claire has been during brunch and now here at the auto show. It is also incredible that I was able to walk away from the Ford exhibit with Bench

Woman right there, on the revolving platform, as she told an audience about the Ford sports car of the future. Of course, Bench Woman does not even know who I am. If I were walking around the auto show by myself, I would not have been able to walk away from Bench Woman. Is Claire a blessing or a curse? Is Claire freeing me from Bench Woman's magnetic pull, which likely will lead nowhere, or is Claire ruining whatever minuscule chance I may have with Bench Woman? Perhaps it is fate that Bench Woman and I see each other here at the auto show today. Of course, I probably would not have come to the auto show today if not for Claire. It was Claire who asked me to go to the auto show to help her look at cars so that she could purchase one soon. Does Claire have a cosmic purpose of showing me that Bench Woman and I should be together or is her purpose to show me that Bench Woman and I have no future? Or is it all just a coincidence that has absolutely no meaning? Claire looks out of the car and points to a mother holding the hands of two little girls who must be identical twins. I look at Claire and kiss her on the cheek in the back seat of the big Lincoln.

## Chapter 27

Claire, alarmed, but I hope, pleasantly surprised by the kiss on the cheek, turns to me and kisses me on the lips. Her kiss to me is not long. It is no more than a peck, but it is more than a friendly kiss. In the rear passenger area of the big Lincoln, with the auto show crowd around us, it was bold and intimate. Without uttering a sound we exit the Lincoln. I exit on my side and Claire, instead of getting out of the car on her side, also exits on my side, which means that she slides across the Lincoln's ample leather upholstery. As I stand outside of the car I see, in the distance, Bench Woman revolving on the Ford future sports car platform. Clearly from there Bench Woman could not have seen either the cheek kiss, which I initiated, or the lip kiss, initiated by Claire. I take Claire's hand with greater strength than before.

I am suddenly overcome by gloom as the reality of the situation hits. Bench Woman would not even care if she saw us kiss in the back seat of the Lincoln. Bench Woman does not know who I am. Even if Bench Woman would see Claire and me make love in the Lincoln, she would not care. If Bench Woman heard that there were two people making love in open view in the back seat of the deep blue Lincoln on display here at the auto show, although she might walk over to see the sight out of curiosity, she would just think it the act of two crazy people. She wouldn't know, or care, that it was me.

Claire tells me that she needs to use the bathroom. I do too. Claire goes to the ladies' room

143

and I go to the men's room. The rooms are right next to each other.

"We'll meet right in front here," I say.

The bathroom of the convention center is large. I do what I have to do, wash my hands, then leave. When I come out, as expected, Claire is not yet out of the ladies' room. There is a line developing for the ladies' room. There was no wait for the men's room. I take a drink of water at the water fountain. The fountain is situated between the two bathrooms. An unusual feeling hits the pit of my stomach because this water fountain is so close to the bathrooms. Is it possible that water from the toilets and urinals mix with water from the fountain? I know that such a scenario is unlikely, so I continue to drink from the fountain. The water from the fountain is mediocre. It is not very cold.

Two older gentlemen walk from the Volkswagen exhibit, which is right nearby, to the bathrooms. As they pass by, I hear the taller, obviously older man say to the shorter, younger man, "The body yearns to go to the ground, but the soul yearns to go to the heavens. That is why we stay on the ground when we are alive, neither flying nor digging into the earth." I hear no more of their conversation because they enter the bathroom.

What exactly does that mean? With Claire still in the ladies' room, I re-enter the men's room, but do not see the two men. Since the two men are not standing at the urinals, they must be sitting down in the stalls. I then hear the older man's voice in one of the stalls. Fortunately, there is an empty stall to his left. The younger man must be in the stall to his right. I go to the empty stall, close the door, and sit. I hear the older man say to his friend in the stall to his right, but loud enough for me to hear,

"That is why we feel so filled with angst and anxiety. It is the tension between our body wanting to go back to the dust from where it came and our soul yearning to go up to the heavens. Those two desires are constantly fighting with each other."

From the other stall, the other man says,

"Could that be why I hate to fly in airplanes, because my body, which wants to go back to the ground, is strongly fighting any rise into the sky?"

"That may well be true. But the opposite is also true. People who enjoy flying in airplanes have souls that want to go to the heavens more than their bodies want to stay on the ground."

I have been sitting on this toilet seat long enough and have heard enough to know that these two men do not know what they are talking about. I exit, but before I do, I flush, just to make my stay in the stall appear legitimate. I also wash my hands before I leave the bathroom. I see Claire waiting for me.

"Were you in the bathroom the entire time?"

Not wanting to tell Claire that I left the bathroom minutes before, only to re-enter and sit on a toilet just to listen to people talk in the stalls next to me about the different yearnings of the body and soul, I tell her that there was a wait in the men's room.

"That's odd, there is no line now," she says.

I go the water fountain for a quick drink. We

145

then head to the Chevrolet exhibit. Claire walks towards a nice small car. She looks good sitting in it.

"I like this," Claire says.

We go to another small Chevrolet suitable in price for Claire. The red four door car on the floor of the auto show looks pretty good and is priced well. It feels like a good car. While sitting in many different cars may help Claire decide what she likes and what she doesn't like, it also muddles the picture. It is getting harder to distinguish or remember the differences between the various cars.

Claire next walks towards another small and nice looking black two door car. I leave her and go towards a red Chevrolet Corvette. I enter the powerful car through the driver's seat. I do not rush out of the car even though there are quite a few people surrounding the car who would like for me to get out of it. I do not rush out. The others will get their turn soon enough. This car is low compared to the other cars. Even the driver's seat is low. I wonder if there is a way to bring the seat up. I don't know if I like the lowness. But the more I sit inside here, the more I grow to like it. It is an intoxicating feeling just knowing that a powerful engine is at my disposal. There is no escaping the exhilarating feeling of knowing all this power is available. I am getting used to the lowness. As the man in the bathroom said, the body yearns to go to the ground. That must be why it feels good to sit down low. Maybe that is why a fast, low car is so desirable. The driver sits down low, to satisfy its yearning for the ground. On the other hand, since the car goes fast, it gives the soul the feeling of going to the heavens.

I exit the Corvette, my body and soul refreshed. I look towards a Chevy family sedan and see Claire talking to a man. This man looks to be my age, maybe a few years older, and the two of them seem to be having a grand old time whooping it up. Perhaps not whooping it up, but they do seem to be having a good time together. He is tall and good looking. Was he just walking around the Chevrolet exhibit waiting to find a sweet girl like Claire and then pounce on her like a tiger as she innocently strolls amongst the new Chevys? He looks like a real smooth operator. I do not approach them, but rather, I lurk behind the blue Chevy minivan and observe the two of them. Claire sees me and calls me over.

"Matthew. This is John. John and I grew up on the same block. We were born within a month of each other. Our mothers walked us together in baby carriages to the supermarket."

I extend my hand to John, Claire's baby carriage companion, feeling unexpectedly jealous at their relationship as babies. I know my feeling is irrational, but it exists nonetheless.

They reminisce. I join in with a smile or comment every now and then. Finally, after what seems a long time, a young woman approaches. She is a tall, slightly chubby blond named Lisa. The leathery mother I met in Las Vegas was also named Lisa.

John introduces Lisa as his girlfriend. By their obvious ease and comfort with each other, I guess that one day, in the not too distant future, they will be husband and wife. I have gotten over my initial jealous reaction to John. I like Lisa. After

147

talking for maybe ten minutes, John asks us if we would like to get dinner with them after the auto show. My internal reaction is initially no, but Claire definitely wants to continue reminiscing with John. She looks up at me and I tell her that it is fine with me if we go. We will meet John and Lisa in two hours at the Ford exhibit and from there we will decide where to eat. It is good that we will meet at the Ford exhibit because that will give me one more opportunity to see Bench Woman before leaving. They head to the BMWs. Claire and I head toward a big white Chevy.

We are drawn to the rear seat of the big white car. Again we find ourselves in the expansive rear seat of a big car. We are only separated by a foot of dark leather. The distance between us shrinks to only a few inches. So far, our time spent in the rear seats of the big American cars has been our most romantic time together, and our time in this big white Chevy is no exception. In the cocoon that is this Chevrolet, we sustain a kiss, and then a few more kisses. I suddenly feel that we are being watched. My intuition is correct as I see a man, woman, and three kids looking inside the car. I don't believe that they mean to watch us kiss. They probably just want to get inside the car to see if it will comfortably fit their family. This car does, indeed, have a big back seat that should comfortably absorb their family. There might even be room to spare. Both Claire and I feel their presence and stop our kissing. I am not upset at the family for wanting to enter this Chevy. They look like good people.

Leaving the Chevy exhibit holding hands, we

make our way through the Nissan, Honda, Toyota, and Saturn exhibits. While these manufacturers make good cars, and they offer many models that Claire may consider buying, the focus of the rest of our time at the auto show is no longer looking for a car that Claire may buy in the future. Rather, in order to find appropriate kissing areas, we seek the rear seats of the large cars. Time is running out fast because we are soon going to meet John and Lisa at the Ford exhibit. At 4:50 p.m. we steal a kiss in a Dodge sedan, which also has quite a comfortable rear seat. Unfortunately, we quickly leave the rear seat of that Dodge knowing that we need to get back to the Ford exhibit to meet our dinner companions.

We walk the floor of the auto show to meet John and Lisa. Going past the sea of cars, I am struck by one thought: How do these cars move? I know that they are powered by gasoline and that the gas burns, but how does that burning gas translate into movement? A building doesn't drive away when it burns. When someone has a backyard barbecue, the grill doesn't drive away. Why should a car? Why does the car have to move just because the gasoline burns? Why doesn't the car burn up with the gasoline? That seems just as likely as the car moving because of the burning gasoline. But since cars do move, I should just accept that the burning of gasoline creates motion. How do the radios inside the cars work? In a car that is moving through traffic, the radio reaches out from the colorless air and brings in radio signals. Amazingly, sound then emanates from the radio. Just flip the dial and suddenly a radio talk show host, the news, or music is penetrating the steel, the glass, and the eardrums, all as the car is moving at sixty miles per hour. It is a miracle that I take for granted.

Claire and I continue our journey toward the Ford exhibit. While moving cars and radios playing in them are miraculous, a more amazing thought overpowers me. Who cares how cars move? How do I move? I know I move with muscles and different body parts working together. But why does it all happen? Wouldn't it be simpler if my body just stopped? What keeps me moving? Why should I even be allowed to move one foot in front of the other and move closer to the Ford exhibit? I feel my blood moving. It is pulsing through my body. I feel strong as I hold Claire's hand. It is good to be able to move. But why should I be so lucky that I can move? It is another miracle. It is good to be alive. But about twenty feet ahead of us, at the Ford exhibit, I see perhaps the greatest miracle of all. Claire's friends, John and Lisa, are speaking with Bench Woman, the Ford spokesmodel, in front of the Ford car of the future. It is just the three of them. Claire and I approach.

## Chapter 28

I slow down as we head toward John and Lisa, who are, to my disbelief, actually speaking with Bench Woman. Because we are holding hands, Claire feels me slow down and asks me why I am doing so.

"Maybe we should wait until your friends finish talking with the Ford spokesmodel," I say.

"Why?" Claire answers, "There is no reason why we can't talk with her also."

My legs are heavy as we approach John, Lisa, and Bench Woman. I've wanted to speak with Bench Woman since I first set my eyes on her at the park during lunch. Yet my dream was not to speak with her in the middle of the auto show with Claire, her childhood friend John, and John's girlfriend. When I awoke this morning, never, in my wildest dreams, did I imagine that I would be right up close to Bench Woman. I am also hearing her voice. Somehow, now that this incredible opportunity is here, I do not want to stand next to her, hear her voice, and be a part of the conversation with her. This is not how I wanted to meet her.

"It was nice speaking with you. Good luck with your modeling and singing career," John says to Bench Woman, just as Claire and I arrive.

"I enjoyed speaking with the two of you. Bye-bye," Bench Woman says to John and Lisa as she walks away.

"Who was that?" I ask John, knowing full well that it was Bench Woman, the Ford spokesmodel. I can't believe Bench Woman told them that she enjoyed speaking with them. That is wonderful for them.

John replies, as if I don't know,

"She was the Ford spokesmodel here today. She is very nice. After I asked her a question about the Ford future car, we just became involved in a conversation. She works for a large modeling agency. Her real dream is to become a singer. She told me her name, but I forgot what it is. She said that she might be coming out with a recording soon and that I should look out for it."

I cannot believe that John heard Bench Woman's name, but forgot it. I don't like him now.

"Lisa, do you remember the spokesmodel's name?" asks John.

"Rebecca Everglades," Lisa says back to John with a slightly harsh tone. John's inquiry apparently interrupted Lisa's conversation with Claire. Don't these people realize that they are talking about Bench Woman?

"That's right," John continues, "her name is Rebecca Everglades. Maybe one day she will be famous."

I now know Bench Woman's name. Rebecca Everglades. That is a beautiful name. I wonder if it is her real name or if it is just the name she uses for modeling and singing. Rebecca Everglades. To me she will always be Bench Woman.

John, Claire's childhood friend, was truly blessed today by having the opportunity to speak with Bench Woman. But he is now absorbed in a conversation with Claire and Lisa about where we should have dinner. Could it mean so little to him to have heard the beautiful voice of Bench Woman, or should I say Rebecca Everglades? John has his arm around Lisa. He looks happy.

We talk about going either to an Indian or Chinese restaurant. Both of those choices are fine with me. I would most like to go to an Italian restaurant, but John and Lisa started off this restaurant discussion by telling us how just last evening they went to an Italian restaurant which, while very good, used too much garlic. I love garlic. How can you use too much garlic? Lisa describes the delicious, but too garlicky, veal and chicken dishes that they had last night.

I'm glad to hear that they are not vegetarians. The worst thing is to go to either an Indian or a Chinese restaurant with a group of vegetarians. While I often have mixed feelings about eating our animal friends, I do nonetheless. But with a group of vegetarians at either an Indian or Chinese restaurant, where everyone is expected to share dishes and not eat meat, there is very little to order. Some vegetarian dishes are good, but to be forced to order a vegetarian dish ruins it for me. What makes it worse is that if the lone meat eater says that he does not like mushrooms, then he is cast aside as a troublemaker. So what happens is that the vegetarians effectively reduce the ordering options to the meat eater by 95%, but if the meat eater says that he does not want mushrooms, he is then shunned. John and Lisa apparently eat meat. I know Claire eats meat since I've seen her do so in the past. All of us going to dinner tonight eat animals. Is that fair to the cows, chickens, and pigs? Are we going to rot in hell because of it?

153

The four of us make a last minute decision not to go for either Indian or Chinese food. Instead, we decide to go to a place that John recommends named Volcano Valley. The name is derived from the specialty drink of the restaurant, which, logically, is called a "volcano." John assures us that the place is very lively, with good American-type food, excellent desserts, and great drinks, especially the volcano. According to John, Volcano Valley opened one month ago near his apartment. We make our way out of the Jacob Javits Center and the four of us get into a taxi cab that will take us to the Upper East Side, to Volcano Valley.

"To First Avenue and 75th Street," John tells our driver.

Lisa tells Claire and me that John took her to Volcano Valley and wanted to get her drunk on the volcano drinks. But she hated the taste of the volcano, and only had a few sips. Lisa drank only soda that night after her sips of the repulsive volcano. She tells us that John fell so in love with the volcanoes that he could barely make the one block walk back to his apartment.

"He was so drunk that he could hardly walk up the two flights to his apartment. He fell asleep in his clothes on the couch," Lisa says.

The quiet cab driver, named Manto according to the plaque in the taxi cab, drives like a madman. We get to the front of Volcano Valley. John immediately whips out his wallet and insists upon paying the entire cab fare. I offer to give him half, but he steadfastly refuses. When we enter Volcano Valley, John opens the door for all of us. It is a nice gesture, but John's excessive politeness upsets me slightly. It is not his gentlemanly acts that upset me. Rather, I am jealous that John actually conversed with Bench Woman, face-to-face, only minutes ago. What a lucky man he is, and he doesn't even know it.

We sit down in a booth in the front bar area of the rather dark Volcano Valley. It is loud in here. There are volcano-type noises at regular intervals emanating from a model volcano that flashes and spews out water vapor every few moments.

A waiter asks us if anyone would like a drink. John convinces Lisa that she should try a volcano again, even though she hated it the last time she was here. John assures her that she must have been in a bad mood on that occasion, or that it was her hormones. John tells Lisa that she will surely like the volcano today. I tell the waiter that I will also have a volcano. With John's enthusiasm directing the drink orders, Claire orders one also.

"Volcanoes all around," John announces happily.

"I can't imagine coming to Volcano Valley and not ordering a volcano," I say.

Almost two minutes later, our waiter, who looks to be very young, as if he is not even old enough to shave, comes back to us with a tray holding the four volcanoes. The volcanoes are a light maroon color. They look appetizing. I do not know what they are made of. They don't look anything like actual volcanoes. Of course, I have never seen a live volcano in action, except on television. Did I expect to see lava rising from these volcano drinks? I ask our waiter, who tells us that his name is Peter, what ingredients make up the volcanoes. Peter tells me that the volcano recipe is top secret. However, he informs me that it contains, in secret quantities, pineapple juice, orange juice, cranberry juice, vodka, and red wine. He warns us that if any of us find out exactly how the volcanoes are made, then that person will have to be killed. Peter leaves us and returns momentarily with four menus.

The Volcano Valley menu is dominated by various hamburgers and assorted sandwiches. The menus are educational too. On the bottom of the menus are photographs of ten different volcanoes from around the world. Above the photographs are the names of those ten volcanoes, but the names are not above the correct photographs. The menus ask us, the Volcano Valley patrons, to match each photograph with the correct volcano name. The menus state that all of the Volcano Valley waiters and waitresses know which photograph goes with which volcano name.

My eyes are attracted to the "Fabulous Fiery Fajitas" section of the menu. I will order a sizzling hot chicken fajita. On second thought, perhaps a beef fajita will be better. It has been my experience that beef fajitas, or beef tacos for that matter, are preferable to chicken fajitas or chicken tacos. The difference between chicken and beef fajitas is not only in taste. It is in the darker color of the beef fajita that makes a beef fajita superior to a chicken fajita. The darker beef fajita is just more enjoyable than the lighter colored chicken fajita. The extra fat in the beef fajita probably doesn't hurt either.

"This volcano is fantastic," exclaims John, who

156

is the first to have some of the drink. He drinks about one-third of his glass by the time Claire, Lisa, and I first taste the concoction.

I take my first sip of the volcano. It tastes mostly like a mixture of fruit juices, which is what it is primarily. I sense the alcohol, in the form of the vodka and wine, more than I actually taste it. I know the alcohol is in there, but this drink goes down so smoothly, it is hard to believe that it is not all juice. A drink with the name volcano should not be so smooth. It should be more explosive. It should almost hurt going down.

"I didn't like it the last time I had one and I don't like this volcano either," says Lisa. "This is the last time I'm ever getting one. What do you think Claire?"

With the sincere expression of someone thinking deeply, Claire declares her dislike for the drink.

"I don't hate it. But I don't like it."

Taking another small sip, Claire says,

"This drink tastes peculiar. I don't think that the wine goes well with the vodka and the other juices. This tastes like bad juice. What do you think Matthew?"

I hate to concur with John, and at the same time go against Claire and Lisa, but I like my volcano. It does not taste bad to me. In fact, it tastes good.

"I must agree with John," I say. "I like it."

Claire says,

"I'm glad you like it. You can have mine."

Lisa, without uttering a sound, just pushes her

volcano away from her with disgust. As our waiter walks by, Lisa says,

"I'll have a Diet Coke."

"I'll have one too please," Claire says.

"Every time I drink a volcano I enjoy it more," says John.

I am envious of John because of his great fortune in speaking with Bench Woman at the auto show. However, we have a common fondness for the volcanoes.

John, just about finished with his volcano, pulls Lisa's maroon drink towards him.

"If you get drunk on these volcanoes again, I'm not going to help you get home," says Lisa.

"Don't worry."

I, too, finish my volcano rather quickly and, upon seeing that Claire has abandoned any remaining desire to finish her volcano, I pull hers towards me. Claire looks at me suspiciously, as if liking the volcano is evil.

"Do you really like these drinks?" Claire asks me.

"I do."

I am not sure what it is about these volcanoes that I like. I start on Claire's volcano. I understand why Claire and Lisa believe that these volcanoes taste like bad juice because, in fact, they do. Yet there is an addictive quality about the volcanoes that captures me. Clearly John has also been captured by that same quality. It's peculiar that both John and I enjoy the volcanoes, while Claire and Lisa do not. Possibly the volcanoes mix particularly well with male hormones and poorly with female hormones. It may just be a coincidence. The waiter comes back.

"Have you decided what you want to order?"

John asks us if we want some appetizers for the table to share.

"How do mozzarella sticks and chicken wings sound?" John asks us. John does not worry about eating healthy.

After affirmative nods from everyone, we order a plate of mozzarella sticks and chicken wings.

"Are you ready to order your main meal or do you need more time?"

We are ready. Lisa begins.

"I'll have a grilled chicken breast sandwich on toasted whole wheat bread."

"That comes with either French fries or onion rings."

"I'll have onion rings."

Claire orders a chicken salad sandwich on pita bread. Instead of the French fries or onion rings, she requests a tossed salad with oil and vinegar. John orders a bacon cheeseburger deluxe, medium rare, which comes with French fries. I order the beef fajita, which our waiter tells me comes out sizzling hot, and is his personal favorite.

During our conversation, we learn that Lisa and John met at a party. They were both on a date with someone else that evening. At some point, they started talking to each other. When each of their dates left them alone for a few minutes, John asked Lisa for her telephone number. That was two years ago. Neither of them knows what happened to their respective dates from that evening.

Lisa looks at me and asks, with a smile, "how

long have you and Claire been going out?"

I don't know what to say. Claire, to save me from having to answer, says, "We are friends from the office."

John then comments, "What do you mean you are friends? I saw you two smooching in a Chevrolet."

The waiter comes to the table with a plate of mozzarella sticks and a platter of chicken wings with four small plates.

"I'll have another volcano," John says.

"Me too," I say.

## Chapter 29

An awkward silence descends upon the table. But Peter, our waiter, soon returns with new volcanoes. Although the subject of the relationship between Claire and me is abandoned, thoughts about it ruminate in my head. This morning I was simply going to the auto show with Claire to help her look at the new cars. Little did I know that we would be kissing in the rear seat of many of the large American cars on display. How did this all happen? And even more miraculously, this all happened on the same day that I stood next to Bench Woman, heard Bench Woman's voice, and even discovered Bench Woman's real name.

John finishes another volcano with barely a breath. I take a rather large gulp of my volcano, taking in about one-quarter of its contents. The conversation has now shifted to the usual-- apartments, jobs, and movies.

It's difficult to understand exactly why both Claire and Lisa dislike the volcanoes. The drink goes down so smoothly. It tastes much more like juice than alcohol. These volcanoes can easily get a person drunk. In fact, I should not drink this volcano too fast because my head already feels woozy. John, on the other hand, motions to Peter, our waiter, to bring him another volcano. Lisa, talking to Claire about her two cats, Tomato and Charlie, gives John a look of disapproval when he orders the additional volcano. John stands up, walks away from the table, and says,

"I'll be back in a few minutes. I need to smoke. It is ridiculous that you can't smoke in restaurants these days."

"Why do you need to smoke? Can't you have a meal without a cigarette?" asks Lisa.

"Calm down. There is nothing as good as a cigarette right after a volcano."

John goes outside to smoke. I see him through the window taking long puffs on his cigarette. He looks satisfied.

Peter comes back to our table with the mozzarella sticks and chicken wings. The chicken wings are lying in a basket and are covered with an orange-colored sauce. There must be nearly twenty small wings in the basket. If chickens have two wings each, I wonder if the twenty wings in this basket came from only ten chickens or whether each wing came from a different bird. Did twenty individual chickens give their lives and wings for this basket of chicken wings or did only ten? The mozzarella sticks, which are fried to a crispy brown, are on a white plate. In the middle of the plate is a small dish with red sauce for dunking the mozzarella sticks. There are eight mozzarella sticks in all. Immediately upon his return from his smoke, John takes a chicken wing. Lisa takes a chicken wing too. Claire and I each take a mozzarella stick. I dip mine in the sauce. It is good. The outside of the stick is crunchy and the cheese inside is hot and stringy. I take a chicken wing. Although it is on the small side, it is meaty and spicy. I take a long sip of my volcano to counteract the wing's spiciness.

"Order that man another volcano," John says to Peter.

I must admit that I am happy to be the

162

recipient of an additional volcano, courtesy of John. The fact that John ordered it for me makes it appear that it is John who is the one who craves these alcoholic masterpieces and that I am just accepting the volcano as his unwilling dupe. Of course, if I really didn't want the drink I could have told John, or our waiter Peter, that I have had enough of the volcanoes. I suppose my silence, and my acceptance of the volcano when Peter brings it over to me in a few moments, will be the equivalent of my asking for the drink itself. Undoubtedly, I am a willing participant in the drinking of the volcano that will soon come my way. By that token, is anyone ever just an innocent dupe? By just going along with something is that follower as bad as the person in charge? Is a soldier who tortures a captured prisoner as bad as his general if he is commanded to do so? And what if the soldier would get killed himself by his commander if he did not follow orders? Is a person guilty by just not being a hero?

My new volcano arrives. I just completed a bite of a spicy chicken wing, so I take the drink to my mouth the moment it is placed on the table. The cold fruity volcano is not only delicious, but it works well at quenching the thirst caused by the spicy chicken wing. Sitting here with Claire, John, and Lisa makes me hungry. With every sip of the volcano, and with every corresponding bite of either a chicken wing or mozzarella stick, I am getting hungrier and hungrier. I look forward to the arrival of my beef fajita.

Claire and Lisa are involved in their own conversation. They must be disgusted by their volcano guzzling companions. John and I talk about baseball. John tells me that he was a pitcher in high school, and quite a good one at that he assures me. He tells me that he hurt his arm by throwing too many curveballs at a young age.

"Two more volcanoes," John tells Peter.

I do not protest, but tell myself that the upcoming volcano will be my last one for the night. I am not drunk yet, but enough is enough. The influence of these volcanoes is sneaking up on me. John tells me that he would like to run for public office one day and that he wants his political career to culminate in the United States Senate. I don't know if John will make it that far, but he does have a kind of charismatic personality. I can't say that I like him, but I see how people might follow him.

In what was only one or two minutes after the last mozzarella stick and chicken wing were eaten, Peter comes, without fanfare, with Claire's chicken salad sandwich, Lisa's grilled chicken breast, and John's bacon cheeseburger. Peter says that my beef fajita will arrive momentarily.

"By the way, I'll have one more volcano," John says.

One minute later, Peter arrives at our table with my beef fajita. Unlike the other three dishes, the fajita is heard, as well as seen. It sizzles. It looks and sounds like a beef fajita that a restaurant called Volcano Valley can be proud of. All four of us look at the beef fajita with admiration. It will be enjoyable, but challenging to eat. It will require that I put the slices of beef, onions, tomato, guacamole, and beans all inside of the fajita. It will be worth it though.

"Be careful, the plate is hot," Peter says.

"That does look good, Matthew," says Claire.

I am pleased that my fajita is making such an impression on the table. By doing so, the conversation between Claire and Lisa is interrupted. Now, possibly, all four of us can be involved in one conversation, not separate conversations for the boys and girls.

We start eating our food. Without a doubt, my beef fajita is the most appetizing dish on the table. In fact, I would say that the beef fajita is head and shoulders more appetizing than the other dishes ordered. As I put together my first fajita, I feel all the eyes of the table upon me. Into the empty fajita I first put some beef. On top of the meat I place some beans, then some onions and tomatoes, and then a small amount of guacamole. The fajita is now filled. I take a good hefty bite so as to get a taste of all of the flavors. It is good. It is as good as it looks.

"Can I offer anyone some of this?" I ask the others.

John, who is almost finished with his most recently ordered volcano, did not even acknowledge the question. He is pleased with his bacon cheeseburger and volcano. Lisa tells me, "No, thank you."

"I'll have a bite," Claire says.

I'm glad Claire wants to try my fajita. The closeness we developed during our time spent in the rear seats of the large American cars at the auto show has been dissipating here at Volcano Valley amidst the volcanoes and John and Lisa.

Instead of handling Claire the fajita so that she can take a bite out of it as she holds it, I take hold of the fajita and move it towards her mouth. She then takes hold of it.

"It's very tasty, but a little too spicy for me."

"I'll have another volcano," John says to Peter.

John drinks the volcanoes as if there is no tomorrow. He drinks them like water. He is still speaking coherently. Yet the look in his eyes and his general demeanor are that of a person who has had too much to drink. One more drink could put him over the edge.

"Why do you have to drink so many of those awful drinks? Stop already," Lisa says to John.

"Calm down," John replies condescendingly. "I'm fine."

John chugs his volcano down.

"Another volcano," John orders with a smirk.

"I'm not helping you home," Lisa says to John.

"I don't care."

The hostile conversation between John and Lisa is in stark contrast to the loving way they were towards each other at the auto show. Their hostility chills the dinner conversation and, except for random comments every few minutes or so, we eat the rest of our meal in silence. Although the silence is awkward, it affords me the opportunity to savor every bite of my beef fajita. It is spicy, yet quite delicious.

No one orders dessert, but I order coffee. Claire orders a cappuccino. Lisa then orders a decaf cappuccino and John orders a final volcano "for the road." We leave the restaurant after our last drinks. The tension between Lisa and John is palpable. Claire tells John that it was nice to see him after all these years, and that it was nice to meet Lisa. I tell

166

them that I enjoyed meeting both of them.

It is almost 8:00 p.m. when we say good night to John and Lisa. Claire has to get back to Queens and I have to go back to the Upper West Side of Manhattan, which is an easy crosstown bus ride.

"I'll take the subway back with you so that you don't have to be alone," I say to Claire.

"That's very nice, but don't be silly. It's Sunday night and it has been a long day. I'm going to take a cab. It is not too far of a cab ride once over the 59th Street Bridge."

"I had a great day," I say.

Neither Claire nor I expected the day to take so many turns. I know that I did not expect to be kissing Claire in different large American cars at the auto show. Rather, I thought that Claire and I would just have breakfast, look at some cars that Claire might purchase in the future, and then go home. Things changed during the course of the day.

"Here's a cab."

The yellow cab, which is a large Ford sedan, similar to one of the cars at the auto show in which Claire and I shared a long kiss, stops for Claire. I open the door for her and we kiss. The kiss lands half on the lip and half on the cheek.

"See you tomorrow," Claire says as she enters the cab.

The cab drives off. I walk uptown ten blocks and then take a crosstown bus.

It is dark outside by the time I get back to my neighborhood. I am not tired. Instead of going right home, I go the Pasture and sit at the counter.

"What can I get for you?"

167

"I'll have to think about it for a minute."

Unfortunately, Ellen is not here now. It would have been nice to have her greet me. The counterwoman who is here now is friendly, but she is more businesslike than Ellen. I have seen her perhaps three times in the past.

"Would you like coffee?"

"No thanks. I'll just have a fruit cup."

The counterwoman brings over a large glass of water filled with ice and the cup of fruit. It is filled primarily with cantaloupe, honeydew, strawberries, and grapes. The fruit cup also contains one or two pieces of kiwi and pineapple.

## Chapter 30

It is just before 10:00 p.m. when I return to my apartment. My body is exhausted. It was only yesterday when I was in Las Vegas. I got practically no sleep before meeting Claire for brunch. Then I went to the auto show and proceeded to have the volcano-filled dinner. It is no wonder I am tired. Yet I feel quite awake, despite my physical weariness. What did the day with Claire mean? We kissed, many times, in the back seats of a great number of cars at the auto show. It was enjoyable. What will it be like between us tomorrow in the office? Will Claire and I be back to our pre-auto show relationship, or will we start sneaking around in closets?

Like a zombie, I take off my clothes and enter the shower. Although I normally take a shower in the morning, this evening-time warm shower soothes my body and mind. As the water hits my skin, cleansing me, I look forward to getting into bed and falling asleep, most probably with the television still on.

I feel good upon exiting the shower. I dry myself well so as not to get the bed wet. I put on the television instinctively. A comfortable heaviness overcomes me. A soda commercial ends as I enter the bed. To my pleasant surprise, the movie The Sound of Music with Julie Andrews is playing on television. Today is not a holiday. I thought this movie only played on holidays. I am content to be in bed watching this movie. It has been a few years since I've seen it. The music is great.

Comfortable in bed, I hear the words to "My

Favorite Things." I hear about raindrops on roses, rich apple strudel, doorbells, sleighbells, schnitzel with noodles, and brown paper packages tied up with string.

Those are nice things I suppose. Not that I even know what schnitzel is. If I did, would it be one of my favorite things? I do, however, know what schnauzers are. I never met a schnauzer I didn't like.

"Girls in white dresses with blue satin sashes, snowflakes that stay on my nose and my eyelashes, silver white winters that melt into spring. . . ."

The movie continues. However, my lack of sleep this weekend is catching up with me. My eyes are heavy. I turn off the television and make sure that my alarm is set for tomorrow morning. I would love to take off from work tomorrow because I can certainly use some rest from the busy past few days, but I cannot do so. I just took off two days last week in Atlantic City. My eyes close. I am truly exhausted, but as the minutes pass, I do not fall asleep.

It is hot in here. It is a hot summer night. The air conditioner is on, but my apartment is still hot. I finally fall asleep, but in what seems like no time, I wake up. According to my clock, it is 1:15 in the morning. Turning over, I close my eyes, but cannot sleep. I turn over again and see that it is 1:29 a.m. My air conditioner is working hard, but it has not broken the heat.

I get out of bed, sit on the couch, and turn on the television. There is a how to be successful show, a how to lose weight show, a home-shopping show, an old movie, and a detective show. These don't appeal to me, so I return to bed, put on the radio, and hear a psychologist discuss insomnia. I change the station to the all sports station. The discussion is about baseball. The subject is the additional round of playoffs for Major League Baseball that was instituted a few years ago and whether it has helped or hurt the sport. Now a team can come in second place in its division and still make the playoffs and possibly win the World Series. The last caller, Mike from Brooklyn, believes that allowing more teams into the playoffs is a good idea. I don't know if I agree. I love baseball, but the average game is sometimes boring. It is the pennant race that is exciting. It is the knowledge that if your team does not come in first place, it might as well come in last. I want to call into the show, but something stops me. I am either lazy or just scared to talk on the radio.

I turn off the radio and close my eyes at 2:25 a.m. But after a few minutes, I get up and put on my gray shorts and one of the shirts that I bought in Las Vegas. I put sneakers on my feet and a baseball cap on my head. I must be incredibly overtired from the weekend. Despite the lack of sleep, I just can't fall asleep.

I walk the short walk to the Pasture. The streets are quiet at this very late hour, but there are some cars and cabs out. There are a handful of customers in the Pasture, which never closes. I sit at the counter, where the counterman, who I recognize but whose name I don't know, greets me with a napkin, a menu, and water. The water is deliciously filled with ice. It is refreshingly cool, even cold, inside the Pasture.

171

"My friend, what would you like?" asks the man behind the counter.

I see the glass cabinet filled with cakes. There are cheesecakes, layer cakes, and assorted pies. They look fresh. But I decide against them.

"I'll have a chocolate milkshake, very thick please."

"One very thick chocolate milkshake coming up."

I see the counterman prepare my milkshake. I ask him for a pen so that I can doodle on my napkin. He obliges and then gives me the milkshake. The straw stands straight up in the shake, proudly showing off its thickness. I take a sip. It is mouth-watering. I take a lengthy second sip without breathing.

I start doodling. I calculate how much money I will have if I save $20 each week until New Years. I calculate how much I'll have if I save $30, $40, $50 a week.

The pen, seemingly with its own mind, writes down the names of women that I know. Next to each name I write down the odds of me marrying that person. For purposes of this game, I assume that each of those women will have me. That, of course, may not be the case. The list reads: Lori: 18:1; Karen: 26:1; Margaret: 15:1; Stacy: 10:1; Helen: 150:1. I don't think these odds are realistic. What about Claire? What are the odds on us getting married? Are the odds 5:1, 50:1, or 500:1? What about Bench Woman? I wish the odds were good with her, but the odds must be 1,000,000:1, if that good. The odds are probably best with a woman that I have not yet met. I'll call her mystery woman with odds of 1:1.

I gulp down the thick milkshake. It is 3:50 a.m. I put the napkin with the doodles in my pocket.

"It was delicious," I tell the counterman.

"Good night," he says.

I walk outside and see an older woman with straight gray hair leave the twenty-four hour supermarket next to the Pasture. She carries two hefty grocery bags. She stumbles on the sidewalk and fruit falls from her bag. I run to her.

"I am so clumsy," she says sheepishly.

"What are you doing on the street at this time?" I ask.

"I always buy my groceries at this hour. I hate the long lines during the day. I live right in that building across the street," the woman says.

The older woman, whose name I discover is Beverly, thanks me for helping her. I ask her if I can carry her bags to her apartment building. She asks me why I am out at this hour and I tell her that I couldn't sleep and went out to the diner. She tells me that she is hungry. She asks me if I will join her for something to eat at the Pasture. I tell her that I will join her, even though I just came from the Pasture and must go to work tomorrow morning, which is only a few hours from now.

We enter the diner. The counterman smiles. We sit at a booth. A waiter approaches.

Beverly says,

"I'll have a cup of decaffeinated coffee and an apple turnover."

I am not hungry at all, but I order a piece of

173

cheesecake upon Beverly's insistence that I eat something. She doesn't want to sit and eat while I just sit and watch her.

I tell Beverly how I went to Las Vegas this weekend with Ken, omitting any reference to Jan English, and how I went to the auto show today, omitting all references to Bench Woman and my kisses with Claire. Beverly, upon finding out that I am not married, tells me that she has a wonderful niece, named Erica. Beverly tells me that she would like me to meet Erica. Beverly does not know Erica's telephone number off the top of her head, so we exchange telephone numbers. Beverly tells me to call her tomorrow night and at that time she will give me Erica's telephone number.

"Erica is a wonderful girl. She lives right in this neighborhood," Beverly says. "You two will get along splendidly."

We leave the diner at 5:00 a.m. Beverly pays the bill and I carry her groceries to her apartment building, where she is greeted by a doorman.

"Call me tomorrow so that I can give you Erica's telephone number."

I get to my apartment, which has finally cooled down from the air conditioner. I have a little more than two hours before I need to get ready for work, but I'm not tired. I empty my pants pocket. I find the napkin with the doodles from the first of my two visits to the Pasture during this late night. I add Beverly's niece, Erica, to the list of women I may possibly marry on the napkin, but put no odds next to her name. She might be "mystery woman" at odds of 1:1.

174

I put on the radio. On the all news station, a man from Russia, who came to the United States five years ago, is being interviewed about winning the $30 million lottery. He says,

> "Since I've come here, I get job, wife, and child. Now with this money, I don't know what to dream about. I am thrilled to win lottery, but it is just icing to top off cake of past 5 years."

That is pretty good icing, I think to myself.

"That's some icing," the newscaster says, "turning to sports, yesterday the Yankees. . ."

# Chapter 31

I close my eyes and the alarm sounds in what feels like one minute. It is time to begin the work week. Exhausted and sleep-deprived, I enter the shower. As the water falls upon my tired body, questions about my new relationship with Claire penetrate my drowsiness. How different, if at all, will things be with Claire today when we see each other at the office? And what will things be like between us as the upcoming Saturday night wedding approaches?

Drying off, I immediately put shaving cream on my face. It is thick. I let the thick white foam sit on my face for a few minutes before shaving. After my last stroke with the razor, I clean my face with cold water in an attempt to wake myself up. I exit the apartment at 8:05 a.m., wearing my charcoal colored suit, white shirt, and yellow and red striped tie.

"The usual," I tell the man who sells me the bagel and coffee.

I am very tired entering the office. What I want to do is close my eyes and sleep, but unfortunately, there is a great deal of work to do, especially since I missed two days of work last week.

I scan the newspaper before beginning the week's work. I have been out of touch with the world these past few days. Nothing much is new in sports. I peruse the editorial section. I finish off with a quick glance at the actual news. Two people, a mother, 29, and son, 6, were found shot in the head yesterday. The sister of the slain woman is pictured in tears on the front steps of the victim's house. In other news, there were two executions around the country, one in Texas, for the killing of a state trooper eleven years ago, and the other in Florida, for the killing of a storeowner during a robbery twelve years ago. In international news, fourteen people were killed in a suspicious explosion and hundreds were lost in a devastating flood. Also, there was a study supporting earlier claims regarding parrots. Researchers believe that the birds might be extremely intelligent. It was found, in fact, that the birds may have a far greater understanding of the words they speak than originally thought. Although some researchers think that parrots merely mimic words, the new studies show that the birds actually grasp the meanings of some words and phrases. That is incredible, but I am not shocked. From what I have seen of parrots on television, it looks to me as if they know what they are talking about.

I look at an office memorandum that was left on my desk about a specific commercial liability policy. It is confusing. Where is Claire? I have not seen her all morning. I see Betty out in the hallway.

"How was your weekend, Betty?"

"Very nice. My Tammy was in a dance recital yesterday. She was so beautiful in her skirt. Blah blah blah. . . How was your weekend?"

"It was very busy," I say. "Have you seen Claire today?"

"No. I believe she called in sick."

Claire rarely calls in sick. Did she call in sick just to avoid seeing me? I hope not. Yet I don't want her to really be sick. Poor Claire. She is either sick or she did not come into work because she feels strange about seeing me after our auto show kisses yesterday. Should I call her? Would I rather that Claire be actually sick or just uncomfortable about seeing me? I don't know. If she is uncomfortable seeing me today, will she feel more comfortable tomorrow? Is Claire just going to keep calling in sick day after day, week after week, month after month, year after year? I doubt it. She is probably simply not feeling well today, although she seemed fine during dinner with her old friend John and his girlfriend Lisa. If anything, of the two of us, I should be the sick one, given all of the volcanoes that I drank with the beef fajita. I wonder how John is feeling today. He drank volcanoes by the gallon yesterday at Volcano Valley.

With lunchtime approaching, I decide to forego an outing by a few of my colleagues to our usual Chinatown eatery. Instead I go to the delicatessen, and order a smoked turkey and tomato sandwich. It is a sunny day, although it is quite hot and humid. The news said it will reach a high of 92 degrees. Armed with the sandwich and a small carton of orange-pineapple juice, I walk, alone, to Battery Park, to the bench where I first set my eyes upon Bench Woman, whose real name I now know to be Rebecca Everglades. In my heart though, she is Bench Woman. Someone as beautiful as Bench Woman cannot be limited by a normal name, even if that name is as unique as Rebecca Everglades. Bench Woman suits her more.

The heat and humidity drain me as I sit on the familiar green bench. Undaunted by the oppressive weather conditions of the day, tourists scurry to the ferries to Ellis Island and the Statue of Liberty. The smoked turkey and tomato sandwich, accompanied by the small carton of cold orange-pineapple juice, makes for a satisfying lunch. The only thing that could make the food and drink more enjoyable would be a glimpse of Bench Woman in the park. With the auto show still in town, Bench Woman may, at this very moment, be revolving on the Ford future sports car platform. Is she revolving on the platform with her pale arm gracefully pointing to the future car, or is she speaking into the microphone as she explains to a throng of admirers why the Ford future sports car is the wave of the future? Whether Bench Woman is revolving and speaking or whether she is not revolving but merely pointing to the car, the people close by her, within viewing distance, are certainly fortunate.

The last bite of the smoked turkey and tomato sandwich is satisfying. My stomach is content. I will get back to the office shortly, but first I'll stroll amongst the people in the park. Two dogs approach as I stand under a tree. They are unleashed, but seem to be well trained. A man is with the dogs. He is wearing denim shorts, a plain white T-shirt and sandals. When he tells the dogs to come, the dogs listen and walk back to him with their tails wagging. Both dogs look happy. They must be mutts, although one resembles a collie and the other looks to be some type of terrier mix. It was my dream as a boy to have an Old English Sheepdog. Will that dream ever come true? What is it like to be a dog? When a dog looks to be happy, either chasing a stick, swimming in the water, or sleeping contentedly in the middle of the floor or wherever it wants, I wish I were a dog. Is it wrong to be jealous of a dog? Is it wrong to want to be a dog?

I finish lunch and get back to my desk. I will call Claire. We shared wonderful moments yesterday and she is sick today. I should find out how she is feeling. But I don't want to call her solely out of obligation because of our kisses. I should call her only if I want to call her. A person should not call another person just because 24 hours earlier the two people were kissing at the New York auto show. Do I want to call Claire because I care how she is feeling, or do I want to call her because I believe that, as a person who spent many moments kissing her lips, it is my responsibility to speak with her? Perhaps it is both of those reasons. Things are rarely black or white. My strongest motivation for wanting to call Claire is, I believe, that I am curious how she will react to my call. Will we talk about our kisses or will we act as if they never took place? There is only one way to find out.

I suddenly realize that I do not have Claire's home telephone number. I call information and get her number. I am nervous. Why do I feel nervous calling Claire? If I were told a few days ago that I would feel tense calling Claire, I would not have believed it. Kissing her in the rear seats of the large American cars at the auto show has certainly changed things.

"Hello. I cannot come to the phone right now. Please leave a message and I'll get back to you as soon as possible."

Is Claire really not at home or is she just screening her telephone calls? I hope that she is not too sick to answer the telephone. Life was better when there were no answering machines. It used to be that if no one picked up a telephone, the caller could assume that no one was there. That is not the case anymore. Now, when an answering machine answers the telephone, it means that the person is not home, or that the person is screening all calls, or that the person is screening only that particular caller's call.

"Hi Claire, this is Matt calling from work. I just wanted to find out how you are feeling. I should be in my office most of the afternoon if you want to call back. Hope everything is ok."

That was a good message. Short and sweet.

Where did the day go? It is already 4:30 in the afternoon. I'll work for another hour and then I'll be out of here by 5:30. As the minutes go by, my mind is preoccupied by two thoughts: What should I eat for dinner and why hasn't Claire called back? Could it be that Claire has not been at her apartment all afternoon and doesn't even know that I called? Should I call her again? I'll call her again tonight.

I exit the office building for the evening. A brilliant thought enters my mind. How could I have been so stupid not to have thought of it earlier? I'll go to the auto show again tonight. The auto show is in town all this week. The odds are high that Bench Woman is still modeling next to the Ford future sports car. I would be crazy to miss this opportunity to see Bench Woman. A happy bounce enters my step as the prospect of seeing Bench Woman fills my body.

I take the subway to 34th Street and 7th Avenue, which is a few blocks from the auto show. Outside of the convention center I wolf down a hot dog from a street vendor. The hot dog is not bad, but I much prefer hot dogs that are grilled on a barbecue to those boiled in water. Yet the hot dog is tasty. I hope it doesn't make me sluggish in front of Bench Woman. I pay the admission fee and enter the floor of the auto show.

I am filled with the anticipation of seeing Bench Woman again revolving on the Ford future sports car platform. Therefore, it is extremely disappointing to see someone else, a thin pretty blond, on the revolving Ford platform talking about the Ford future sports car. I have nothing against tonight's Ford spokesmodel. However, I wanted very much to see Bench Woman again tonight. With a heavy heart, I walk away from the Ford exhibit. If Bench Woman is not here, I do not have much of a desire to look at the cars. I just saw them yesterday. I didn't actually examine all that many cars yesterday because once Claire and I started kissing in the rear seats of the large American cars, we then stopped examining the cars themselves. After aimlessly walking for a few moments, I walk back to the Ford exhibit and ask a Ford representative, a young man wearing a name tag that says "Carl Miller," if he knows whether yesterday's spokesmodel will be back at any time during the remainder of the auto show this week. Carl Miller eyes me suspiciously and says that he doesn't know. Most likely he believes that I am a deranged lunatic spying on yesterday's Ford spokesmodel. Am I?

I leave the auto show hungry. That one hot dog I ate prior to entering the auto show was not enough for dinner. Once I get back to my neighborhood I stop at Tony and Joey's Pizza, which is my favorite pizzeria. The pizza is delicious here when they serve it piping hot fresh out of the oven. Unfortunately, many times they just serve a lukewarm slice of pizza that has spent too much time behind the counter. In those situations I always ask them to heat it up. "Make it very hot," I tell them. They are nice enough at Tony & Joey's, but they seem taken aback when I inform them that I want the lukewarm pizza heated up hot, as if they know better than I do at what temperature I like my pizza. Is there anything unusual about wanting to eat a hot slice of pizza?

"Hi. I'll have two slices and an iced tea."

"It will be a few minutes. There's a fresh pizza in the oven."

"Great."

Joey takes the fresh new steaming, cheese bubbling pizza out of the oven and cuts me two slices. Hot cheese slides off of the pizza's edges. It is perfect. It is just the way I like it as it burns the roof of my mouth. There is nothing as good as a fresh, hot slice of Tony & Joey's pizza.

"Take it easy."

It is hot in my apartment, so I immediately put on the air conditioner. There are two messages on the answering machine.

The first message is not a message at all. Someone called but hung up. There is a second message, though.

"Hi Matthew, it's Claire. I'm sorry I didn't call you back at work. Please call me back tonight if you can."

# Chapter 32

"Hello."

"Hi Claire, this is Matt, how are you?"

"I'm fine. I'm sorry I didn't call you back at the office today, Matthew, but I didn't sleep very well last night, so I slept most of this afternoon. I was too tired to answer the telephone. I feel much better now."

"Why couldn't you sleep last night?"

"Matthew, I'll tell you, but only if you promise not to think that I'm strange."

"Don't worry. I promise that I won't think that you're strange." Although I say that to Claire reflexively, is it really possible to promise someone not to think they are strange? If what she tells me makes her strange in my mind, there is nothing I can do.

"I had a dream last night. The dream kept me in a half awake and half asleep state from about 2:00 in the morning to 7:00 in the morning. Do you promise that you won't think I'm strange if I tell you about it?"

"I won't think you're strange. Tell me about your dream."

"I went to sleep at midnight after I watched a television documentary about a mass murderer in England at the turn of the century. The show was interesting, but it made me anxious. I must have fallen asleep quickly because what I remember next was looking at the clock and seeing that it was 2:00 a.m. I turned around in bed and there, lying next to me under the blanket, or so I thought, was a human arm. I did not actually see the arm, but the blanket next to my side was shaped as if there were an arm under it. Then, slowly, I moved my hand to what I thought was the arm. I moved very slowly to it, and when I finally touched it, I recoiled in terror. It felt fleshy to me. I did not know what to do. There was no body connected to the arm, at least I didn't see any. As I lay next to the arm, many thoughts came into my half awake mind. I thought that the British murderer from the television show was in my apartment and was going to kill me, and that he deposited an arm next to me to frighten me. I also thought that the murderer was in my apartment and killed the person to whom the arm belonged, but that the body was left somewhere on the floor of my apartment. I even thought for just a moment that I killed someone in my sleep and brought the victim's arm into bed with me."

"Who did you think you killed?" I asked.

"I don't know. It was a female arm, but whose I don't know. I was so overcome with fear that I was afraid to move or make noise because I believed that the murderer was in the apartment and I did not want him to know I was awake. I was afraid to put on the light or scream or use the telephone."

"You could have called me," I say.

"No I couldn't, Matthew. I was afraid to make noise or move. I must have been half awake and half asleep because I stayed in bed, but sat up against the wall, just lying next to the arm."

"That sounds terrible."

"I stayed motionless in bed the rest of the night. I tried not to move at all."

"What time was this?"

"It was 2:00 in the morning when I first thought that I saw the arm. I didn't move for the rest of the night. My only movement was slight turns of my head to look at my clock or to look at what I believed was the arm underneath my blanket right near my head. Hour after hour I just lay there in bed, thinking that a murderer was keeping an eye on me and that a disembodied arm was next to me. Finally, at 7:00 in the morning my alarm clock sounded. The alarm startled me so that I screamed and literally jumped up. When I jumped up, I grabbed hold of my blanket and pulled it violently off of me. To my relief, when I jerked the blanket an arm did not go flying across the room. There was nothing under my blanket at all."

Stating the obvious, I tell Claire that it would have been much more horrible if an arm without a body connected to it actually were there and flew across the room when she pulled her blanket.

"I suppose so. But I just cried when I realized that I had spent the last five hours up in bed, thinking that an arm without a body was lying next to me and that a murderer was in my apartment. I could not come to work. You must think I'm strange, don't you?"

"I don't think you're strange, although I do think that you had a strange dream," I tell Claire.

"You don't really understand. The dream was so vivid. But that is not all. When I was twenty years old I used to have very realistic dreams that kept me from sleeping soundly. They were bad dreams, although not always as horrifying as the dream last night. For almost an entire year I was plagued by the dreams. I do not know why they started. I went to a therapist for six months. Then one night, almost one year after the first dream, I simply stopped getting the dreams. Since that time I've had some dreams, like everyone else, but nothing like the bad dreams that I used to get. The year that I had all of those dreams was a nightmare. I am afraid that it will start happening again."

I've never heard Claire open up so much. I've never even heard her talk this much. I wish that I could do or say something to put her mind at ease. Could our kisses at the auto show have brought upon Claire's nightmare? How could the kisses have done that?

"Maybe it was our kissing at the auto show that brought on your dream?" I say, attempting to lighten the mood.

"I don't think it was that," Claire says.

I am not sure whether I should have mentioned our kisses at the auto show. Claire changes the subject and asks me about the day at work. I tell Claire that it was a dull day and that she did not miss anything. Claire tells me that she is afraid of going to bed tonight.

"Do you want me to come over?"

"That's very sweet, Matthew. But no thank you. I can't imagine what you are thinking. Thank you for listening though. I'll see you at work tomorrow. Good night."

Poor Claire. What happened to her last night sounds pretty bad. I hope her past sleeping problems don't come back to haunt her. Claire opened up to me in a way that she never would have done before our auto show kisses. What brought on her nightmare? Was it something I did? Was it any particular kiss in any particular rear seat at the auto show? Did something happen, perhaps a chemical reaction in her brain, during one of our kisses in the Lincoln, the Chevrolet, or the Dodge that brought on the nightmare?

It is 10:45 p.m. Claire and I were on the telephone for quite a long time. I am now sleepy. As I undress, I straighten out various papers on my desk and come across the telephone number for Beverly, the older woman I met last night. I was supposed to call her today to get her niece's telephone number. It is probably not too late to call her. Given that Beverly was grocery shopping yesterday at 2:00 in the morning, she is likely awake at 10:45 at night. Is it right to get her niece's telephone number when Claire and I may be starting a relationship? Against a part of my instincts, which part I do not know, I dial Beverly's telephone number.

"Hello."

"Hello. This is Matt. I met you yesterday and we went to the Pasture and . . . ."

"Of course I know you. I wanted you to call. Let me give you my niece Erica's telephone number. She is a wonderful girl. I spoke to her today and told her that I met a nice young man for her. Her telephone number is (212) 838-3115."

"I hope I didn't call you too late."

"Don't be silly Matt. In fact, I was just going to go to the supermarket at the corner to buy some grapefruit. Would you care to meet me for a cup of

189

coffee at the Pasture?"

I am very sleepy. Yet there is something about Beverly's kind request that makes it difficult for me to refuse. Despite my sleep-deprived state, I tell her that I will meet her at the Pasture.

"Very good. I'll even bring a photograph of Erica so you can see for yourself how pretty she is. Let us meet at the Pasture at 11:15."

"Ok," I say, "but I won't be able to stay out too late because I have to get up for work tomorrow."

"Don't worry. I won't keep you out too late."

# Chapter 33

Drowsiness overcomes me after my brief telephone conversation with Beverly. When I next look at the clock, I see that it is already 11:16 p.m. I am one minute late for my meeting at the Pasture with Beverly. I jump up and put on a short sleeve shirt, denim jeans, and sneakers. I do not have time to put on socks. I also don a baseball cap. I quickly rinse my mouth with mouthwash to get rid of the bad taste that has entered my mouth. It is 11:18 p.m. when I shut the door closed. I enter the Pasture a few minutes later and I see that Beverly is just sitting down at a table.

"Hello."

"Hello Beverly," I say. "I'm glad that you just got here. I thought that you were going to be waiting for me."

Is it proper for me to call Beverly by her first name, as opposed to Mrs. Something? I don't know her last name. She is much older than I am. However, Beverly introduced herself to me as "Beverly," not as Mrs. Something, so I call her Beverly.

Beverly orders a grilled American cheese and tomato sandwich on whole wheat bread with a cup of tea. I, wanting to eat something light and healthy, order a slice of honeydew melon and a decaffeinated coffee.

"Before I forget, Matt, let me show you a picture of my niece Erica. You should call her tomorrow. I do not normally play matchmaker, but after sitting with you last night, I am sure that the two of you will get along famously."

Beverly opens up her pocketbook and takes out an envelope. In the envelope is the picture of her niece Erica, which Beverly takes out with slow, but steady progress.

"The picture was taken at a barbecue at a cousin's house in New Jersey earlier this summer. I am standing next to Erica. Next to me is my sister Rose, who is Erica's mother."

I look at Rose and see her resemblance to Beverly. The two of them look like sisters, which is appropriate, since they are sisters. Erica, Beverly's niece, also has similar features, but is much younger. Erica is pretty. She looks to be about 5'2" tall. She is a little chubby, and has a wonderful looking smile. Beverly tells me that Erica is twenty-eight years old. She is just my age.

"She's very pretty," I say to Beverly. "She has such a beautiful smile."

"She is a wonderful girl," Beverly replies. "She is my favorite."

There are a lot of people in the background of the photograph. Beverly tells me the photograph was taken at a college graduation party for her cousin's son. Beverly says that she did not know many of the people there. I look at the right hand corner of the photograph and, unless my eyes are playing cruel tricks with my brain, I believe that I see Bench Woman in the background. Beverly senses my distraction and asks me if something is wrong. I tell her that someone in the background looks familiar.

"Do you know who that person is? I think that I know the one in the right corner, wearing the pink blouse."

"I have no idea who she is," Beverly says.

I do not want to be rude, but I cannot help but stare at the photograph. I should be looking at Beverly's niece Erica, who is right in the middle of the photograph, and the reason that I am being shown this photograph in the first place. But my eyes automatically move toward what looks to be Bench Woman in the right corner in the distant background. Bench Woman, or the person I believe to be Bench Woman, is standing, with a smile, with another woman. Bench Woman is holding a plate filled with food. Because Bench Woman is a good distance from the main subjects of the photograph, it is impossible to discern what food is on her plate. It looks as though there may be both a hot dog and a hamburger on her plate, although it is impossible for me to determine this with certainty. If I were a cow and knew that my fate were to be devoured by as wonderful a creature as Bench Woman, would that make the knowledge of my impending slaughter any easier to deal with? I doubt it. Do cows know that they are going to be slaughtered?

Not wanting Beverly to think that I am primarily preoccupied with the possible image of Bench Woman in the photo's right corner, I hand the picture back to her, and repeat how pretty her niece Erica looks. That is true. Erica looks as nice as Beverly says. Her smile is especially warm. However, if I call Erica tomorrow, what about Claire? Are Claire and I involved in a relationship? Who is to say? Should what happened with Claire at the auto show stop me from calling Erica?

Our food comes. My honeydew melon is huge and the cup of decaffeinated coffee is piping hot. What does the waiter think? For the second straight night Beverly and I sit here together at the Pasture for a late night snack. The waiter, who also served us last night, might think that Beverly is my mother, grandmother, or aunt, or that we have some odd relationship.

"So Matt, how was your day at work? What exactly do you do?"

After briefly detailing my day, I tell Beverly about the dream Claire had about the dismembered arm. Of course, I do not tell her my relationship with Claire. In fact, I do not refer to Claire as "Claire." Instead, I refer to my friend who had the dream as "Jeff." If Beverly knew that just yesterday Claire and I kissed at the auto show, then she would not want me to meet her niece. Beverly tells me that the dream may indicate that my friend Jeff is either very troubled or that he may have just eaten some disagreeable food before going to bed.

Beverly tells me that her normal sleeping time is from 3:00 a.m. to 8:00 a.m., and that she gets sluggish if she sleeps more than those five hours. My normal weeknight routine is going to sleep at 11 or 11:30 p.m. and waking up at 7:00 a.m., but I have had much less sleep over the past week. Surprisingly, I feel alert. Our conversation moves through a variety of subjects--Beverly's upbringing in the Bronx, my childhood, and her marriage. Once she got married, Beverly stopped working as a secretary for a big shot at the stock exchange because her husband Charles, may he rest in peace, who was quite a number of years older than she when they married after a one month courtship, made a good deal of money manufacturing bricks. "There is always a need for bricks," Beverly says, telling me what Charles had said to her innumerable times.

It is late. The time is now 12:20 a.m., and while I am enjoying myself, I should go home and finally try to get a good night's sleep. However, when the waiter places the bill on the table, Beverly asks for more hot water for her tea bag. I, in turn, ask for a refill of the decaffeinated coffee. The waiter walks towards us with our refills. He has a pot of hot water in one hand and a pot of decaffeinated coffee in his other hand. As our waiter pours the hot liquids, one at a time, I take the last bite of the very moist and refreshing honeydew. The melon, however, while refreshing, could have been a little sweeter.

"I had a nice time," Beverly says as she finishes her tea. She also grabs hold of the bill and insists on paying it in total.

"Do not insult me by offering to pay. It is my pleasure," she says.

I walk Beverly to the front of her building, where the doorman lets her in.

"Good night, Matt, and remember to call Erica."

My body feels the full effects of not sleeping sufficiently over the past few days. I plop into bed with my clothes on, turn off the light, and close my eyes. But after no more than five minutes I realize that my alarm clock is not turned on. I get up and turn it on. Then I close my eyes once again, for what I hope is a good rest. Sleep, however, does not come easily to me. My mind keeps seeing the photograph of Beverly, her sister, and her niece Erica at the barbecue, with Bench Woman possibly eating in the background. Yet even my curiosity about Bench Woman at that barbecue is, within five minutes, overwhelmed by drowsiness as I fall asleep.

I sleep soundly but then awaken. It is only 5:10 in the morning. The alarm clock has not yet gone off. I will stay in bed until 7:00 a.m. no matter what. I wonder whether Claire had a recurrence of the nightmare of an arm in her bed, or did she have a different nightmare featuring another dismembered appendage? If I were to have a nightmare in which only one body part was to be laying next to me, I suppose that an arm would not be the most objectionable.

I see the book of short stories that I purchased at the Las Vegas airport. I turn on the light on my bedside table and open the book to a very short story.

Street Scene   by Emil Tursy
It was late evening when I began that disgusting walk to my lodging. The streets were dark and gloomy, with only a light here and there shining through the heavy mist. I walked rapidly, my coat collar standing stiff around my neck to shield me from the cold. That wretched feeling soon left me, and now that I was nearing my destination, I felt a warm glow of satisfaction within. Suddenly, my eyes were attracted toward the figure of a man, the first that I was consciously aware of. He was standing alone, shivering in the cold. He stood there loitering over a sewer grating, trying to warm himself from the

196

steam that came out of its apertures. I hastened on without another thought. The mental picture soon fled.

Oh God, what has become of us? Have we become so immune to human suffering, so passive to signs of trouble and misery, that we are able to look on such things without sympathy or pity? Good God, if ever man were imperfect, if ever man were shown to be less heavenly, less noble, less spiritually honest, it is truly in such manifestations of his utter self-centeredness.

## Chapter 34

I look out the window and see the beginnings of a bright blue sky. The air outside is cooler than it has been in weeks. I am happy to be awake. The radio tells me that a cool high pressure front from Canada has landed here and will provide, for two days, a break from the heat and humidity that has settled in the city all summer. "Enjoy the cool," the radio weatherman says. "Humid heat should come back for the end of the week and the weekend." The crispness outside is apparent by the coolness in my apartment. For the first time in a long time, my skin is chilled upon my exit from the shower. It feels good. It is an enjoyable feeling to actually crave warmth. I know that I have to get ready for work, but I crawl into bed and put the cover halfway over my head. It feels outstanding to be clean, yet cool, from the shower. I am under the covers getting warmer. It is only 7:01 a.m., so I have enough time to stay in bed for fifteen more minutes.

I jerk my head, look at the clock, and see that I fell asleep for another hour. I spring out of bed. My suit goes on without a struggle after a cursory shave. I pick up a bagel from the bagel man near the office. Entering the office I go directly to my desk to scan the newspaper.

"Come in," I say to the person knocking on my office door. It is Claire. This is the first I've seen of Claire since the auto show and the dinner at Volcano Valley with John and Lisa. Somehow our kisses in the rear seats of the large American cars at the auto show seem like the distant past, even though it was only two days ago.

"How are you?"

"Fine, Matthew. I want to thank you for listening to me last night. I can't imagine how I must have sounded to you."

"You sounded like someone who had a bad dream. How did you sleep last night?"

"Fortunately I did not have any nightmares. But I barely slept. I was worried about falling asleep because I did not want to have a repeat of the previous nightmare. At 2:00 in the morning I turned on the television and watched a documentary about penguins in Antarctica. It was fascinating."

"That sounds interesting, and much better than believing that a dismembered arm is lying next to you all night. I've never met any penguins personally, except at the aquarium, but they seem like fine birds to me."

"They lead a difficult life," Claire says. "Thousands of penguins live together. They have to find their mates, lay eggs, and guard the eggs so predatory birds don't steal them. They keep their eggs warm by just sitting on them for weeks. Even the males sit on the eggs. They live as though they are in good marriages. Every season they have the same mates. Anyway, Matthew, I have to get back to my desk. I'll speak to you later."

"See you later," I say.

I look at the stack of papers on my desk. The pile is high, but most of it can be discarded with a quick glance. I need a real vacation. My recent sick days spent in Atlantic City and then the unexpected weekend in Las Vegas were good, but I have a lot of vacation time left for this year. I should take a week off some time in the next month or two. Where should I go? Today at lunch I'll go to the travel agency. I'm not going to book any trip, but I'll pick up some brochures. I don't have enough money to take a lavish trip, but I will, if possible, go on a plane somewhere. I'll put in for vacation time for September. The weather should be good almost anywhere at that time.

It is 12:20 p.m. already. The day is just speeding away. The unclear nature of the new relationship with Claire makes me unsure how to act with her. Because it is approaching lunchtime, I ask Claire what she is doing for lunch. She tells me that she did not bring lunch with her and has not thought about what she is going to eat. I tell her that I am going to go to the travel agency, which is only a block away, where I will try to figure out what to do for a possible upcoming vacation. We decide to go together to the pizza place near the office, Pizza Castle, and then she will accompany me to the Freedom Travel Agency.

Claire and I take the elevator down the thirty-six floors to the lobby and join the mass of humanity on the busy downtown street during this cooler than normal sunny summer day. The deep blue sky and lack of humidity is a welcome change from the grayness and humidity of recent weeks.

The last bite of my second slice of pizza from Pizza Castle goes down easily. The slices are not awful, but they are mediocre at best. They are far from delicious. I don't understand why so many people at the office love this place. People swear by the pizza here. Even Claire likes it a great deal. Claire only ordered one slice, and she is now eating the crust. It took her longer to eat the one slice than it took me to eat two. However, Claire's slice was topped with broccoli. Who in their right mind would ruin a slice of pizza by putting broccoli on top of it? No wonder Claire has been plagued by nightmares.

"Ready to go?" I ask Claire.

"Ok, let's go."

We exit Pizza Castle and, as we do, the bulk of the lunchtime crowd enters. Mediocre pizza or not, Pizza Castle does a healthy business. In one minute, Claire and I reach the entrance to the Freedom Travel Agency.

We are greeted by a receptionist who asks us if we want to be helped by a travel agent. I tell her that I am not sure where I want to go, and that I would just like to take some of the brochures hanging on the wall. The receptionist tells me that I can take as many different brochures as I want.

"If you two want to travel to the Caribbean, we have some wonderful specials at romantic hideaways on many of the less crowded islands."

The receptionist believes that Claire and I will be traveling together as a couple. Awkwardly, I tell the receptionist that I will be traveling alone.

"Oh well. Take whatever brochures you want. But remember, make sure you come back to us to book whatever trip you decide upon."

There is a wealth of brochures hanging on the wall. The receptionist, now with the belief that Claire and I are not a couple, asks if I would like a brochure for a resort for single people in the

Caribbean, or perhaps a cruise for single people to the Caribbean.

"We have some excellent deals on cruises this coming September," the receptionist tells me.

"I would love to go on a cruise," I tell Claire. "Have you ever seen the cruise ships headed for Bermuda that dock on the West Side piers? They are huge. They are like cities on the water. And from what I hear, a passenger can eat all day and night on these cruises. But I wouldn't want to go myself. A cruise to me seems like something to do on a honeymoon."

Despite my belief that I would not want to take a cruise by myself, even a singles cruise where others would be traveling alone, I take a brochure for the Harmony Cruise Lines, which has a cruise geared for single people leaving on the second week of September. It leaves from Miami and goes to five different Caribbean islands. The price of the cruise includes the airfare to Miami. Since it is a "singles" cruise, the company will put you in a cabin with another person, or you can get your own cabin. A private cabin costs a lot more money.

Claire looks at a brochure for Bermuda.

"I would love to go to Bermuda," Claire says. "But I do not think that it is a place to go alone."

I, too, would like to go to Bermuda. But as Claire says, it is not a place to go by myself. Should I ask Claire if she would like to go with me? That would be crazy. Would I be asking her as a friend, or as a date? Our relationship is too murky after just one afternoon of kisses at the auto show to ask her to go on vacation. Today it seems like we are back to being platonic friends, although I cannot know for sure. Imagine if Claire and I traveled to Bermuda together. It would be the scandal of the office. Who cares about the office?

Another interesting brochure shows train trips across the country. I would like to go by train across the country and watch the greenness of the east change into flat farmland, to the plains, to high rocky snow capped mountains, to desert, and then to the Pacific. One day, perhaps, I will take a long train trip. Unfortunately, my upcoming September vacation will be too short, only one week, for such a journey. But there are shorter train trips that can be done, such as the train trip on page 36 of this brochure, which goes to Montreal and Quebec City, Canada. The idea of traveling by train is appealing.

Claire holds out two brochures, one of Italy and the other of Spain. "They look beautiful," Claire says. She does not want a response. She is simply making an observation that they look to be beautiful places.

The pictures of Spain are spectacular. However, because I enjoy Italian food, Italy is high on my list of places to go in Europe, although I am sure there is excellent food in Spain. What I like most is garlic, so if there were a country called Garlic, then that might be the most enticing destination for me. Actually, places called "Chocolate Chip Cookie" or "Yodel" or "Mallomar" would be my first choices, if those places existed.

A jolt of romance runs through my veins as I look at the brochures. When we exit the travel agency, I use my free right hand to grab hold of

203

Claire's free left hand. This surprises Claire, I think, but she takes hold of mine with a squeeze. Our grip loosens only when we get very close to our office building. We finally let go, realizing that at any moment we could be spotted holding hands by one of our co-workers. Before arriving back at the office I pick up a banana from an outdoor fruit vendor. The banana is perfectly yellow. It is neither green nor brown. It looks perfect, at least to my eyes. I will eat it sometime later this afternoon for a snack. While I would prefer an afternoon snack of a donut, specifically a chocolate cream filled donut, I will eat the healthy snack of a banana instead.

Claire and I enter the building, and after our trip up the elevator, we go our separate ways. Claire has an afternoon of work she must complete for Mary Pinnyon, and I have a few business calls to make. I glance again at the brochure of Bermuda before starting the afternoon's work. It would be wonderful to go to Bermuda with a woman that I love. Could that woman be Claire? A picture in the brochure shows an almost pink sand beach with crystal clear blue water. A man and a woman stroll hand in hand with their feet just at the point where the blue water meets the pink sand.

As my mind wanders, I close my eyes and see my face as the face of the man in the picture. But I am not holding any hand. I am alone. My serene walk on the beautiful Bermuda beach is disturbed by a scream. I look out and see Claire struggling in the deep water. She needs my help or she will drown. I rush in the water, but as I do, I hear another scream, coming from a different direction, but also in the water. It is Bench Woman. She is also fighting for her life in the suddenly, and surprisingly, hostile water. I am paralyzed with the dilemma. Do I save Claire or Bench Woman? By some miraculous occurrence, clearly of divine intervention, my body changes into the bodies of two distinct dolphins. One of the dolphins is bigger than the other. The bigger one swims to Claire and the other to Bench Woman. The two dolphins, emanating from my body, bring each of them back to the sand, and when their job is complete, they combine into one and I reappear. I am exhausted as I lay on the sand next to the two saved women. Claire and Bench Woman look at each other, amazed that their lives were saved by two dolphins. They ignore me completely. They don't realize that the dolphins that saved them emanated from me. Claire and Bench Woman leave the beach together. I remain on the sand alone, on the one hand pleased that I saved their lives, yet unhappy that I received no credit for it.

That depressing daydream is interrupted by the telephone. The caller is the owner of a company that installs carpeting and wood tiling and has a question about one provision of the insurance plan that he recently purchased from me. His question demonstrates that the policy provision is very confusing.

# Chapter 35

The afternoon moves quickly. The banana I purchased during lunch is, when accompanied by a cup of coffee, a welcome late afternoon snack. Claire is very busy this afternoon, but when I pass her desk we exchange secretive smiles. We do not want to risk the office finding out about our relationship, whatever it is. I am about to leave for the evening. It is 5:15 p.m. Claire is leaving too. For the second time today, we enter the elevator together and go down the 36 floors. Once outside, Claire goes left to catch her subway and I go right to catch mine. When we go our separate ways I want to kiss her, but I don't. Things are awkward, but there now exists the possibility of new and bigger and better horizons between us. Once on the subway, I am filled with one pervasive question: What will I eat for dinner?

I am only halfway home when I reach the subway stop at 34th Street. Without thinking, I exit the subway car even though this is not my stop. The auto show is still in town, and will be in town through this weekend. If I go to the auto show again tonight, it will be my third straight day there. That is excessive, even for auto aficionados. Of course, going to the auto show for me holds the promise of seeing Bench Woman on the revolving platform of the Ford future car exhibit.

I walk to the convention center. On my journey I am given religious material by one person standing at a street corner. At the next corner I am given information about a new large strip bar. I take both pieces of paper. After a quick glance, I deposit them in a garbage can. I am one block from the convention center when I realize that I need food. Tonight I am hungrier than usual. The auto show is open until 11:00 p.m., so I have plenty of time to eat. I see a diner on this block called the Green Cabin Diner. I am happy to go to a diner, armed with the knowledge that a new meeting with Bench Woman might soon be at hand. Of course, disappointment looms for the second consecutive evening if Bench Woman is not revolving on the Ford exhibit.

A large waitress--tall and broad--stands over me and places down a large menu and a heaping glass of water. She has a smile on her face, which is a good thing because without a smile she would be imposing. She is an imposing presence even with a smile. She asks me if I would like a beverage, and I tell her that water is enough.

The menu is typical diner fare. It is big and imposing, like the waitress. The choices are dizzying. I want to eat enough to satisfy my hunger. On the other hand, I do not want to eat too much just in case I see, or possibly even speak with, Bench Woman. The worst scenario of all would be seeing Bench Woman and then speaking with her, but feeling so full of heavy greasy food that I would be incapable of looking my best or feeling confident enough to sweep her off her feet. Could I ever sweep someone like Bench Woman off her feet? With that consideration in mind, I order a simple dish of scrambled eggs with rye toast. The eggs come with a side of home fried potatoes, making it a greasy meal, but I will eat only a small portion of the potatoes. The eggs may not be the best choice for my arteries, but they will not make me feel full of grease. The eggs should not hurt my chances of charming Bench Woman.

"Would you like anything to drink with your eggs?" the waitress asks.

"I'll have a cup of coffee. Thanks."

The waitress's voice is deep. She has a voice that matches her physical appearance perfectly. It is deep, but not too deep. If it were a bitter cold winter day and I needed a hot cup of coffee or hot chocolate to be served to me by a waitress, this waitress would be perfect. Of course, it would be even better to share the hot beverage under a blanket with Bench Woman next to a roaring fireplace.

The coffee is delivered to me in less than one minute. I take a sip. It is very dark coffee, darker than the average coffee served in diners. I like this cup of coffee, which is strong, but not too strong. Since I hope to be bold if I meet up with Bench Woman, a strong cup of coffee is preferable to a weak cup. As I sip the strong coffee, the waitress places the eggs and rye toast on the table. However, the "toast" is barely toasted at all. It is hardly browned. I had planned to put the scrambled eggs on top of the bread, so the bread needs to be toasted. Therefore, I ask that the bread be toasted more. The waitress, whose name I do not know, accommodates my request pleasantly. She even concurs, with a nod, that the bread needs additional toasting. The waitress gives excellent service and in one minute she brings to the table not only two perfectly toasted pieces of rye bread, but also a refill for my cup of coffee.

"Enjoy," she says.

I am filled with optimism as the eggs and toast make their way into my stomach. I envision myself sharing future breakfasts with Bench Woman. I know it is only a pipedream, but that pipedream is a luxury I will afford myself right now. There is the possibility of future breakfasts with Claire. The situation between us is unusual. I finish the eggs and toast. I do not want any more coffee. The home fries are not too greasy, but I do not finish them. I give the waitress a generous tip and leave the diner.

"Have a nice evening," the waitress says.

The huge glass convention center stands before me for the third straight day. While hundreds, and even thousands, of people pour into the building to get a look at the newest and the best that the world's auto manufacturers have to offer, I have another purpose in mind--to see Bench Woman on the revolving platform at the Ford exhibit. As I pay the entrance fee and enter the floor to the auto show, I hesitate to approach the Ford exhibit. In fact, upon my entrance, I move quickly to the other side of the convention center floor. I do not want to be disappointed if Bench Woman is not revolving on the platform with Ford's future sports car. As physically far away from the Ford exhibit as possible, I find myself looking at the exotic sports car section, surrounded by Ferraris, Lamborghini's, and Bugattis, some of which cost more than many houses. These are interesting cars to look at and the crowd around them ogles with approval. Yet if these cars were to cost only one-tenth as much as they do, then they undoubtedly would receive only one-tenth as much attention.

Because I did not come to the auto show this evening to examine cars that are well beyond my financial reach, I make my way slowly towards the Ford exhibit. But I go to the bathroom before I get there. It is critical that I wash my face to look refreshed before possibly seeing Bench Woman.

Fresh cool convention center water from the bathroom sink hits my face. It is as if the water is stripping away an entire layer of residue from my skin. There is an extra special freshness to the water pouring out of this sink, and I feel tingly clean when it goes on my face. Afterwards, I see in the mirror a fresher, cleaner face, which is ready to look up at Bench Woman with confidence. I exit the bathroom standing very straight and begin my walk directly to the Ford exhibit.

I pass the Volkswagen display. Inside the Volkswagen minivan, I see in the back seat a young couple, no older than eighteen to twenty. They are kissing passionately right in full view of everyone, as if there is no tomorrow. Do they have to do that here? Not that I object to their public kissing in the back seat of a minivan at the auto show. Who am I to talk? It was only Sunday that Claire and I did the same thing, except that we had the good sense to do it in the rear seats of the large American cars, not in the rear seat of the Volkswagen minivan.

People look at the amorous couple disapprovingly. The couple appears oblivious to the people going in and out of the front seat of the minivan. I can only speculate that the reaction of people watching Claire and me kiss must have been just as negative, if not more so, because Claire and I are probably a decade older than these two. People are likely more willing to tolerate this spectacle from a younger couple. Why couldn't I have been an eighteen-year-old last Sunday instead of a twenty-eight-year-old? In ten years from now, will I wish to be a twenty-eight-year-old instead of a thirty-eight-year-old?

I walk past the kissing couple in the Volkswagen and approach the Ford exhibit. Specifically, I go to the revolving platform of the Ford exhibit on which stands the Ford future car. A woman is on the platform talking into a microphone about the car's many virtues. She has long hair, but at this point in her rotation I can only see her back. It may be Bench Woman based on the hair in back. The woman revolves into view and, to my bitter disappointment, it is not Bench Woman. She is quite attractive though and, in fact, has features similar to Bench Woman. But she is not Bench Woman. I leave the Ford exhibit quickly and walk to the Cadillac exhibit, where I sit behind the wheel of an empty blue sedan, alone with my sadness about not seeing Bench Woman.

I sit alone behind the steering wheel of this blue car. Thoughts of Bench Woman leave me as the loving young couple from the Volkswagen minivan open the rear doors of the Cadillac and sit inside. They speak in hushed tones for maybe three seconds and then kiss. It is very comfortable for me behind the steering wheel of this car and I don't want to get out, despite the heavy breathing in back. I don't know if the couple even knows that I am sitting up here. I hear their conversation.

"Eric, I have to tell you something."

"Yes Gina?"

"I'm pregnant."

I am dumbstruck by Gina's announcement. Eric says nothing for a few seconds. Then he hugs Gina.

"We'll get married Gina. I'll move back to the city and go to City College. Or you can transfer to school upstate."

Before Gina has a chance to respond, Eric goes down on one knee on the floor of the rear seat of this blue Cadillac, takes Gina's hands, and says, "Will you marry me?"

Gina, with tears in her voice, says,

"I love you Eric. Yes, I'll marry you."

Gina and Eric laugh in the Cadillac's rear seat. I leave the Cadillac. As they hear the door thump closed, I catch a glimpse of Eric, who turns around. I give him a smile.

Uplifted by the scene between Gina and Eric, but weakened by my own bitter disappointment at not seeing Bench Woman, I walk to the subway station. The subway arrives after a one minute wait. I pick up a box of chocolate chip cookies at the grocery store and make my way home. I lay on my bed with the cookies and watch television, but I cannot concentrate. These chocolate chip cookies are soft, chewy, and truly delicious. They are filled with fat though, and are destined to clog up my arteries. One day in the future I will surely pay for the enjoyment of these cookies now. But I enjoy them anyway.

Next to my alarm clock I see Erica's telephone number, which Beverly, my recent late night diner companion, gave to me. I should call Erica, despite the very real chance that Claire and I are on the precipice of a relationship. Claire and I did hold hands on the street today after leaving the Freedom Travel Agency during lunch. Of course, it is always better to keep as many options open as possible. With that in mind, I dial Erica's telephone number.

"Hello, you have reached Kate and Erica. We are unable to come to the phone now, so please leave a message at the tone."

"Hello Erica. This is Matt. I was given your telephone number by your Aunt Beverly. If you can, give me a call. I hope to hear from you soon. Take it easy."

That was pretty smooth. After I put down the telephone, I realize that I did not leave Erica my telephone number. I will call back tomorrow.

It is 10:17 p.m. when I close my eyes for the night. However, at 10:53 my telephone rings, waking me up from what was a sound sleep.

"Hello Matt. This is Beverly."

"Hi," I say to Beverly.

"My niece Erica called me tonight and told me that you left a message for her. She also told me that you did not leave your telephone number. But don't worry about it. Give her another call tomorrow night. You sound sleepy, Matt. Go to bed. Good night."

"Good night Beverly."

## Chapter 36

I wake up feeling good after a restful night of sleep. As I shave my face, the mirror reflects a man with dark circles around the eyes, despite a night of sound sleeping. Are the circles around my eyes due to the fact that I have been quite busy over the past week? I feel refreshed. I don't see why I should have these dark rings around my eyes. I examine my face more closely and see small wrinkles at the corner of my eyes. Is it normal to be twenty-eight years old and have little wrinkles like these? Are the wrinkles near my eyes appropriate for someone my age or do I possess wrinkles that are appropriate for a forty-year-old? Maybe most or all twenty-eight-year-olds have these small wrinkles. I splash my face with cold water to take off all of the shaving cream. I now have a clean, shaven face with little wrinkles. Has Claire noticed the wrinkles? What would Bench Woman say if she saw them? Unfortunately, I do not think Bench Woman will ever get close enough to my face to see the wrinkles.

Most of the faces surrounding me on the crowded subway have some wrinkles. Most people old enough to work have some wrinkles. But the two guys standing next to me, who look like they just graduated college, seem free of wrinkles. Yet one of them, even with his apparently wrinkle-free baby face, is beginning to lose his hair. This subway ride has energized me. Everyone, for the most part, has some wrinkles. My wrinkles are not so bad. I don't want them to get much more pronounced, but because I see the same thing on other people who are approximately my age, I don't believe the wrinkles are terrible. Even the two just out of college wrinkle-free subway riders will get a wrinkle or two in the near future. Not that I wish wrinkles to descend upon them.

My wrinkled face and the rest of my wrinkling body enter the office. Claire gets off the elevator. I see her from a distance. She is wearing what looks to be a new outfit, or at least it is an outfit that I do not recognize. It is a mostly beige dress, but it has small blue and violet colored flowers on it. As she walks this way, the dress comes into sharper focus. I like it.

"Hello Matthew, how are you?" Claire says. She stands in front of my desk, with her new dress in all its glory.

"I'm fine. That's a very nice new dress. You look great."

"That's very nice of you to say, Matthew. However, I've had this dress for two years and have worn it before. It is nice though to hear that you think it is pretty."

That's interesting. I never noticed Claire wearing that dress before. Did my failure to recognize the dress offend her? I doubt it, especially since I told her how nice it looks. Now that Claire and I have exchanged kisses at the auto show I must be seeing her in a different light, and in this new light I notice her appearance more. This dress is very flattering to her. It is simple, but colorful and not plain, and it shows that she has a body underneath. The dress is far from being skin tight, but Claire's other clothes tend to just hang down on her, like drapery against a window.

I start the day's work. Our department's monthly 10:00 a.m. meeting lasts fifteen minutes and encompasses the usual topics, no more, no less. Ken and I speak for a moment after the meeting and decide to eat lunch together. If I'm having lunch with Ken I don't want to ask Claire to join us. With the status of my relationship with Claire so up in the air, Claire and I do not need to have lunch together every day. We don't need to invite questions from everyone here. Who is to say that Claire even wants to have lunch with me anyway?

"Matt."

"Ken, what's up? It's too early to go to lunch now, isn't it?" I look at my watch. It is only 11:35.

"Sorry pal, but I can't go to lunch. I was just saddled with a pile of Don McSherry's work. He had an emergency appendicitis last night."

"Is he okay?"

"He's fine. His wife just called from the hospital. But I've been elected to finish a project of his. I'm skipping lunch."

With Ken out of the lunch picture, maybe I should ask Claire if she wants to go to lunch. We could go for a burger. I walk to Claire's desk to ask her if she wants to go to lunch. I am happy at the prospect of having lunch with her and not Ken. My happiness is nothing against Ken, and of course, I am not happy that Don McSherry had his appendix removed.

"Hi," I say to Claire. "Would you want to go get lunch? We can go to The Starlight for a burger."

"Just two minutes ago Mary Ann and I decided to go shoe shopping at the Fabulous Shoe Shop.

There is a clearance sale. I need a new pair of shoes for the wedding Saturday night."

"That sounds fun. Have a good time."

Both my friend Ken and my possible future girlfriend Claire have abandoned me, leaving me to fend for myself for lunch. The choices are at once enormous, but limiting. There are many places to eat lunch in this area if someone is so inclined. I decide to eat a fast food double cheeseburger with french fries. I rarely eat hamburger-type fast food. My fast food of choice is normally pizza, but once in a blue moon I eat fried chicken. But my mouth waters for a greasy double cheeseburger accompanied by greasy and salty french fries. I am salivating at the thought of the upcoming lunch.

I enter the fast food joint slightly before the maddening lunch crowd. I sit eating this double cheeseburger, which is quite good. I watch people stream into this large eating establishment like cattle. How many days ago was it that the hamburger I am now eating was actually part of a living cow? What percentage of the cow is contained in the burger? Can one cow make 100 hamburgers or 1000? There is something extremely satisfying about how the meat, the grease, the cheese and the salt come together. I add some pepper to the salty french fries, which makes them perfect.

I exit the fast food restaurant and walk the crowded lunchtime streets. I do not have to get right back to the office. As I walk, I feel why I do not routinely eat double cheeseburgers and fries. The food sits like lead in the stomach. Yet it was satisfying, extremely satisfying.

My afternoon work proceeds smoothly. Similarly, the double cheeseburger and fries apparently move through my digestive tract without incident. Claire comes into my office.

"Before you leave today I want to show you the shoes that I bought at lunch for the wedding."

"Why don't you show them to me now?"

"I'll be back."

Claire leaves my office. She comes back in about one minute with a bag in hand. The shoe store bag is a lime green color and the lettering on the bag reads "The Fabulous Shoe Shop." It gives the address of the store in the city, along with addresses of their two other stores in New Jersey.

Claire's thin, nicely manicured fingers open the box. She takes out a pair of black shoes, with what look to be medium high heels by female shoe standards, and there is a strap in the middle of the shoe. The shoes come to a sharp point and so, to my eyes, look as though they will be uncomfortable. They are attractive and I tell that to Claire. However, if the truth is to be told, I cannot get very excited about shoes. It is good to see Claire so happy with the shoes. She genuinely likes them and believes that they will go perfectly with the dress she is going to wear to the wedding. There is another box in the lime green bag from The Fabulous Shoe Shop, and Claire says that she also bought a pair of light brown, almost beige, flats. She shows me that pair also. Claire likes the flats, but she loves the shoes that she will wear to the wedding. The difference in her optimism between the two shoes is evident. She bought the black wedding shoes because she fell in love with them, while she bought the light brown flats because she needed a pair and the price was right. Claire leaves the office with her lime green bag filled with shoes.

In what feels like almost no time at all since Claire left the office, I look up and see Claire standing in front of my desk, carrying her lime green bag containing her two new pairs of shoes. My watch reveals that it is 5:15 p.m.

"Matthew, we will have to discuss when and where we will meet to go to the wedding. But we can talk about that tomorrow or Friday. Good night."

"See you tomorrow."

I need to work late today. I feverishly examine various documents related to the JTJ Construction commercial general liability policy. Time moves quickly and by 7:45 p.m. I have done all that I can do in one day. It is 8:05 p.m. by the time I actually leave the building. This is the latest that I have worked in months.

It is wonderful outside. The downtown streets are much quieter than they are when I usually leave at approximately 5:30 p.m. Limousines are lined up in front of many big office buildings in the area. Surprisingly, I am not even very hungry, despite not having eaten since the double cheeseburger and fries at lunch. Instead of going directly to the subway to take me home, I walk into Battery Park to stroll by the water. The sun is setting on this comfortably warm summer night. The sky is orange with wisps of maroon behind the Statue of Liberty. The colored sky makes the water look orange.

Strolling slowly along the water's edge I

219

approach the bench where I first saw Bench Woman. I sit on that bench now, as darkness descends, contemplating how Bench Woman actually sat here, next to me, only days ago, and how she was also at the auto show, revolving on the Ford future car exhibit. Should I go to the auto show again tonight to see if Bench Woman is there? I go to the subway pondering that possibility. However, hunger suddenly permeates my body. While the temptation is powerful to get off of the train at 34th Street, which would mean a visit to the auto show, I stay on the train and head uptown to my apartment. That decision means that there is no way that I will cast my eyes upon Bench Woman tonight. She probably isn't at the auto show anyway. I decide to treat my tastebuds to my favorite dish from the Indian restaurant nearby, the Bombay Terrace. A succulent dish called chicken saag will be mine. It is chunks of white meat chicken served in a spicy spinach sauce, with white rice.

I go to the restaurant and order the dish to take home. Once at home, I sit on the couch and put on the television. The chicken saag is especially spicy tonight, requiring that I drink lots of water. Usually I tell the restaurant to make it medium spicy. Tonight, however, I said nothing about the spiciness issue. Accordingly, it is more spicy than usual, although with each bite the additional spice is gratifying. The rice is also very good tonight. It is just plain white rice, but it is extremely enjoyable. Comfort fills my body as the last of the chicken saag enters my stomach. On my table, I see the telephone number of Beverly's niece, Erica. I decide to call her.

"Hello."

"Hi. This is Matt. I'd like to speak with Erica."

"This is Erica," the voice says.

"Hi. I got your telephone number from your Aunt Beverly."

The phone conversation with Erica is awkward. She is pleasant, with a lilting voice, but we do not seem to have too much to say to each other. Of course, we don't know each other. Things might be much better if we meet face-to-face.

"Would you like to get together?" I ask.

"Sure."

"How about tomorrow night for dinner?" I ask.

"That would be great."

Erica and I live in the same neighborhood. We decide to meet in front of a restaurant at 8:00 p.m. tomorrow night.

"Do you like Italian food?" I ask.

"I do, but just this evening I ate Italian food," Erica says.

"What about Indian food? Erica continues. "There is an Indian restaurant that I love called the Indian Gourmet. Would you like to go there?"

"Indian sounds terrific."

Erica tells me where the Indian Gourmet is located. I have actually passed it many times but have never eaten there.

"See you at 8:00 tomorrow night."

"Good night."

"Good night Erica."

It looks like tomorrow night I will have more Indian food. Perhaps I will eat chicken saag for two consecutive nights.  But will the chicken saag at the Indian Gourmet be as good as the chicken saag that I brought home tonight from the Bombay Terrace?

# Chapter 37

I am groggy in bed. I have been in bed for nearly two hours already. It is now 1:30 in the morning. Although tired, I cannot sleep. Images fill my mind as my body lays here. I see Claire's new pair of black shoes that she will wear to the wedding. The black leather straps in the middle of those shoes stand at attention. Now the straps intertwine with each other. They do this repeatedly, first slowly then frantically. It is difficult to tell if the shoes are engaged in some sort of mating ritual or if the two shoes are fighting. Just as one of the black shoes appears to be in a superior position to its twin, and looks as if it might stab the other to death with its strap, Claire's other new shoes, the nondescript brown flats, circle the feuding dress shoes and begin a rain dance. Around and around the brown shoes circle the fighting black dress shoes. Rain descends upon the four shoes. The shoes all look to the heavens with awe, and then, out of nowhere, the lime green bag from The Fabulous Shoe Shoppe devours them all, leaving emptiness. The lime green bag is satisfied by eating its hearty meal of shoes. The alarm clock rings. It is morning.

I take a very quick shower. I don't shave. I will shave after work before my date tonight with Erica. I will also take another shower before meeting her at the Indian Gourmet. With yesterday evening's chicken saag from the Bombay Terrace coursing through my veins, I believe that I will order a new and different Indian dish tonight to expand my horizon in the Indian food world. Tonight, with Erica,

I will order something other than chicken saag. Perhaps I will order a curry dish.

Even though I worked late at the office yesterday, the pile of papers I see on my desk this morning instantly reminds me of how much work there is left for me to do today. Suppose I do not do any of it. Would it get done? Who would do it? And what if no one did it? Would the earth cease to exist? I don't think so. However, to avoid the possibility of the catastrophe that could accompany my failure to do the work, I begin my tasks for the day. I, and the millions of people in this city and country, and the billions in this world, all toil thanklessly in our daily tasks because of the universal fear that if our tasks are not performed, then the universe, as we know it, will come to an end. Perhaps things are not done totally thanklessly. For example, it is because of my daily work here that I am able to pay for tonight's upcoming Indian dinner with Erica, as well as pay for yesterday's Indian dinner of chicken saag. It is only because of my work here that I sat in Battery Park during lunch and glimpsed Bench Woman for the first time. Very few things could be more rewarding than that. Likewise, my kisses with Claire in the rear seats of the large American cars at the auto show only took place because I met Claire at work. Who knows the countless other daily enjoyments, big and small, that I take for granted everyday, which emanate from my toil.

The minutes fly away and my lunch, which consists of a turkey sandwich on a roll, takes me no more than five minutes to eat at my desk.

"Claire, come in."

"Matthew, you've looked so busy today that I didn't even ask you if you wanted to go to lunch. I hope that you are looking forward to the wedding."

"I really am. I have not been to a wedding in almost a year. Last year, I went to quite a few weddings, but this is the first wedding for me this year. Where is the wedding again, by the way?"

"The ceremony will be at the Come Together Church on 56th Street and Second Avenue. The reception afterwards will be at the Nottingham Hotel only a few blocks from the church. It should be very interesting. The bride is officially Catholic. The groom is officially Jewish. However, they met at the Come Together Church, which, from what I have learned, has a very loyal following that puts together different aspects of different religions. The ceremony will be unusual."

"Sounds great," I say.

There is tension between us. Not a bad tension, but just a tension arising from the fact that since our afternoon spent kissing at the auto show, we have not kissed again. Also, we have barely spoken about or acknowledged those kisses. But we did hold hands two days ago during lunch, which is something that we never would have done before the auto show kisses. Saturday night will be a big night. A relationship between us will develop, or it will not.

"I can see that you are very busy. Tomorrow we can discuss where and when we will meet on Saturday. The ceremony begins at 7:00 p.m."

Claire leaves. I have a good feeling about what will happen with Claire. My good feeling, however, dissipates with each insurance report examined, insurance rate calculated, and phone call made to a customer. Nonetheless, despite the energy drain, the afternoon hours go by quickly. It is 5:00 p.m. and I will leave shortly. When I get home tonight I will shower and shave for my blind date with Erica, Beverly's niece.

"Good night Matthew. See you tomorrow."

"Good night," I say to Claire.

I leave the building five minutes after Claire. I deliberately do not take the elevator ride with her. If Claire were to ask me what I am doing tonight I would be compelled to make up a story about meeting an old friend for dinner. I certainly cannot tell her that I have a blind date.

The subway going uptown is, as usual, extremely crowded. There is no available seat on this rush hour train, but I am fortunate enough to have secured a position against the door. The subway is packed, literally. It is astonishing that, as a passenger on a crowded subway, it is socially acceptable for people to have their bodies pressing up against perfect strangers. Luckily for me, being against the door affords me a bit more privacy, so to speak, in that my back is making contact with the door, only my front is making human contact. But standing next to the door is not ideal. At each subway stop, a mass of people leave the train and a new mass enters. If the stream of bodies going out and then coming in is not too great, it is possible to stand firm by the door, while not blocking the movement of the human traffic. Sometimes, though, it is impossible to keep a position by the door because there are too many people. That presents a dilemma. While it is enjoyable to have a standing position by the door on a crowded subway, it is stressful trying to maintain that position.

Exiting at my subway stop, I decide to buy a chocolate chip muffin at a small grocery store. I am not meeting Erica at the Indian restaurant until 8:00 p.m. and I am hungry now, at 5:50 p.m. Therefore, the muffin, a prepackaged chocolate chip muffin wrapped in clear plastic with the name Aunt Harriets's Old Fashioned Chocolate Chip Muffin, should hold me over until the Indian food meal with Erica.

After peeling the suit off of my body, I peel the plastic off of the muffin. Aunt Harriet's Old Fashioned Muffins are good when they are fresh, or at least fairly fresh. This muffin, unfortunately, is not fresh. It is hard and stale. I eat only about a quarter of it. The rest goes in the trash.

It is 6:30 p.m. when I enter the shower. The water wipes away the grime that gathered on my skin. I rarely take showers at this time, but I want to be refreshed for my date with Erica. It might be smart to shower at this time every day. It is invigorating. It is better than just sitting on the couch with the television on, with only the day's accumulated sweat to keep me company.

I put shaving cream on my face. The mirror is steamed up from the shower. Each stroke of the razor wipes away shaving cream, along with the day's accumulated stubble. I feel fresh and clean for meeting Erica. What should I wear? While The Indian Gourmet is not a fancy establishment, I decide to put on a suit. It is a safe bet to wear a suit on a blind date. Erica will assume that I went directly to the restaurant after a long day of work. She will have no idea that I took a refreshing shower right before meeting her. There is no harm in that deception.

# Chapter 38

It is not a long walk from my apartment to the Indian Gourmet. My pre-date emotions are a mixture of hope, excitement, and nerves. The telephone conversation that Erica and I had last night was uninspiring. It was not her fault. We just did not say much to each other. Things may be entirely different when we meet at the Indian Gourmet. A small plate of chutney, some Indian bread, and some Indian beer or wine may cause us to talk with each other like the best of friends or, more optimistically, the newest of lovers. A small crowd is gathered on the street corner two blocks from The Indian Gourmet. Not a crowd, but a group of five people are huddled together. A woman apparently fell to the ground. That person is being helped to her feet. Everything is fine.

It is a beautiful evening. It is warm, but not too humid. Erica does not know what I look like, but I know what she looks like, having seen her standing in the photograph with Beverly at their family gathering. That picture taunts me. What was Bench Woman doing in the corner of the photo? Was it even Bench Woman I saw in the corner? I know what Bench Woman was doing. She was eating. It's hard to believe that Bench Woman does simple things, like eating at barbecues. But why was Bench Woman there? Who did she know? Did Erica meet Bench Woman at that barbecue? Without having possession of that photograph, I cannot ask Erica about the possibility of her knowing Bench Woman. Even if I did have the photograph, under what pretense could I ask her about the woman eating in the corner? My unconditional love for Bench Woman would be exposed. I must wipe from my mind any thoughts of Bench Woman and focus on Erica and whether we enjoy each other.

I see Erica standing in front of the Indian Gourmet. She is wearing jeans and an off white blouse. She is wearing a light blue jacket over the blouse. It is not a jacket for warmth. It looks very lightweight, as if it is part of a summer outfit. She is dressed casually, but neatly, and is appropriately dressed for a blind dinner date at the Indian Gourmet. Given her state of dress, I feel overdressed as I approach her in my suit. Yet my decision to wear a suit was a good one, and acceptable for this occasion.

"Hi Erica. I'm Matt."

"Hello Matt."

We smile. The Indian Gourmet has outdoor seating, which is somewhat unusual for an Indian restaurant. Given the ideal weather conditions, we take an outdoor table.

Erica is no taller than 5'2". She appears slightly shorter because of her chubby physique. Her face has a rounded look. She has medium length brown hair. She also has, just like in the photograph, a beautiful smile that makes her pretty face glow. Her smile is contagious. We sit right next to the sidewalk and have a good view of the people walking past us.

"Have you been here before?" I ask my dinner companion.

"I come here quite often," Erica says.

The sun sets behind Erica. It is a spectacular sunset, although much of it is blocked by the city's buildings. As I look straight ahead, past Erica, the horizon is a deep maroon, and the falling sun an orange disk to the right of Erica's head. While I do not want to interrupt Erica as she speaks to me--in a lively and convincing way about why she enjoys Indian food, especially here at the Indian Gourmet--I need to tell her about the sunset behind her.

"Turn around and look at the sunset behind you," I say to her. Erica turns her head and body westward.

"It is fantastic," Erica says admiringly. "Look at the moon over there."

The almost full moon looks down on us. Even though it is not fully dark yet, the moon is extra big and bright and looks particularly close tonight. While the moon may be a barren, airless, uninhabitable place, it looks like a big friendly companion. It is quite a good omen, I suspect, to have our friend the moon watch over my first date with Erica. The sunset and big moon start the date off right. It also makes me hungry.

"I'm quite hungry tonight," Erica says to me.

It is refreshing for her to tell me that she is hungry. Many women, especially on the first date, hesitate to actually eat, or they eat only a small amount.

"Everything is delicious here Matt. Do you like to be called Matt or Matthew?"

"Matt is fine. Most people call me Matt, but some call me Matthew. Erica, should I call you Erica?"

231

Erica smiles at my little joke.

Because of our respective hungers, we each carefully examine the Indian Gourmet's menu. This is the first time in my life that I have eaten outside at an Indian restaurant. What is most conspicuous about eating outside at the Indian Gourmet is the absence of Indian music playing. Every other time I've eaten in an Indian restaurant, I've heard Indian music playing in the background. There is, most likely, Indian music playing for those patrons eating inside the Indian Gourmet, but for those of us eating outside, the only music is the sounds of the pedestrian and vehicular traffic on Amsterdam Avenue.

"I think we should order an appetizer or two," I say.

"That is a good idea. The breads here are marvelous."

Erica is very knowledgeable about Indian food. She tells me that she never had it until she moved into her own apartment. Once she discovered it, she fell in love with the unusual blend of spices. She tells me, however, that her love of Indian food has not removed her love of Italian, Chinese, Mexican, delicatessen, or other food.

"I love all food," Erica says with a smile. "But I like seafood the least."

Being that both Erica and I have expressed our desire to eat a lot, I restate my suggestion that we order some appetizers. Erica does not hesitate again to notify me that the breads here at the Indian Gourmet are marvelous. I am not an Indian bread connoisseur, so I defer to Erica's wishes. Accordingly, we examine the Tandoori bread section of the menu. Next to each item on the menu is an explanation. Therefore, it is easy to decide what to order. We know what breads we will order by the time our waiter, a soft-spoken, thin, dark Indian man arrives at our table. Erica tells the waiter that, under the bread section of the menu, we would like to start with an aloo paratha, which is, according to the menu, a whole wheat bread stuffed with potatoes. We also order an onion kulcha, which is a naan stuffed with seasoned onions. Nann, according to the menu, is an unleavened white bread. We also order a samosa from the appetizer section of the menu. A samosa is defined in the menu as a flaky pastry stuffed with lightly spiced peas and potatoes. I order an Indian beer. Erica orders a Diet Coke. I tell the waiter that we have not yet decided what entrees we will order, but we will do so shortly. He replies that we should not hurry.

Erica asks me where I grew up and what I do for a living. I tell her. She listens, seemingly fascinated by my existence in the insurance world, which is, I gather, far different from her daily existence as a social worker. Erica likes her work, but finds it frustrating. She is reluctant to talk about any of her particular cases. Our waiter comes back with my Indian beer, called Calcutta Ale, and Erica's Diet Coke. Unfortunately, he has yet to bring forth the appetizers.

"Are you ready to order your entrees?" he asks.

"A few more minutes," I reply.

"Take your time."

I sip my beer. Erica drinks her Diet Coke with gusto. I learn that Erica has absolutely no interest in professional team sports, but she likes to ice skate. One of her favorite things to do is ice skate in Central Park on a brisk winter night.

"You must go skating there. It's beautiful with the skyline of Central Park South in the background. It's like a postcard, especially if there is snow covering the park."

"I will go this winter. It has been years since I've ice skated. As a kid I used to go to a community park with my best friend. Neither of us could really skate, but my friend was fearless. He would just fly around the rink and not care whether or not he fell on the hard ice. At the time, I thought my friend was crazy, but now, in retrospect, I wish that I had skated around the rink with that kind of abandon. What would have been the harm? I had a hard head back then. I am sure of it."

"Then when you go skating this winter, make sure you skate fast, without any fear," Erica says.

"But my head is softer now."

Erica tells me that she ice skated indoors one time last year, but did not enjoy the experience.

"The fun of skating is being all bundled up in a hat, scarf, and sweater. It is not the same skating indoors."

We look at the Indian Gourmet's menu to order our entrees. As opposed to the Bombay Terrace, where my favorite dish is chicken saag, here, at the Indian Gourmet, that same dish is called chicken saagwala. It is, nonetheless, the same dish, chicken with spiced spinach. Whatever its name, tonight I will not order it. I will try something new.

I now notice Erica's eyes, which are a stunning green. It is no exaggeration to describe them as remarkable. They are, as the sun sets in the background, like no other eyes I have ever seen.

"I can see you are looking at my eyes," Erica says to me.

I feel embarrassed for doing so. I certainly do not know her long enough to be staring lovingly into her green eyes.

"I'm sorry," I say.

"There is no need to be sorry. It's a compliment."

"Your eyes are the most unusual shade of green that I have ever seen. I didn't mean to stare."

Erica starts to giggle. She has an adorable giggle.

"I hardly know you, but already I have a confession."

"What?"

"I am wearing contact lenses. Just two days ago, I bought these green colored lenses. Today is the first time I have worn them. Close your eyes."

I sit with my eyes closed for ten seconds.

"Open your eyes."

Erica sits before me, but her left eye is now a simple plain brown. Her right eye is the dramatic green of the contact lens. It is unusual to see a person across a table with two different colored eyes.

"I just bought the colored lenses to try something different. Now I think they are silly."

"No," I tell Erica. "The green eyes are nice. Not that there is anything wrong with your brown eyes."

"Thanks," Erica says, looking a little embarrassed.

Erica puts her left contact lens back on her eye. Again I am confronted by the two spectacular green eyes. Is it wrong to deceive someone about eye color? For all I know, Erica may suddenly rip off a mask from her face, which may reveal the face of a monster. I doubt that will happen. Besides, beauty is what is inside a person. Did I like Erica more when I believed that she had the overly dramatic green eyes? Actually, I don't think so. I think the green eyes intimidated me. The simple brown eyes underneath the lenses are more comforting. They look like chocolate pudding. But for tonight, I will look across the table from a green-eyed Erica.

Our waiter comes back to the table.

"Are you ready to order your entrees?"

"Another few minutes," I reply.

"Take your time."

"Do you know what you are going to order?" I ask Erica.

"I'm going to order the chicken saagwala. It is delicious. It is my favorite Indian dish."

I am taken aback. What is the likelihood that Erica's favorite Indian dish is my favorite dish? I do not tell Erica about my fondness for chicken saag, or chicken saagwala, as it is called here. Instead, I listen attentively as Erica describes to me the tasty dish of chicken saagwala. Little does she know that I ate chicken saag last night, but from the Bombay Terrace.

"That sounds good," I tell her. "But I'm going

to try the chicken jalfrazie."

Chicken jalfrazie is described in the menu as a deliciously flavored curried chicken with onions, tomatoes, and green peppers.

"I've never eaten that. But it sounds good too," Erica says.

Erica informs me that the vegetarian dishes here are excellent, especially the dal makhani, which, according to the Indian Gourmet's menu, is black lentils simmered for many hours in a charcoal oven, and blended with ginger and tomatoes.

"When I bring Indian food home, I often bring home one of the vegetarian dishes," Erica notes.

Erica informs me that she is too hungry tonight for dal makhani. She believes that the chicken saagwala is a better choice than a vegetarian dish to satisfy her strong hunger.

The waiter comes to our table with the samosa, the onion kulcha, and the aloo paratha. They look and smell luscious.

"We are ready to order our main dishes," I tell the waiter. "One chicken saagwala and one chicken jalfrazie."

"Very good," says the waiter.

Erica and I sit with the appetizer, the breads, and our drinks.

# Chapter 39

The breads are steaming and hot to the touch. I split our appetizer, the samosa, into two, and the smell from that flaky pastry stuffed with lightly spiced peas and potatoes fills me with anticipation of what the rest of our meal at the Indian Gourmet has in store for us. The breads, as Erica predicted, are scrumptious and, taken with a large sip of the Calcutta Ale, make me want to consume more food. Erica, too, enjoys the food on the table, but her Diet Coke certainly does not supply the extra kick that is provided by my Calcutta Ale.

"Would you like to try some beer?"

"I'll have a sip," Erica says hesitatingly. "I never was able to drink beer. After one glass I get sleepy. I also hate the taste of it," Erica says after a sip of the Calcutta Ale.

Erica tells me that her mother and her Aunt Beverly have always been extremely close. They have been especially close since the death of Beverly's husband, Erica's Uncle Charles, the brick manufacturer. Erica loves her Aunt Beverly a great deal. She doesn't object when Beverly sets her up on blind dates. According to Erica, Beverly believes that it is of vital importance that Erica meet the man she will marry by age thirty, and that she and this man be married before Erica turns thirty-two. Erica does not necessarily believe in this timetable, but she is not necessarily adverse to it, so long as it is with the right man.

I am Erica's third blind date through Beverly. The two other dates never progressed beyond a first meeting. The first time Beverly arranged a date for Erica was one year ago. The man's name was Ted, and he was the son of one of Beverly's neighbors. He was forty-two years old at the time. According to Erica, Ted was filled with such zeal to get married that he overwhelmed her. The day after their date, which included dinner at a very, very expensive French restaurant, La Monique on 67th Street between Fifth and Madison Avenues, Ted sent two dozen roses to Erica's apartment. Erica describes the food at La Monique as a "revelation." But she did not enjoy it as much as she should have because Ted implied to her that he would marry her that night, if she gave the go ahead. Erica was uncomfortable because Ted spent so much money on the dinner. Ted, she tells me, was a very successful bond trader, who lived in a large home that he purchased in an exclusive area of Port Washington, Long Island. Ted drove a large black Mercedes. Erica did not know whether it was his pushiness or not, but she knew that she did not want to date him a second time. After receiving the two dozen roses, Erica received three telephone calls from Ted. During each call she made up a reason why she could not see him that week. Ted was generally nice, Erica says, but she knew that she did not want to see him. Just this week, Beverly told Erica that Ted married a woman he met in a video store, and that the two of them departed on a two month long honeymoon, taking them to Morocco, Portugal, Spain, Italy, and France.

"Aunt Beverly says that I blew it big time."

Erica's second blind date arranged by Beverly took place about three months ago, with a doctor

Beverly met at New York Hospital. Beverly met the young resident, Dr. Ben Arnold, while visiting her longtime friend, who was hospitalized for a week due to some undiagnosed stomach ailment, which ultimately cleared up just as mysteriously as it came. Dr. Ben Arnold appeared out of the blue as Beverly sat in her friend's hospital room. "Dr. Ben," as Beverly called him, was making his rounds when he entered her friend's room. Beverly instantly believed that Dr. Ben needed to meet her niece. Beverly apparently worked Erica's name into her conversation with the strapping six foot tall doctor until Dr. Ben asked Beverly if he could call Erica. Beverly insisted that Dr. Ben give his number to her so that Erica could call him at her convenience.

"When I called Dr. Ben two days later," Erica says, "he seemed very excited to meet me. We met the following Sunday for brunch. Dr. Ben was very good looking, just as Aunt Beverly had told me. However, after only a few minutes into the brunch, Dr. Ben, without any prompting on my part, began telling me about the many, many women he had dated in the past, and how the landscape of the Upper East Side of Manhattan was littered with the hearts of the women he had stopped dating. Then Dr. Ben spoke about one woman whom he dated for a year. Her name was Evelyn. Their relationship ended about three weeks before our date. I was his first date since their breakup. Dr. Ben was obviously distraught over her, despite his confident appearance and his assertion that it was a mutual decision to split up. It was clear to me that Evelyn must have dumped Dr. Ben. Our date quickly turned into a therapy session. I felt as though I were at work, except that instead of listening to the problems of a battered child, I was listening to the troubles of a spurned doctor. I don't think Dr. Ben asked me a single question about myself. It was as if he forgot I were there. Dr. Ben called me a few days later. I was utterly surprised when I came home to my apartment and there was a message on the answering machine from Dr. Ben, asking me if I wanted to have dinner with him that weekend. Since I did not want to be his therapist during another meal, I did not return his call. He never called again."

"What did Beverly say about me?"

"Aunt Beverly told me that she believes we will get along splendidly. She believes that she knows you much better than she knew either Ted or Dr. Ben, and she is more confident in our compatibility. She likes you. She enjoyed the time that she spent with you at the coffee shop late at night."

Erica is nice. She speaks with a smile, and that smile, in conjunction with her fake green eyes, make the Indian breads and the Calcutta Ale a satisfying experience. Our waiter arrives at our table with Erica's chicken saagwala and my chicken jalfrazie.

"I've talked your head off, haven't I?" Erica says to me.

"Not at all. It's very interesting to hear how I fit in among Beverly's suitors for you."

"Have you had any unusual blind date experiences recently?"

"Let me think," I say.

Obviously, I cannot talk about my recent brunch and auto show date with Claire since Claire can possibly be called my girlfriend, or my potential girlfriend. Besides, I knew Claire when we had the brunch and auto show date, so under no circumstances could it be considered a blind date. And then there was my time spent last week in the Atlantic City hotel room with Jan English. However, the Jan English bubble bath incident is not something I should tell Erica. In any event, it was not a blind date. Maybe I'll tell Erica about it when we're old and gray together, and have shared countless evenings of married life together.

"Give me a second to think of a memorable blind date. In the meantime, this food looks and smells great, doesn't it?"

"Indeed it does."

Our entrees do, in fact, look fantastic. My chicken jalfrazie is an enticing ensemble of chicken, tomatoes, peppers, and onions. It is pleasing to the eyes, wonderful to the nose, and, upon my first bite, which is taken with white rice, a joy to the tastebuds. It is tasty, but not overly spicy. It has an unusual, but delicious, flavor that I have never had before. I have, in my life, had peppers, tomatoes, and onions before, but there is something about this chicken jalfrazie that sets it apart from things I have eaten before.

"Mine is great. How is your chicken saagwala?"

"It is wonderful. I have had it before, but it is especially delicious tonight. Please, try some."

I take a forkful of Erica's chicken saagwala,

courtesy of the Indian Gourmet's kitchen. Only last night I consumed chicken saag, but prepared from the chef at the Bombay Terrace. As I move the fork full of chicken saagwala closer to my mouth, there is a significant difference in color between this dish and last night's dish. Last night's chicken saag was more yellow in color. This chicken saagwala, while recognizable as the same basic dish, has a greener color. There is something they put in the sauce here, at the Indian Gourmet, that is absent at the Bombay Terrace. Or is there something put in at the Bombay Terrace that is absent here? In any event, the difference in taste is apparent. This is not as spicy hot as the chicken saag to which I am accustomed, but it is spicy nonetheless, with a sweet flavor emanating from it. Whether I like this chicken saagwala more or less than the chicken saag I usually buy from the Bombay Terrace I cannot tell from only one bite. Perhaps next week I will conduct a comparison taste test.

"Your chicken saagwala is excellent," I tell Erica. "Would you like to try some of this chicken jalfrazie? It is also excellent."

"I'll have a little," Erica says with a smile.

I take hold of Erica's fork and put some chicken jalfrazie with rice on it. Unfortunately, as I pass her the fork, some of the chicken jalfrazie falls into her glass of Diet Coke.

"This is good," Erica declares. "It certainly will make the remainder of my Diet Coke even more flavorful."

I see our waiter.

"I'll have another Calcutta Ale."

I also order another Diet Coke for Erica.

"Thank you Matt. Before our orders came you were about to tell me about an unusual blind date. Why don't you tell me about it?"

I've had an assortment of blind dates over the past few years. Which one should I tell Erica about? How I wish one of those blind dates would have been with Bench Woman. Of course, due to Bench Woman's beauty, she probably has never had a blind date. Potential paramours must flock to her as she walks down the street. But suppose Bench Woman and I were set up on a blind date. When I first arrive at her home, armed with a dozen roses, I would be unable to speak because I would be so struck by her incredible beauty. Then, upon seeing me for the first time, Bench Woman would take my roses and say, "I originally wanted to go out to dinner with you, but why don't we just say inside here. You just sit in my penthouse 50th floor apartment couch. Wait for me." I would wait for Bench Woman to summon me. She would go to a different room and then close the door behind her. I would sit on her remarkably comfortable blue silk couch and look out upon the city's evening lights shimmering far down below.

"Come in," Bench Woman would beckon to me from the other room.

Bench Woman would be lying in a large bed with beautiful sheets, pillows, and blankets. She would be wearing nothing but the twelve red roses that I bought for her, placed on different areas of her body. I would hope that the thorns would not hurt her. "Take these roses off of me with your teeth," Bench Woman would say to me.

That would have been a wonderful blind date. Unfortunately, it did not, and will not likely ever happen. Of course, even if it did, I would not tell it to Erica on this, our first date.

I start to tell Erica about my blind date with Brenda, whose last name I do not recall. The date took place sometime last fall. We first saw a movie. I believe the movie was called "Lights of Ember," which was a slow-moving film about the trials and tribulations of a wealthy family in the early 1900s. Brenda liked the movie, but I did not. Afterwards, we went to an Italian restaurant called Marsala Roma. It served good food with a man playing the piano in the background. When we arrived at the restaurant it must have been after 10:00 p.m. We hung up our coats on a long coat rack near the bar, which was in the front of the restaurant. Brenda wore a long khaki colored overcoat. The dinner was delicious, but we had a very difficult time talking to each other. Despite the deliciousness of the food, Brenda had minor complaints about the service throughout. It was nearly midnight by the time we finished our late meal. When we got to the coat rack, Brenda's coat was not there. There were, however, at least three very similar overcoats still on the rack. Someone obviously took her overcoat by mistake. Brenda became so enraged that I thought she would take the head right off of the restaurant manager's neck. The manager offered her $100 on the spot to pay for the coat just to shut her up. I asked her to calm down, especially when she told me that the coat was not even worth $100. It was, after all, most likely an honest mistake. As the manager noted, the person who took the wrong coat might very well bring it back to the restaurant. Rather than calm down, Brenda called her father on the telephone, at midnight, to tell him what happened. What exactly this thirty-year-old woman expected her father, who lived in another state, to do, was beyond me.

Once outside, I offered Brenda my coat to wear until we made it back to her apartment, which was only a short cab ride away. It was warm enough that a coat was not even necessary. Brenda refused my offer, and was very unpleasant on the cab ride back to her apartment, as if the coat fiasco was my doing. I said good night to her in front of her apartment building. I saw her in Central Park about a month ago. She was lying down on a blanket sunbathing. I don't think she saw me as I walked past.

"I once had dinner last autumn at Marsala Roma and I took home the wrong khaki colored overcoat," Erica says.

"I don't believe you."

"I cannot fool you."

Our waiter arrives with my second Calcutta Ale and Erica's second Diet Coke.

## Chapter 40

My second bottle of Calcutta Ale and Erica's second Diet Coke come at the perfect moment. The chicken jalfrazie, although delicious, makes my mouth ache for more Calcutta Ale. This is a nice Thursday night, sitting at the outdoor section of the Indian Gourmet with my date, Erica. As I sit here making small talk with Erica between bites of the tasty chicken, onions, tomatoes, and peppers, I think of my relationship with Claire. What will the wedding Saturday night bring? Will it bring passion and love or passion and emptiness? Will the promise of the auto show kisses disappear leaving not even a friendship, or will a strong platonic friendship develop, with the auto show kisses a funny memory? Whatever happens with Claire, I now sit across from Erica, and see a wonderfully smiling person in front of me.

Two women sit at a table next to us, and one of them, with very blond hair wearing a deep blue blouse, tells the other that it is her tenth wedding anniversary in two weeks, and that she and her husband are going on a cruise in the Caribbean. Both Erica and I cannot help but listen to their conversation. The women, if I were to venture a guess, are likely friends who rarely spend time together. When the blond woman mentions the date of her ten year anniversary, Erica's expression becomes downcast.

"What's wrong?" I ask.

"Nothing. Something has just snuck up on me. I did not even think about it this year until I heard that woman. This Saturday, two days from now, is the eighth anniversary of my father's death. I'm sorry to put a damper on our conversation. I just heard that woman mention the date of her wedding anniversary. I am fine."

Not sure what to say, I ask Erica if she wants to talk about it.

"There is not much to talk about. My father was going on a business trip to Texas, just like the many trips he had taken in the past. It was a summer day, so I was at home for college vacation. He was supposed to be away for three days. The day he left, my mother and I went to the beach together, just the two of us. It was a weekday so the beach was not very crowded. We had a great day. Mom and I hadn't spent an entire day like that together since I had started college two years earlier. We sat on the beach talking and laughing. We didn't listen to the radio on the car drive back to our house. We just talked with each other. When we arrived home, there was news about an airplane crash in Houston, but no additional news was released. Shortly thereafter we found out that it was Dad's plane that crashed."

Erica's eyes watered up.

"On the one hand, I cannot believe that the accident happened eight years ago. It feels like yesterday. I can still hear his voice as if it were yesterday. Yet at times it seems as if it were an eternity ago when I spoke with Dad, as if it were a prior life."

That is a horrible story. I wish that there is something I can do to ease Erica's eight-year-old pain, but there is nothing to say. On the theory that misery loves company, I could tell Erica about how I lost my own father, just three years ago. Yet I am at a loss about what to say about it. My father's death came about due to sudden illness. There was no great crash from the sky to the earth. There were no news reporters or rescue crews searching for living beings within a tangled heap of fallen machinery. It was an ordinary death, I suppose, as deaths go. One day he was here, the next day gone. It was something that happens every day, countless times, all over the world. There was a week off from work, and sympathy and well-wishes from friends and relatives. But for me things had turned upside down. When I went back to work the next week, I wanted to scream out to the world that things had changed, but for the masses on the subway, life was as usual. All of a sudden I was a twenty-five-year-old without a father.

"My father died three years ago," I tell her.

"I'm sorry," she replies.

We leave that topic. Erica had apparently said all that she wanted to say on the subject of the plane crash, and she must have noticed how I did not elaborate on my father's death.

For the next few minutes, Erica and I spend our energy concentrating on our food. The food is good, though. The combination of chicken jalfrazie and white rice, then followed by a swig of Calcutta Ale, is not a bad way to spend a lull in conversation.

Hardly any topic of conversation seems important after a discussion about death, especially a discussion about the death of a loved one. The funny thing is that we don't even know what happens after death.  Perhaps there is just nothing, or perhaps there is, as some have claimed to experience, a brilliant white light that fills the soul with a great warmth and contentment.  If that is the case, there should be no reason to mourn the dead and no reason to fear death.  Although I fear death, I think that there is a reasonable chance of a life after this life, and of happiness there.  There have been billions and billions of people who have lived and then died.  One day I will experience what they have experienced.  Of course, maybe I will be the first person not to die.  I doubt that.

Despite that my better instincts tell me not to talk about death, I tell Erica that I hope to be the first person in history not to die.  It is possible that there are people who live forever, but keep their identities secret.  Erica tells me that she also plans on living forever.  We go back to eating the Indian dishes that are before us.  Confident in our immortality, we decide that, after our Indian feast, we will go for dessert at Café Chocolate, which is a nearby cafe specializing in unbelievably rich chocolate desserts.  It also serves non-chocolate desserts.  The last time I was there, which was about six months ago, I had a piece of apple pie.  Because Erica and I have decided that we will live forever and, accordingly, cannot be harmed by fat and cholesterol, I will order a slice of cake with extra chocolate tonight.  I should even ask Café Chocolate to put additional fat in whatever cake I order.  Although the apple pie that I had six months ago at Café Chocolate was good, no sane person would order apple pie over chocolate cake, no matter how delicious the pie. I still regret ordering that slice of apple pie.

The anticipation of going to Café Chocolate immediately after the meal does not lessen my enjoyment of the remaining chicken jalfrazie. That is quite a testament to the savory flavor of the food here. I am satiated from the meal, as is Erica, but we concur that there is still some room left in our stomachs for our upcoming dessert.

"Was everything to your satisfaction?" our waiter asks me with a heavy Indian accent.

"Everything was excellent," I reply.

Erica notes how the waiter only asked me about the quality of the meal.

"Obviously your opinion is the only important one," she says.

"Would you like anything else?" the waiter asks, again directing the question only to me.

The bill arrives. It is quite reasonable, even with the appetizer, breads, drinks, and entrees. I pull out my credit card and when the waiter walks by, I hand him both the bill and my credit card. Erica says she wants to contribute, but I tell her that I invited her to dinner and that it is my pleasure to take her out.

We walk the three blocks to Café Chocolate on this very comfortable summer Thursday evening. The air is warm, but not too humid. The bars are busy with Thursday night revelers, but the bars hold no attraction for Erica, who does not care much for drinking alcohol. I too am much happier going to Café Chocolate than any of the crowded bars.

Erica and I enter Café Chocolate. It is bustling with people enjoying post-dinner desserts. The smells of cappuccinos, espressos, and herbal teas linger in the air. Near the Café Chocolate entrance is a glass cabinet showcasing many chocolate cakes and pastries. There is also a smattering of fruit pies, cheesecakes, and assorted other pastries.

"Come this way," says the tall, red-haired hostess.

The hostess sits us down at a corner table. Here we have an excellent view of the whole scene. She puts two menus down on the table. The menus are as large as small books. There are two entire pages devoted to their trademark chocolate and pastries, and a final page describing their "Non-Chocolate Wonders." My eyes head to the chocolate dessert pages. Erica, by contrast, has a keen interest in the beverage page. She tells me that she greatly enjoys different flavored coffees and teas, and marvels at the options available here at Café Chocolate.

"I love to people watch," Erica says.

Café Chocolate is, indeed, a great place to sit, relax, and watch other people sit and talk with each other. Erica and I are here primarily for something sweet to eat, which will compliment perfectly the Indian food that our bodies are presently digesting. Of course, Erica and I are here for more than simply chocolate. We are here to continue our evening together--an evening that, at least for me, has so far been enjoyable.

Our waitress comes by, but we tell her that we need additional time to review the long menu. The many coffees, teas, cappuccinos and espressos do not appeal to me. As far as a beverage goes, I am quite simple and boring. I will order a standard coffee, a "caffe Americano" as the menu calls it, which should go perfectly with a chocolate dessert. Erica says that she will order a decaffeinated hazelnut cappuccino. It is the cakes that present a dilemma for me. Yet it is a pleasurable kind of dilemma, and one that I will resolve by ordering a black and white chocolate mousse cake. To my surprise, Erica orders a pie that has no chocolate inside of it. She orders the mixed berry pie, which is filled with blueberries, raspberries, cranberries and other berries.

"No chocolate?" I inquire.

"That berry pie looks so good and colorful. I cannot resist it."

The mixed berry does look good through the glass counter in front. I can, therefore, understand Erica's desire for it. It looks colorfully delicious. We decide that we will taste both desserts. In this way Erica can eat both her fruit pie and my chocolate mousse cake, and I can have some of her fruit, in addition to the mousse. The berries will add a somewhat healthy component to my dessert.

Erica tells me that she often creates a fictional world and makes up stories about the people around her in restaurants. For example, there are two men in their late twenties or early thirties sitting a few tables away engaged in a serious looking discussion. Erica suggests that the two men are gay lovers who have had a love affair for the past year and that the shorter dark-haired one, whom Erica refers to as Ed, is in the process of informing the taller, light-haired one, referred to as John, that he wants to break off their romance because he has started dating a woman by the name of Jacqueline. John is shocked by Ed's announcement.

"Very interesting theory," I tell Erica. "But to me they look like two people who have lived all their lives as brothers, but the taller one is about to tell the shorter one that they are not biological brothers, and that their parents kept the shorter one when he was left in a basket on their doorstep as an infant."

"Fascinating, but unlikely," Erica says.

Erica and I continue playing this game. We create a Café Chocolate in which we are surrounded by ultra-rich and ultra-powerful people, who have destroyed the lives of others, and whose lives, in turn, are being destroyed by others even more powerful.

Our waitress arrives with our beverages. Erica's decaffeinated hazelnut cappuccino and my caffe Americano come in very attractive deep blue mugs. The waitress comes back momentarily with the black and white chocolate mousse cake and the mixed berry pie. They look so good that Erica and I cannot help but grin upon their arrival.

The white chocolate and the normal colored chocolate taste so good in my mouth that I almost do not want to swallow. The combination of sugar and fat is delicious. The only consolation is that there is plenty of cake left on my plate. Erica's mixed berry pie is a beautiful combination of the colors of the different berries. Erica gives me a forkful of her pie. It is sweet and virtually explodes with the tastes of the different berries. It is very good, but I do not believe that it has the same appeal, at least to me, as the mousse cake. Erica loves both my mousse cake and her mixed berry pie, but she concentrates her efforts on the berry pie. She believes that too much of the mousse cake would keep her awake at night.

The chocolate, the occasional piece of berry pie, and the coffee all come together in a perfect mix, especially with the prior taste sensation of the chicken jalfrazie. We have fun eating the desserts. The time moves quickly.

Erica and I finish the desserts and exit, full and happy, from Café Chocolate. We walk to her apartment building. When we arrive, I tell her that I had a great time, which I did. She concurs and, slightly taking me off guard, asks me if I would like to get together this weekend. Realizing that I will be attending the wedding with Claire Saturday night, I tell her that I would enjoy getting together Sunday night, for perhaps dinner and a movie. We decide to speak by telephone early Sunday afternoon to make exact plans. After a very quick kiss good night on the cheek, Erica enters her building.

I stroll leisurely on my ten minute walk home. There is a message on the answering machine when I get there.

"Hello Matt. This is Erica. Please give me a call when you get in."

I just left her. What could she want? I call immediately.

"Hello Erica, this is Matt. What's up?"

"Matt, I don't think that we should go out Sunday. I just don't think that we should see each other again."

"Why? I thought we had a great time tonight."

"Matt, you are a nice guy, but I just do not want to go out with you again. Take care."

I am dumbfounded after getting off of the telephone. It was only minutes ago that Erica and I shared desserts and laughed at Cafe Chocolate. And it was Erica, not I, who at the end of our date suggested that we see each other this weekend. What made Erica ask me to do something this weekend and then, in the course of the few moments that it took me to walk home, decide that she did not want to see me again? I need to know.

"Hello."

"Yes Erica, this is Matt. I don't want to bother you, but I want to confirm that it was you, not me, who suggested that we see each other this weekend. Isn't that true?"

"Yes."

"So what happened?"

"Matt, I simply do not think that we should go out on another date. Good luck to you."

I get off the telephone. I am tired and go into bed. I determine that Erica is insane, like many people I know. What will I say if I bump into Erica's Aunt Beverly? I'll tell her the truth. What will Erica say about me to her Aunt Beverly?

## Chapter 41

I get into bed perplexed from the events of this evening. Didn't things go well between Erica and me? I was there. Things did go well. Why did Erica ask me to do something this coming weekend, but then, during the short time that it took me to walk back to my apartment, change her mind and decide never to go out with me again? My eyes are heavy as my head hits the pillow.

Sunlight streams through the apartment window. It is Friday morning. Although I slept soundly, I am not refreshed. It looks as though it is a beautiful morning outside. My seat of the pants forecast is confirmed by the radio meteorologist, Mike Henry, who tells the radio listening world over the airwaves that it is presently 68 degrees, and will reach a high of 83 degrees under a clear blue sky.

How can the radio, just sitting on a small table next to my bed, reach out and pluck the radio waves from the surrounding air around me, bring them inside, and put them back together so that I can hear the weather report? It is a miracle that I experience every day, but one that I take for granted.

I replay the evening with Erica in my head as the shower water cascades down upon me. Was there something in the way I left Erica in front of her apartment building that made her decide not to see me again? Was my posture bad as I walked away from her? No answers come easily to mind as I pour more shampoo on my head than usual. I allow myself to relax under the shower a long time.

I look at my skin as I dry off. This is skin that

Erica has decided she does not ever want to see again. It is not horrible skin. Certainly there is worse skin. Of course, there is also better. It is, though, the only skin that I own. It is the shell that protects me from the cold and the hot, all the while keeping my inner organs running at a fairly constant temperature. If Erica has decided that my skin is not good enough for her to look at, or spend any time with, even just to get a future cup of coffee with, then so be it. I don't want her anywhere near my skin.

Maybe it wasn't my skin that was rejected by Erica. She may have liked my skin. It could have been my soul that Erica did not like. What is a soul and what is so unacceptable about mine that warranted such a rejection by Erica? How could Erica even know about my soul? Did she learn everything she needed to learn about it as I ate chicken jalfrazie and the black and white chocolate mousse cake? Was it that she hated both my skin and my soul? Did she hate them in equal parts?

Perhaps it is somehow to spite Erica, but I put on my maroon paisley tie today, which looks especially good. If, by chance, I bump into Erica at some point today and she sees me with my stunning maroon paisley tie, she may regret her decision to reject me. Even if I do not see Erica, it feels good to wear this good looking tie.

It should not be a particularly difficult day at work. Fridays tend to be the most relaxed days in the office, and summer Fridays are the most relaxed of all. A low stress day will be nice. The only stress will be when Claire and I discuss our plans for going to tomorrow night's wedding. But there is no reason why such a discussion should be stressful. To the contrary, it should be fun and enjoyable talking about tomorrow night's wedding.

I look down upon my paisley tie. I did not make the connection, but now I realize that it may have been fate that Erica spurned me, which influenced my decision to wear my maroon paisley tie today. I will go to the auto show again tonight directly after work. The auto show is still in town through this weekend, and tonight Bench Woman may again be revolving on the Ford platform. She may catch a glimpse of the maroon paisley tie and fall in love, not only with the tie itself, but also with me, the person wearing the tie. Can the maroon paisley tie, or any tie for that matter, cause as beautiful a woman as Bench Woman to fall in love with a man? Probably not. However, a stunning tie certainly cannot hurt. Does the tie make the man?

I am flooded with client calls even though it is a Friday. Today has also brought with it the news that I sold a policy to a large company, Gigantic Foods Inc. I worked very hard for this sale for the past two months. It is a good way to end the week. It makes me confident for tonight's visit to the auto show, where it is possible that I will see Bench Woman. Although this time if I see Bench Woman, I must, somehow, make her aware of my presence.

Claire and I have barely spoken today because I have been so busy. We still need to make plans for tomorrow night's wedding. It is 4:30 p.m. when I finish all the work that I will do for this week. I see Claire at the coffee machine. We decide to discuss the wedding plans in my office.

I ask Claire what she is doing this weekend besides the wedding. She tells me that she plans on relaxing, and that she looks forward to doing so. She then asks me the same question, and I tell her that I, too, have no real plans except for the wedding. I tell her that I plan on watching baseball on television tonight. Of course, I actually plan on going to the auto show tonight to search for Bench Woman, but that is not something I want to divulge.

"Matthew, I have a few more things I need to do before the end of the day. Why don't we get a quick dinner tonight? We can discuss the wedding in Chinatown."

I am surprised by the invitation but, because I just told Claire that I am only going to go home to watch television, I cannot tell her that my plan is really to look for Bench Woman at the auto show. The truth is, going to dinner with Claire tonight is a good idea. It will set a tone, either romantic or platonic, for tomorrow night. And we can finish early enough for me to still go to the auto show, which closes at 11:00 p.m.

"Dinner is a good idea."

Claire and I decide to go to Chu Fat Ho. I have never been to this restaurant for dinner, but I have been there for lunch. It is always very busy during lunch. It is colorfully filled with gaudy plastic Chinese ornaments. I like the decor. The food is always good.

It takes us fifteen minutes to walk from the office to Chinatown. Our relationship is strange. Since the kisses in the big American made cars at the auto show, we have done nothing to continue any type of physical relationship, except when we held hands briefly on the street during one lunch. Although I have the desire to hold her hand on this walk to Chinatown, I do not.

I open the door to Chu Fat Ho for Claire. The restaurant is busy, but we do not have to wait for a table. Immediately upon sitting down, a waiter gives us menus and glasses of water. Ten seconds later, another waiter places down on the table a bowl of fried Chinese noodles and two small dishes. One is filled with duck sauce, the other with Chinese mustard.

We are oddly quiet with each other. We should talk about what has happened between us. Maybe we shouldn't, despite the fact that it has been a most unusual week for us. Instead we decide what we should eat. Claire orders hot and sour soup. I order wonton soup. We order an appetizer of scallion pancakes to share, and two entrees to share. One of those entrees is shrimp with lobster sauce and the other is sesame chicken.

The food arrives without incident. First we eat the crisp, but greasy, scallion pancake and the hot soups. Then the entrees arrive. We receive one small dish of brown rice for Claire and one small dish of white rice for me. Everything is tasty. We decide to meet tomorrow at 6:30 p.m., one half-hour before the wedding ceremony is to begin, right in front of the church. Meeting at the church makes the most sense. As Claire notes, it does not make sense for me to go from my apartment in Manhattan into Queens by subway to pick her up, just to have us both go back into Manhattan to go to the church.

Small squares of pineapple with toothpicks standing up in them are placed on the table, along with two fortune cookies. I take a pineapple square. It is juicy and delicious. Claire breaks open one of the fortune cookies. It tells her that "The winds of change are soon to be upon you." That is interesting. I bite into the remaining fortune cookie. It says: "Life is like a budding flower." That is disappointing. First of all, it is not a fortune. Whether life is actually like a budding flower is not a fortune. It is simply a statement. It is a nice sentiment, I suppose, it is certainly better than "your life will turn into a piece of garbage with each passing day." However, telling me that "life is like a budding flower" in no way predicts the future, like a legitimate fortune cookie should.

It is 7:30 p.m. when we exit Chu Fat Ho. Nothing romantic takes place between us at dinner. We just make the meeting arrangements for tomorrow night's wedding. When we walk outside Claire tells me that she still hasn't decided on the type of car she wants to purchase. Upon seeing a billboard advertising the New York Auto Show, Claire tells me that she will go back there again right now to seriously examine the cars.

"I am in no rush to get home," Claire says.

This puts a wrench into my plans. I want to go to the auto show tonight also, but I want to go there to see, and speak with, Bench Woman. I was hoping to see Bench Woman revolve on the Ford exhibit. But now if I go to the auto show, I will have to go with Claire. Of course, if I go with Claire, it will be impossible for me to seek out Bench Woman. What choice do I have if I hope to have any chance to see Bench Woman tonight? I must go to the auto show with Claire.

"Would you mind company at the auto show?"
"Certainly not Matthew. Let's go."

## Chapter 42

Claire and I stand on the platform awaiting the subway to take us to the auto show. However, our motives are quite different. Claire wants to re-examine the new cars on display. I want to catch another glimpse of Bench Woman revolving on the display of the Ford future car. I want more than a glimpse of Bench Woman. I want to be with her. I do not, of course, disclose my motives to Claire.

A man approaches as we wait for the subway. He wears very old jeans and a dirty shirt with the front buttons open. His white skin is marked with time spent living on the streets. His hair is black and gray and long. He wears no shoes.

"You are a lucky man," he tells me, "to be standing next to such a lovely woman."

"Thank you," I reply.

The man's comment is based on his reasonable assumption that Claire and I are a couple, not just co-workers in an uncertain relationship.

"Got any change?" the man continues.

"If you give me fifty cents, I'll tell you and your lady the meaning of life."

I want this man to go away, but he is persistent. He is an extremely friendly panhandler.

"Here," I say, giving him two quarters. "What is the meaning of life?"

Claire and I listen carefully to the man.

"Life is a plum," the panhandler says.

Claire and I look at each other after hearing those words.

"A plum?" We ask this man in unison.

264

"Yes, a plum," he repeats. "Life is like a plum."

"What kind of plum?" I ask. "Is life like a purple plum or a red plum?"

The man says, "A purple plum, of course, that is obvious."

The man walks away with my fifty cents, but leaving us with the knowledge that life is like a purple plum.

"Why, if life is like a plum, must it be like a purple plum?" Claire asks me.

"I don't know."

Armed with the knowledge that life is like a purple plum, Claire and I enter a subway car and then exit at the station stop closest to the auto show.

A good feeling comes over me as we go through the revolving door of the convention center. I take hold of Claire's hand.

The auto show is busy on this Friday night. This is the second, and last, weekend that the show is in town, and it is humming with activity. I buy the two tickets for admission. Claire thanks me. We hold hands upon entering the floor of the show. The enjoyment of holding Claire's hand momentarily makes me forget about my main purpose in going to the auto show tonight--to see Bench Woman. However, I am immediately reminded of that mission when, as I glance at the Pontiac exhibit, I see a spokesmodel for Pontiac's van of the future. The spokesmodel is not Bench Woman, but just the appearance of the model reminds me that Bench Woman may be here among the cars. That reminder jolts me physically and makes my hands sweat.

Unbeknownst to me, over the past few days

Claire has narrowed her upcoming new car purchase to one of two models. She will buy either a Toyota or Mazda. We decide to concentrate our time at those exhibits. However, when we see the big Cadillac sedan, we head straight for it. Not only do we head straight for the Cadillac, but since no one is sitting in it, we go to the back seat of the car. We want to kiss in the big cars, just like we did on Sunday. We are filled with passion at the auto show. I enjoy our kisses, but we are constrained by the fact that we are in public. We have to exit the Cadillac because other auto show patrons want to sit in it. We go from large car to large car, always in the rear passenger compartment, never for more than a few minutes at a time. Cadillac, Buick, Mercury, Chrysler, and many others follow. Claire jokes that she can write a book about the most comfortable new cars in which to kiss.

I enjoy each new kiss in each new car. I assume that Claire is having a good time also, since she is a willing accomplice. Thoughts of Bench Woman depart from my mind with each embrace. I must admit, however, that whenever we go to a new exhibit, I sneak a glance at the spokesmodel displaying that manufacturer's special car. There is no sighting of Bench Woman.

What is it about the auto show that has this effect on us? Whatever it is, the good feeling continues as we exit the auto show, arm-in-arm. It is after 10:00 p.m. and I am happy to be here walking on the street with Claire. Not seeing Bench Woman has not put a damper on my time. If anything, the time spent kissing Claire in the back seat of the large cars at the auto show has made me forget about

Bench Woman.

Claire tells me that she is going to take the subway back to her apartment in Queens. While it is not that late at night, I feel uncomfortable with Claire taking the subway alone at this hour, so I tell her that I will accompany her to her home and then I will take the subway back to Manhattan. She offers meek opposition to that suggestion. It is true that I do not want her to travel alone on the subway at this hour. I also know that I want this night to continue. Who knows what will happen when we get to the front door of Claire's apartment building? Will I enter her apartment? What is going through Claire's mind?

We enter the subway platform and wait. A train enters the station in less than five minutes. We are holding hands as we sit down. The train is not very crowded, but there are other people seated near us. I want to kiss Claire right now, right on this subway train, and I believe she feels the same way. But for now, while we sit on the train, I am content to sit next to her. The train makes its last stop in Manhattan, and it now moves again, taking us with it into Queens, and with each passing subway stop we move closer and closer to Claire's apartment.

"My stop is next," Claire says to me. "I'm glad that you came with me. I don't like being on the subway when it is this late and not too crowded."

Claire is not holding my hand as tightly as before. Her grip is looser, as if she does not know whether she wants to hold it or not. Her sudden ambivalence may be because we are now approaching her subway stop, meaning that we are approaching

267

her apartment. She may be nervous or confused as to whether she wants me to come into her apartment. If I am invited inside, where will that lead?

We exit at her subway stop.

"It is a four block walk to my apartment building," Claire says.

With my right hand holding Claire's left hand, we walk slowly to Claire's apartment building. We talk about the calm beauty of the night.

It is a few minutes before 11:00 p.m. when we get to the front of Claire's building. It is a standard looking brick apartment building, nine stories high, on a quiet, clean, tree-lined street.

"This is home," Claire declares.

"Very nice," I say.

"Matthew, I am happy that we went out tonight. I look forward to tomorrow night's wedding."

"I do too."

"Things are a bit confusing between us, aren't they?" Claire says.

"They are, but I think they don't really need to be. I have a wonderful time being with you. Maybe it just took an auto show to make us find out," I say.

I did not plan to make such a bold pronouncement. But I mean those words as I stand here with Claire in front of her building.

We enter Claire's building. The grip of our hands strengthens. The elevator door opens, and a woman in a nurse's uniform exits. She must be on her way to a hospital for the midnight shift. Claire and I enter the elevator together. We are alone when Claire presses the button to get us to the sixth floor. She lives in apartment 6C. Once the elevator door closes shut, our lips meet strongly with our arms around each other tight. We are bound more tightly together now, in this elevator, than at any time in any car at the auto show. In what feels like both an instant and an eternity, the elevator opens to the sixth floor. While I, for one, look forward to entering Claire's apartment, I do not want us to leave the elevator just yet. Since no one is coming into the elevator from the sixth floor, I press the "door close" button. As we embrace, the elevator moves downward. The elevator door opens to the lobby. There stands a man with a nice looking dog, which looks to me as if it is a Labrador retriever-collie mix, if such a thing is possible. Claire gives me a nudge to exit the elevator. She obviously does not want this man to know that we traveled down the elevator without reason. She knows this man and his dog.

"How are you, Harry?" Claire says smiling to the man as she pets his dog. "And how are you, Svengali? You are my favorite dog in the building."

"Have a good evening," the man says as he and his dog, Svengali, enter the elevator, while Claire and I exit the elevator.

A few seconds later, we press the elevator button, which arrives almost immediately. This time we press the button for the sixth floor and, when the door opens to our destination, we exit the elevator.

Claire opens her apartment door with her key and, upon entry, turns on the light, which reveals a moderate sized living room connected to a kitchen. Claire has a one-bedroom apartment that is larger than my small studio apartment. Her apartment is neat, simple, and comfortable looking. There is not much time, however, to examine all the furniture because, within five seconds of being inside Claire's apartment, we grab hold of each other and start to kiss. These start out to be soft kisses, like many of the tender ones we shared at the auto show, but soon they grow to be heavier and deeper. We stand in her living room. I am still wearing my suit from work, and Claire is in her skirt and blouse. We make our way out of the living room and into her bedroom, and land on her bed. The bed is neatly made. We do not put the light on in the bedroom, but light comes in from the living room. I am very warm, as I am still wearing my suit jacket, which I finally take off. We each take off our shoes. Claire touches my chest over my shirt, and she takes off my tie and unbuttons my shirt. She then puts both hands underneath the bottom of my undershirt and pulls my undershirt up over my head. She rubs her fingers up and down my chest. We continue kissing and I take off Claire's blouse and then her bra. We slowly touch each other.

"That feels good, Matthew," Claire says.

After savory kisses all over each other, we both lie on her bed without any clothes. Claire, shyly, asks me if I have "a thing" for protection. I am slow to understand. She then asks me again if I have any protection with me. I realize what she means, and then I tell her that I do not have a condom. We rest from our kisses. Claire informs me that right on the corner of Queens Boulevard, which is the main street in her neighborhood, and only two blocks away, is an all night drug store.

"I'll be right back," I say to her.

# Chapter 43

I quickly put on some of my clothes for the short journey to the 24 hour drug store. Unfortunately, the only clothes I have with me at Claire's apartment are the clothes that I wore to work. On go my suit pants and dress shirt. I rush, and so I only partially button my shirt. I put on my suit jacket and my dress shoes, without socks. Finally, I grab my wallet. Anyone who sees me on the street will see a disheveled character. Something hits the hard wood floor of the bedroom.

"Here are my keys," Claire says, giddily.

Claire waves good-bye to me. Only her head and hand show through from under the covers.

The street is quiet as I make my way to Queens Boulevard. My dress shoes are not meant to be worn with bare feet. Indeed, the shoes are not at all comfortable without the protection provided by my socks, which are now somewhere on the floor of Claire's bedroom. However, I happily endure the emergence of a blister so that I can make this purchase.

Queens Boulevard, unlike Claire's quiet street, is busy with cars even at around midnight. There are quite a few stores still open. But I only need the drug store.

There are two other customers in the drug store. It is uncomfortable to buy condoms, but to purchase them now, the way I am dressed, is even worse. Why should I care? There is nothing wrong with buying this product and I do not know the cashier. Yet I feel compelled to buy more than the package of condoms. Accordingly, I take a basket and fill it with not only the condoms, but also with shaving cream and disposable razors. I do not need the other items right at this moment, but they will not go to waste. Upon paying for the goods, I realize that the cashier, a man around forty-five years old, could not care less what I buy.

I exit the store with my purchases. Two stores down from the drug store is a diner, also open twenty-four hours, called the Clocktower. Despite my desire to get back into bed with Claire and use my purchase, I am overcome with hunger. It seems like hours and hours have passed since Claire and I had our Chinese dinner at Chu Fat Ho. I walk into the Clocktower for a very quick bite. I will need my strength for Claire.

I sit at the counter. I tell the waitress who greets me that I do not need a menu. I order a toasted corn muffin, no butter, but with jelly on the side, a cup of coffee, and a glass of water. The Clocktower is not very crowded at this hour. There is one booth of four teenage boys, two booths with couples who appear as if they are on dates, and one couple that looks as if they are married. There is one older man sitting at the counter. He is three seats to my left. He looks my way and I smile. He eyes me suspiciously, does not smile back, and turns away.

The toasted corn muffin, coffee, and water arrive. I do not want to sit here at the Clocktower for more than a few minutes while Claire waits in her bed. This is a large corn muffin. Although I am hungry, I do not want to be too full when I get back into bed with Claire. It is a fresh muffin, despite the fact that it is the middle of the night. I wolf down the muffin. The coffee is hot, but I drink it quickly. Claire is waiting. She must be wondering what is taking me so long. Certainly she did not expect me to stop off at a diner on the way back to her apartment from the drug store. The counterwoman refills the coffee mug with steaming hot black coffee. I take a few more swigs of the coffee, and then leave $5 on the counter, which covers the bill and tip.

It is beautiful outside. Unfortunately, after walking almost one full block on the way back to Claire's apartment, I realize that I am not carrying the plastic bag from the drug store that is filled with the condoms and the other products. I must have left the bag under my seat at the Clocktower Diner's counter. I quickly go back to the Clocktower. There, right where I left it, on the floor under the seat of the counter, is the bag from the drug store. I walk into the diner and pick it up from the floor. I again exit the Clocktower.

It is quiet on Claire's street. My pace quickens because I look forward to getting back into bed with Claire. Once at her building, I take Claire's key chain out of my jacket pocket. There are five keys on her chain, and one of them will open the door to the front of her building. I use the correct key after two unsuccessful attempts. I take the elevator to the sixth floor and go to her apartment.

I slowly enter the dark apartment. I take off my clothes in her bedroom and put the box of condoms on the floor next to the bed. Claire is all snuggled up and comfortable. She grabs hold of me tightly. Despite the darkness I can see a smile on her

273

face.

"Matthew," Claire says with a light, but very tired sounding voice. "I am happy. We don't have to rush everything. What you bought tonight we can use some other time soon. I'm so sleepy now."

With that, Claire falls asleep. She looks serene. She is right. It has been a wonderful night and there is no need to rush. What I bought tonight can be used another time, possibly tomorrow night after the wedding, or for other nights after that. I close my eyes.

## Chapter 44

It is such a beautiful night that the bedroom is a perfect temperature even without the air conditioner. The open window provides the right amount of circulating air. It is a good feeling seeing Claire sleep next to me in the darkness, and hearing her breathing and feeling her warmth. I am sleepy too and so I close my eyes, comfortable under the covers with Claire.

I suddenly see a glimmer of light streaming in from under the pulled down window shade. There is a clock radio next to the bed. It informs me that the time is 9:10 in the morning. I am surprised that it is as late as it is, although it is not that late. I slept like a rock. It is only now, after being awake for a few moments, that I am fully oriented to my surroundings and remember that I am in Claire's bed. Claire is not in bed with me, but I hear her movement outside of the bedroom.

I enter the bathroom next to the bedroom. I would like to brush my teeth, but unfortunately, I do not have a toothbrush. I take a small amount of Claire's toothpaste and put it on my finger, which I move briskly around in my mouth, then wash out with cold tap water. I also take a small amount of Claire's mouthwash. My breath is now fresh. It would be nice if I had some other clothes to wear besides my suit. I go back into the bed contemplating my next move. In a few minutes I will put on my pants and greet Claire in her kitchen, but I just want to stay in the bed a little longer.

Claire must have heard me move because she

enters the bedroom about two minutes after I got back into the bed. She looks adorable. She is wearing shorts and a colorful T-shirt emblazoned with animals and the words "The Bronx Zoo." Claire tells me that I look very comfortable under the covers. She is right. I am comfortable, although there is a slight awkwardness between us. I suppose that is not so strange. Neither of us imagined when we awoke yesterday morning that the next morning-- meaning now--I would be in her bed.

To break the awkwardness, and because I am feeling a little frisky, I grab Claire, who is standing right next to the bed, and ask her to join me in the comfort under the covers. We are now both under the covers. What started, though, as just cuddling, turns more and more passionate until we find ourselves in the same position we were in last night before I went to the drug store. But now, unlike last night, right next to the bed sits the drug store plastic bag filled with the condoms. I open the box and, with a mixture of excitement, nervousness and haste, take hold of the first condom out of the box. After some difficulty opening the wrapping, Claire and I look at each other. We are both--to put it mildly--surprised at what we are about to do. Then Claire and I embark on putting on the condom.

We are able to put the condom on successfully and everything works out from there. I am amazed that we just had sex. I am sure that Claire is just as surprised. Afterwards we hold each other tightly. We smile as we both look at the used condom filled with liquid. Perhaps we should keep it for posterity and show it to our grandchildren one day. Is that the

276

kind of thing grandparents should show to their grandchildren? I don't think so.

"Matthew."

"Yes."

"I am having a wonderful time with you. That was the first time I ever slept with a man. I'm happy it was with you."

What? This is a big deal. I'm pleasant enough I guess, but why did Claire choose me? And why now? Did something happen in the Buick at the auto show last night that made Claire want to sleep with me? Or was it in the Mercury?

Claire's head is on my chest. I lay contentedly next to her. We are huddled together. We tell each other that it would be nice to stay in bed like this all day.

I close my eyes and fall back asleep. I wake up and see that it is 12:40 in the afternoon. Claire is no longer in the bed next to me. She then comes back to the bedroom, wearing the shorts and shirt she wore earlier in the morning.

"Come into the kitchen. I made breakfast."

I am hungry. Claire exits the bedroom, and I lumber out of the bed and put on my pants and shirt. On the kitchen table are two big glasses of orange juice and a stack of big healthy golden pancakes. There is a pot of coffee percolating.

"This is incredible," I tell Claire.

Claire gives me four of the big pancakes, but gives herself only two.

"Two of these are more than enough for me," Claire says.

The pancakes are excellent. They are

extraordinarily light and fluffy. The sweetness of the imitation maple syrup heightens the experience. I had no idea that Claire is such a good cook.

Eating this wonderful breakfast tantalizes my hopes of future evenings and mornings with Claire. We confirm our plans to meet in front of the Come Together Church at 6:30 p.m. It would be nice to stay here now with Claire and go to the wedding together, but I need to go home because my clothes for the wedding are there, and Claire has things to do before getting ready for the wedding. Based on the events of last night and this morning, I am sure that we will spend tonight together after the wedding reception. We will likely then have another breakfast tomorrow morning. I kiss Claire at her apartment door and leave.

"See you later."

The streets in Claire's neighborhood look very different in the bright sunlight as compared to their appearance in the middle of the night. As I approach the subway station on Queens Boulevard, I walk by the all night drug store that made this morning possible. The breakfast Claire made was exceptional. Her pancakes were so light and fluffy that they were undoubtedly superior to those that can be had at most diners. But the coffee she brewed was an unpleasant gourmet coffee called "Almond Desire," which I did not enjoy. I did not tell Claire that I didn't like the coffee, especially given the unbelievable pancakes and the fact that we just had sex. Notwithstanding the great time with Claire, I now need a real cup of coffee, not "Almond Desire." I enter the Clocktower Diner.

The staff at the Clocktower is completely different than the late evening skeleton staff. It is very busy here now, far different than in the middle of the night. The booths and tables are packed with people eating late breakfasts and lunches. All I want is coffee at the counter.

"Do you need a menu?" I am asked by the counterman, who brings me a glass of water, silverware and a napkin.

"I'll just have a cup of coffee."

The coffee arrives momentarily. It is a deep black, and steaming hot, exactly the way good diner coffee should be. As I drink it--and it is as good as it looks--I realize that it was much more fun drinking the unenjoyable "Almond Desire" coffee with Claire than to be drinking this good cup here at the Clocktower alone.

"Would you like a refill?"

"No thanks. Just the check please."

I leave the Clocktower and walk to the subway station.

# Chapter 45

The thirty-five minute subway ride to my neighborhood is painless. Once back in my apartment, I immediately take off the suit and shirt that I wore to work yesterday, then to the auto show with Claire, and then again this morning. It is already 2:00 in the afternoon when I get back home. I am meeting Claire at the church at 6:30 p.m. I will have to leave my apartment at 6:00 p.m. to get there on time. I will allot one hour to shower, shave and get dressed, which is more time than I actually require, but I will give myself that amount of time nonetheless. Therefore, I get into bed, set my alarm for 5:00 p.m. and close my eyes. Although I had a good sleep at Claire's apartment, followed by the unexpected sex and the deliciously light and fluffy pancakes in the morning, I want to take a nap. Perhaps the reality of this relationship with Claire has made me sleepy. It is a good, fulfilling sort of sleepy. It is not a heavy uneasy sleepy. I close my eyes, grateful for the prospect of seeing Claire again in only a few hours.

My eyes open after a restful sleep. It is 4:30 p.m. I want to look extra good for Claire tonight. Claire sees me wear a suit every day at work, so it will not be anything special for her to see me wear a suit tonight. As the water from the shower cascades down upon me, I decide that I will buy a new, especially fantastic tie just to wear for this occasion. I will leave my apartment a little early, and on my way to the church I will go to the nearby department store and buy a tie that will go perfectly with my suit.

Price will be no object when it comes to the tie that I select. I want Claire to love the tie so much that she will be thrilled to see me with my tie on, and then later, when we are alone, she will be thrilled to see me without my tie, and without anything else on for that matter.

I depart from the shower with a renewed sense of vitality. My darkest charcoal gray suit, almost black, emerges from the closet. I had the suit dry cleaned and pressed for tonight. As I put the suit on, I am becoming more and more excited about seeing Claire soon. A recently pressed, deep blue shirt goes perfectly with this suit.

I exit my apartment at 5:15 p.m., giving me more than one hour to meet Claire in front of the church. But I left my apartment without a tie because I am going to buy one at the store.

The men's department presents a dizzying array of ties, ranging in price from $15 to $75. Ties are laid out on table after table. Floral ties, striped ties, solid ties, and other ties are displayed. On the table to my right are cartoon-character ties and to my left are ties adorned with geometric shapes. I pick up a striped tie and place it so it runs down from my neck. I go to another tie. A young saleswoman approaches.

"Would you like help?"

"I'm going to a wedding tonight and I need a great looking tie to go with the shirt I'm wearing."

"Let's see," the pretty saleswoman says. "That's a nice looking suit. It will be easy to match with most every tie. Do you want a conservative tie or a brighter party tie?"

"I want a beautiful tie. It should not be too conservative and boring. At the same time it should not be so wild that it is inappropriate for a Saturday evening wedding."

"I see."

Strategically leading me to a table of the more expensive ties, the saleswoman and I stand in front of a table of extremely nice looking $50 to $60 ties. Some of the ties are very conservative and not what I want for this evening. The saleswoman picks up a mostly maroon tie with circles in it.

"How does this look?" she asks me seductively. Her smile alone almost convinces me to buy the tie.

"It is very nice, but not extraordinary," I reply.

"I see," she responds, her face still wearing its enticing grin.

I then grab hold of a blue and red tie, which is quite nice, but also too dull for this evening. Out of the corner of my eye I see, on the $30 tie table, the perfect tie for this evening. It somehow straddles the line of bold, but understated. With its deep red and yellow combination of rectangles, it looks stunning with the dark charcoal gray suit that I am wearing.

"Very nice," the saleswoman says.

I go to the counter to pay.

"No bag necessary. I'll be wearing the tie out," I tell the cashier. I put on the tie, using a store mirror to help me put it on straight. I leave the store happy with my new tie.

It is still only 6:10 p.m. when I arrive at the Come Together Church. Claire is not supposed to arrive for another twenty minutes. I am filled with energy so I take a walk. I do not walk far, but the walk up one street then down another is a good way to expend my excess energy. I arrive back in front of the church at 6:25. At exactly 6:30, I see Claire emerge from the subway. She walks up the block to the church. She looks great. She is wearing a black sleeveless dress that modestly reveals her figure underneath. I am amazed that until our kisses at the auto show I never really thought about Claire's body. Now that I have seen and touched what is beneath Claire's dress, and am aware that it is smooth and soft, I cannot help but stare at her.

"You look great."

"Thank you Matthew. So do you."

We greet each other with a somewhat tentative kiss on the lips, and hold hands.

"Do you want to go inside now?" Claire asks.

"Before we go in, I just want to show you something that is in a store window on the next block. It will only take a minute," I tell her.

"What is it?" Claire asks.

"You'll see."

We cross the street and are now one block from the church. I grab Claire and tell her that she looks beautiful. I tell her that there is no store window for her to see, but that I just wanted to walk with her on the street for a moment to be alone with her before we go to the wedding. We kiss, and then go back to the Come Together Church.

"Is that a new tie, Matthew?"

"Yes."

"I like it."

## Chapter 46

A friendly, distinctively high pitched voice calls to Claire only two or three steps before we enter the Come Together Church.

"Claire, is that you?"

Claire turns around, but keeps hold of my right hand.

"Wendy, how are you?  It's great to see you."

Claire lets go of my hand and the two of them, almost in unison, say it has been such a long time since they last saw each other.  They knew each other as camp counselors years ago.

Wendy is tall and robust.  Her size greatly contrasts with the squealing tone of her voice.  In contrast to Claire's sexy but reserved jet black dress, Wendy is wearing a flowery dress.  It is pretty, but she looks comical compared with Claire.  I am truly amazed at how I just recently—only since the auto show and, more specifically, since the time we spent together last night and this morning--realized how beautiful Claire is.  Not stunning in a movie actress way, but beautiful, in a girl next door way.  Wendy stands next to a man, who is slightly shorter and less robust looking than she.  After Claire and Wendy spend a few moments determining that they have not seen each other in six years, they realize that they must introduce each other to the men at their sides.

"This is my boyfriend Gary," Wendy says to Claire.

It is now Claire's turn to introduce me to Wendy and Gary.  Since Gary was introduced as Wendy's boyfriend, it would make sense for Claire to introduce me similarly. And based upon what happened last night and this morning, it would be suitable for Claire to introduce me as her boyfriend. Claire hesitates for a moment, perhaps feeling that it is premature to introduce me as her boyfriend. Claire then says, enthusiastically,

"This is Matthew."

"Hello Wendy, Gary. Nice meeting you."

Claire left the status of our relationship up in the air, which is appropriate at this stage. Wendy, Gary, Claire, and I enter the Come Together Church. Wendy and Gary are holding hands. Claire and I are also holding hands.

The Come Together Church is, from the outside, a plain gray stone building that blends in, without any pretense, on a block of beautiful brownstone homes. The inside maintains the simplicity of the outside. It looks more like a small school auditorium than a church. There is a small table near the entrance to the building, and on the table there is a box filled with brochures. I pick up one of them, which describes the Come Together Church.

The Come Together Church was founded in 1982 by an Episcopalian minister from Baltimore, a Buddhist monk from San Francisco, and a Jewish Rabbi from Brooklyn, who all found that their particular religious practices needed teachings from other religions to be complete. They formed this church to be open to all faiths, so long as the basic tenet of those who joined was that people should treat all others with compassion. What started with an initial congregation of twenty is now up to nearly

285

600, and the church counts among its members people who belong to all the major world religions, as well as those who do not know if they believe in any higher power. Services are held every weeknight at 8:00 p.m., and on Saturday and Sunday mornings at 9:00 a.m. The prayers said at services are taken from different religions, but there are also some prayers that have been written by members of the church. The present leader of the church is Albert Permanding. He joined the church ten years ago and was made its leader one year ago. The church is a non-profit organization with a yearly membership fee of $400. However, if money is a problem for a congregant, that person can pay less, or nothing at all. Donations are always appreciated. There are donation boxes throughout the chapel.

We all sit in a row of chairs. Claire and Wendy are engaged in a conversation, trying to catch up with their lives. Gary is at the end of the row. Claire sits to my right and an older man sits to my left. A woman who looks to be his wife sits next to him. Claire and Wendy wave to another woman a few rows in front of us. That woman's name, Claire tells me, is Elise, who is another old friend from their summer camp days. Claire informs me that Elise got married one month after college graduation, but divorced one year after that. The seats fill up. Two female violin players play classical music. The piece of music is familiar, but I do not know the name of it. Will I ever be so in love with someone that I will walk down a wedding aisle? No one has yet started to walk down the aisle, but I assume that the actual ceremony will begin at any moment. The music is beautiful.

There is a stage with four steps leading up to it. Two men walk down the aisle, up the four steps, and onto the stage. Claire tells me that she was informed by Debbie, the bride, that in a concession to each set of parents, both a Priest and a Rabbi will conduct the ceremony. Claire refers to them as a "pseudo" Priest and a "pseudo" Rabbi.

"What do you mean 'pseudo'?" I ask Claire in a whisper.

"That was the word Debbie used to describe them to me. She said that a serious Priest or Rabbi would not officiate a ceremony here at the Come Together Church."

With the two men on the stage, the members of the wedding party make their way down the aisle. The men of the wedding party, in black tuxedos, and the women, in deep blue dresses, walk together to the stage. Once on the stage, the men go left and the women right.

The two men conducting the service--the pseudo Priest and Rabbi--are surrounded by the three men of the wedding party on one side, and the three women of the wedding party on the other side. The violin players continue playing music as the groom, accompanied by his parents, walks down the aisle. The groom is smiling, as are his parents. The smiles on the faces of his parents, especially the father's smile, look forced. Perhaps they are just nervous that their son is getting married, or perhaps it is that they are unhappy with the nontraditional surroundings here at the Come Together Church. But both groom and parents make it to the stage successfully. The music suddenly stops. It then begins again and the bride and her parents make their way down the aisle.

Everyone turns their necks to view the bride. Claire and Wendy remark to each other that Debbie's wedding dress is beautiful. Three quarters of the way down the aisle the bride and parents stop walking. At that point the bride is kissed by her father on one cheek and by her mother on the other cheek. The parents walk away from their daughter and go onto the stage. The groom walks down from the stage and over towards his bride. When he reaches her, the two of them walk back on the stage. Claire and I hold hands. Our grip strengthens as the ceremony progresses.

The bride and groom stand on the stage with their backs facing us. The pseudo-Priest says a prayer that lasts maybe fifteen seconds. The pseudo-Rabbi says a short prayer in Hebrew. The pseudo-Priest moves to one side and the pseudo-Rabbi moves to the other. From the first row of the audience, a man walks to the place on stage just vacated by the pseudo-Priest and Rabbi. He says:

"Welcome all of you to the wonderful occasion of the wedding of Debra and Richard here at the Come Together Church. I am Albert Permanding and I am pleased that you are all here to join us in celebrating the union of two wonderful people, from different backgrounds, who met, came together, and fell in love right here in this very church."

Mr. Permanding goes on to tell everyone how the church brings together people from all different religious backgrounds and cultures and how, in the case of the bride and groom, two people from different religious backgrounds were afforded the opportunity to worship together and, in the process, fall in love. He tells us that, in front of his very eyes during services at the Come Together Church for the past one and one-half years, he has witnessed friendship and love blossom between the bride and groom. I look at the parents of the bride and groom and speculate that they do not appreciate everything that Permanding is saying. They are probably thinking that their children were brainwashed by a cult.

Permanding's words seem sincere to me, and I am happy for the couple. The place does not feel like a cult to me, whatever it means to be a cult. In fact, the last page of the pamphlet describing the Come Together Church shows a New York Times article discussing the church and its good works for different communities in the city. The article praises the church.

The service concludes with the bride and groom reciting their vows to each other. The groom says that today, his wedding day, is one of the two best days of his life. His other best day was nineteen months ago when he first looked across the Come Together Church during a Saturday service and his eyes fell upon Debbie. The groom, in a light moment, says that it was not until two weeks later that he had the courage to speak with Debbie. He says that he pretended to accidentally bump into her after services. The bride tells the congregation that she was lukewarm about Richard during most of their first date, which consisted of dinner at an Italian restaurant after a Friday night service at the Come Together Church. However, during dessert Richard opened up his wallet and showed her a photograph of his dog, Wally, a mangy gray haired mutt, the light of Richard's life. Debbie says that she fell in love with the dog. She decided to go out with Richard a second time because of the dog. "If Richard loved this lovable looking homely dog, he had to be worth more time," Debbie says to everyone.

"I now pronounce you husband and wife," Albert Permanding says.

## Chapter 47

The bride and groom kiss immediately upon being pronounced husband and wife and the guests burst into applause. After the newlyweds, along with the rest of the wedding party on stage, leave the chapel of the Come Together Church, the groom's brother comes back into the chapel to announce: "The cocktail hour is starting as soon as you arrive in the Gold Room on the third floor of the Nottingham Hotel, which is only two blocks away, on the corner of 62nd Street and Second Avenue."

It was a nice ceremony, especially because it was not too long. I have been brought to near tears at some weddings in the past, but this wedding ceremony, although enjoyable, did not have such an impact on me. Perhaps it was because I do not personally know the bride and groom. By contrast, the ceremony had a real emotional impact on Wendy, who needs many tissues to capture all the teardrops streaming down her face. Gary, her boyfriend, sits next to her, and tries to comfort her by rubbing her shoulders.

"That was a nice ceremony," I say to Claire.

"Yes Matthew, it was."

Claire and I stand up when Elise, who was sitting a few rows ahead of us during the ceremony, walks over.

"How are you Claire?" Elise says. "It has been a long time."

The two women hug. Wendy, now fully recovered from her teary emotional release, also greets Elise with a hug. All five of us--Claire, Wendy,

291

Elise, Gary, and I--walk out of the Come Together Church together, and make our way to the Nottingham Hotel for the wedding reception. The three old friends walk next to each other and reminisce, leaving Gary and myself to their right, walking next to each other.

"That was an interesting ceremony," I say to Gary. "I've never been to the Come Together Church."

In the few block walk to the Nottingham Hotel, I learn that Gary, at twenty-three years of age, is five years younger than his girlfriend Wendy. He grew up in a home where his parents were committed to a small alternative religion called Chutoma, whose home base was in a small town in the middle of the Allegheny Mountains of Pennsylvania. Although Gary grew up in upstate New York, his family used to make a two-week trip each summer to the main Chutoma base. They also went for two weekends in the winter. He loved the long car rides in what he remembers as blizzard conditions. Dozens of families made it to the Chutoma summer enlightenment weeks, as they were called. The Chutoma Church also had small churches in different cities, one of them being in Syracuse, New York, where he, his younger brother, and his parents went almost every Sunday.

Gary tells me that he used to love going to the summer and winter getaways at the headquarters of the church, which was located at a campsite with a mountain lake. Gary never found the actual religion of Chutoma very compelling, although that church, like the Come Together Church, offered a less structured way of praying than traditional churches. But Gary fondly recalled the two-week summer mountain retreats when he was twelve, thirteen, and fourteen years old. During those retreats Gary snuck off into the far isolated end of the lake with a girl named Violet, who was two years older than he. She also came to the retreat with her family. The two of them would sneak off to swim naked at the isolated north end of the cool mountain lake. Gary remembered his disappointment when he and his family came back one year, but Violet and her family were no longer there. He never saw Violet again.

The three women, Gary, and I, enter the distinguished looking Nottingham Hotel. We take an elevator together to the Gold Room on the third floor. Chandeliers illuminate the beautiful dark-paneled room. There is a large bar in the front of the room, and there are many tables where the guests are congregating with drinks. Waiters walk back and forth in the crowded room holding platters containing varied hors d'oeuvres. Claire tells me that 200 people are expected at the wedding. The five of us sit together at a table during this cocktail hour. All five of us have been assigned to sit together at table 7 during the main dinner in the nearby Medallion Room. But the main dinner in the Medallion Room will take place after this cocktail hour in the Gold Room. Unlike the main dinner, there are no assigned tables during this cocktail hour.

Gary and I decide to go to the open bar. Before walking there, we ask the women what they want to drink. Claire wants a glass of white wine, Wendy a Diet Coke, and Elise a Tom Collins. Gary tells the bartender what the women want, and then he orders himself a beer. I, too, order a beer. The two of us carry the five drinks back to the table. A waiter approaches with a platter of small meatballs. They look good.

"Would you care for some meatballs?" he asks.

I, for one, definitely would like at least one meatball. I take a toothpick that is also on his platter and pierce a meatball with it. The meatball is as good as it looks. Before he leaves, I take another, as do the others. There are many waiters parading the floor of the Gold Room. I look forward to trying different foods. Given the number of people here, and the opulent surroundings of the Gold Room of the Nottingham Hotel, I deduce that this is quite an expensive wedding reception. Another waiter comes to our table. He is holding a platter filled with what appears to be small fried egg rolls.

"Care for a spring roll?" he asks.

Elise takes one, followed by Gary, Claire, and me.

"None for me, thanks," says Wendy.

The spring roll, although fried, is not very greasy. To the contrary, it is hot, crispy, and unexpectedly tangy. It is small, however, so two bites finish it off. Fortunately, the waiter is still nearby, giving me the opportunity to take another one before he goes off to another area of the Gold Room. Following the spring roll, a veritable parade of waiters come to our table, allowing us to sample bite-sized quiches, bite-sized pizzas, bite-sized hot dogs, fried potato pancakes, fried shrimp, deviled eggs, stuffed mushrooms, which I do not eat, teriyaki chicken breast slices, and finger-sized roast beef and turkey sandwiches. For me, the meatballs are the highlight of the cocktail hour. Very few foods satisfy like a good meatball. Happily, the meatball waiter comes back to our table a number of times.

The three women spend much of the time at the cocktail hour reminiscing about their days as camp counselors. I enjoy listening to them, especially as I eat the hors d'ouerves and drink the beer. Gary and I stand up from the table to get ourselves a second beer. None of the women want a refill of their drinks. After three steps towards the bar, I inform Gary that I will meet him back at the table because I need to use the bathroom. In response, Gary tells me that he also wants to use the bathroom before getting his second beer.

We walk to the bathroom together. I feel as though we are at a high school dance leaving our dates for a few moments so that we can talk about them in the privacy of the bathroom. Of course, that is not why Gary and I go to the bathroom. However, once in the bathroom, Gary talks about Wendy. Although Gary just met me, he must need someone to talk to. Gary tells me that Wendy is very nice, but that he must end their relationship of ten months. He tells me that he is only twenty-three years old and that, unlike Wendy, who is twenty-eight, he is not at all ready to get married. He informs me that Wendy has been his first real girlfriend and that he is not ready to commit to a permanent relationship. Wendy, on the other hand, has had many prior boyfriends, and she believes that they will get married.

We now stand next to each other at the large

sink washing our respective hands. Gary tells me that he has wanted to break off their relationship for the past two months, but has chickened out repeatedly. The past month he felt that he could not break off their relationship because he knew that Wendy was looking forward to going with him to this wedding. Gary says that Wendy has done nothing bad to him, and that she is a wonderful person, but he just does not want to be her boyfriend anymore.

"She thinks I am going to ask her to marry me in the next few months, but soon, maybe even after this wedding, I'm going to tell her that our relationship is over."

"That's too bad." I say.

Gary says that he has made feeble attempts to distance himself from Wendy, but she has not noticed. Gary says that the men in Wendy's past have not treated her well and that when he came into her life she fell head over heels in love with him because he was so much nicer.

"She deserves someone ready to commit. I am just not that man," Gary says to me as we exit the bathroom.

We stop at the bar to get our second beers. When we arrive back to the table, Wendy gives Gary a loving kiss on the lips. He sits on the empty chair next to her, and then she places her hand softly around his shoulder.

"I love you," Wendy whispers to Gary, although loud enough for me to hear without trying. She then kisses him on the cheek.

The waiter with meatballs comes back to our table. I avail myself of two hot juicy meatballs.

Claire, who is not a big drinker, notifies me that she is going to get a second glass of wine. She asks the two other women if she can bring them back drinks. Wendy asks for a Diet Coke and Elise asks for another Tom Collins.

"I'll go with you," I say to Claire.

We go to the bar together, and we lightly kiss upon our arrival. Claire then orders the drinks. Claire tells me that Wendy expects Gary to propose to her sometime before her birthday on September 25, and that Wendy will plan on having an outdoor wedding the following June. Wendy told Claire that the reason she cried so much at this wedding ceremony was because she was envisioning herself and Gary walking down the wedding aisle in the near future.

"That's nice," I say weakly.

## Chapter 48

The bride and groom are conspicuously absent from the cocktail hour. They are taking pictures. If I ever get married, I would not want to take pictures during the cocktail hour because the cocktail hour is, I believe, the best part of any wedding reception. The two female violin players who played their violins during the wedding ceremony are playing here now. They add a sense of formality as the guests indulge on the meatballs, quiche, and spring roll hors d'oeuvres.

"Matt, I'm going to get another beer, do you want one?" Gary asks me.

I have already had two beers. But I decide to have one more.

"Sure, I'll have one more. Thanks."

I am slightly buzzed from the first two beers. The many hors d'oeuvres are also lightening my mood. While I am not an avid dancer, I actually look forward to dancing with Claire during the main part of this wedding reception that will take place in the Medallion Room right after the cocktail hour. Claire tells me that there will be a six piece band playing. Just as Gary comes back to the table bringing my third beer, a waiter arrives with a platter of hot new spring rolls. All of us at the table take one. This new batch of spring rolls is greasier than the prior batch. Both Gary and I, whether motivated by the beers, hunger, or just gluttony, crave the hot grease surrounding the spring rolls. We both take a second spring roll before the waiter leaves to go to another table with the remaining spring rolls on his platter.

A man in a tuxedo next to the violin players then announces that we should exit the Gold Room and enter the Medallion Room for dinner. We all follow the instructions.

Claire and I hold hands as we make our way with the others from the Gold Room to the Medallion Room. The Gold Room was quite a handsome room. It was dark, even with the overhead chandeliers, and quite formal. The Medallion Room, by contrast, is stunning. It is brilliantly illuminated by chandeliers, which pick up the dynamic colors of the varied flowers in the large centerpieces that stand in the middle of the approximately twenty tables. The tables surround a large dance floor, and there is room for a band in the front of the room.

We sit at table 7. The band has not yet started to play, but two men in tuxedos, who look to be members of the band, are setting things up. There are nine seats at our table, which means that four other people are going to sit at the table besides myself, Claire, Wendy, Gary, and Elise. In fact, only seconds after the five of us sit at the table, two unmarried friends of the groom, Don and Vincent, arrive. They know the groom from the groom's hometown. A single woman, Angela, a friend of the groom's family, also sits down at the table. Another woman, Annette, also sits down. She works with the bride. Everyone is cordial. There is no doubt that the bride and groom arranged this table with the hope that some romance might emerge. I can't help but notice that Annette instantly catches Gary's eye. Of course, Gary is not supposed to become interested in one of the single women. Rather, Gary is seated at this table with Wendy as part of a seriously involved couple. Wendy, who mistakenly believes that her engagement to Gary is imminent, is oblivious to Gary's quick, perhaps even unconscious, eye movements in Annette's direction.

The Medallion Room fills up. The guests take their seats. The man in the tuxedo, who only minutes ago announced that we should all enter the Medallion Room, then tells everyone to stand and give a rousing welcome as the bride Debbie and groom Richard make their first appearance together as husband and wife.

Claire and I kiss when he says this. I am truly happy to be here with Claire and I hope that our relationship grows. I think it will.

The wedding guests applaud as the newlyweds enter the Medallion Room and embrace in the middle of the dance floor. The man in the tuxedo then says that the bride and groom will dance their first dance to "I Love You Just the Way You Are."

The band begins playing. A female voice fills the Medallion Room with song. At first I cannot clearly view the singer because a large man from the table between my table and the band stands directly in front of me. There is something about the faceless voice that is familiar. I move two feet to my left to get a clear view of the singer. Unfortunately, at that same time the big man also moves in the same direction. Quickly I then move two feet back to my right, back to my initial position.

"Why are you moving around so much?" Claire asks me.

"I just need to get a better view. I can't see the

singer."

"You know," Claire says, "there is something about the singer that looks familiar."

I then get a clear view of the singer. There is a reason the singer looks familiar. Claire saw the singer when we were together at the auto show. Claire should remember her as the Ford spokesmodel talking to her friend John. The band singer at this wedding reception is Bench Woman.

Blood leaves my face and rushes to my extremities, causing my face to become white and my hands to sweat. My pulse rate doubles. Claire must feel the changes in me since we are holding hands.

"Matthew, are you all right?"

"Sure."

During Bench Woman's rendition of "I Love You Just the Way You Are," the man in the tuxedo asks the guests to please join the newlyweds on the dance floor to share this first dance. Despite the initial shock of seeing Bench Woman as the band's singer, I regain my composure and ask Claire if she wants to dance.

"I'd be happy to," she replies.

Claire and I dance tightly together to this romantic song.

"Matthew, I am having a wonderful time," Claire whispers in my ear, which she follows by a caress of my neck.

"Me too," I say, as Bench Woman's voice fills the Medallion Room with song.

# Chapter 49

"There is something familiar about that singer," Claire says to me again, as we sit down at the table to begin eating the fruit cup that has been placed down on our plates.

Trying to be nonchalant, I tell Claire that the singer, Rebecca Everglades, was the spokesmodel that we met briefly at the auto show with her old hometown friend John and his girlfriend Lisa.

"Yes, I do remember," Claire says.

The band plays softly during the fruit cup, which is followed by a mixed green salad and then a steaming hot and thick vegetable soup. There are times, though, when the band plays a dance tune, and Claire and I go to the dance floor. Bench Woman's voice and body movements are at their most seductive during the slow songs. At those times, I have the need to be on the dance floor, as close to Bench Woman as possible. Claire and I hold each other closely when dancing to the slow songs, as Bench Woman's voice fills the room. I tell Claire that she is a great dancer, which she is. She is certainly a far better dancer than I. While I enjoy dancing with Claire, my thoughts are with Bench Woman. Claire, of course, does not know this. I cannot share with her my feelings about Bench Woman, who sings with the band while wearing a red dress, looking as astonishing as ever.

The wedding dinner proceeds at a normal pace. The vegetable soup is followed by the main course. Our waiter tells us that we can have either prime rib of beef, roasted chicken, or filet of sole. I order the prime rib, medium, while Claire orders the fish. Although the cow deserved a better fate than to be eaten at this wedding, I need to eat the red meat at this time. Small roasted potatoes and asparagus are served with the entree. The band plays softly during the main course. Bench Woman sings a few slow songs, and the band plays one or two instrumentals without Bench Woman's accompaniment. Once most of the guests near completion of their entrees, the master of ceremonies has the bride throw the bouquet, which is caught by Wendy, much to Gary's chagrin. Afterwards, the band plays more lively music, and the master of ceremonies encourages dancing. Claire and I oblige. It is, however, when Bench Woman sings a slow song that I most want to be on the dance floor. When I dance the slow songs with Claire and my eyes close, I see Bench Woman as my partner. Everyone who sees Claire and me on the dance floor must believe that we are madly in love. Claire says, and I agree, that it will be wonderful when we are alone together tonight. How would anyone know that my true love is not the woman I am dancing with, but rather, is the woman singing the love songs no further than twenty feet away from me?

Our dancing stops when the desserts arrive. On each table the waiter places down two large platters of assorted cookies and pastries. He also asks if we would like coffee. I say that I would, as do all of the men at the table. Annette, Claire and Wendy ask for hot water for tea, and Angela asks for decaffeinated coffee. Elise does not have any hot beverage. The pastries are quite good, especially the puff pastries with custard in the middle. Claire and I feed a pastry to each other. In addition to the one custard pastry placed in my mouth by Claire, I eat two chocolate chip cookies and a cookie with varied colors and chocolate on top. Right after the varied color cookie goes down my throat and into my stomach, Bench Woman, with the band accompanying her, starts to sing the song "The Party's Over."

This wedding reception is coming to an end. People are saying their good-byes to the bride and groom. Claire and I also go to say good-bye to them. They tell Claire that it was great to see her. They tell me that it was wonderful to meet me and they hope we can all get together after their honeymoon. Claire and I exit the Medallion Room, and stand with her friends in the lobby, whereupon Claire tells me that she is going to the bathroom.

Something compels me to leave the lobby area and re-enter the Medallion Room. When I do, I see Bench Woman, and the other band members, talking amongst themselves. I walk towards Bench Woman. Precisely at that moment the other band members carry their band equipment out of the room, leaving Bench Woman alone. Without thinking I walk closer to her.

"Yes?" Bench Woman says to me.

"You sing wonderfully," I tell her.

After thanking me for the compliment, she asks me if there is something I want. I ask her if she remembers me. After she tells me that she does not, I tell her how I was with other people who spoke with her at the auto show the weekend before. She says that she does not remember me there. The words then pour out of my mouth like a raging river. I tell Bench Woman about the first time I saw her in the park when she sat down on the same bench next to me when I was eating my lunch in Battery Park. I tell her that I saw her beautiful face and hair glimmering in the bright sunshine as I ate my lunch and at that moment believed that we were meant to share a life together. I tell Bench Woman that the feeling was heightened when I then coincidentally saw her revolving on the Ford exhibit at the auto show and how, as if destined from above, she is the singer at this wedding. Bench Woman looks at me strangely, and tells me that she noticed me dancing closely with a woman at the wedding.

"What about that woman?" Bench Woman asks.

"That is Claire," I tell Bench Woman. "She is great and I like her a lot, but I haven't been able to get you out of my mind since the first time I saw you on the park bench. I know this makes no sense at all, but . . . ."

Bench Woman's face looks very serious.

"I want absolutely nothing to do with you," she says, and she turns her back to me and walks out of the Medallion Room. I stand motionless for a moment. When I turn around, I see Claire in the Medallion Room, only about ten feet behind me. It is clear from her expression that she heard much, if not all, of what I just said to Bench Woman. There is nothing for me to say.

"Good night Matthew," Claire says, walking quickly out of the Medallion Room.

# Chapter 50

It is nearly 1:00 in the morning when I exit the Nottingham Hotel, alone. I walk the city streets in the direction of my apartment, which is a fairly long walk away. I should hail a taxi cab. But on this comfortable summer evening, walking relaxes me. The hurt feelings apparent on Claire's face are etched on my brain as I walk. Was it wrong to tell Bench Woman that I love her? It must have been fate seeing her at the wedding. How could I not have exposed my true feelings? Of course I should have been more careful when doing so. There was no reason Claire had to hear me tell Bench Woman those feelings. Yet how could I have spent the rest of the evening with Claire when I would have thought only of Bench Woman? What am I thinking? Can I really be this stupid? How could I have treated Claire so badly?

I walk to 86th Street and Fifth Avenue and then hail a taxi cab to take me home across Central Park. I am not sleepy, despite it being 2:00 a.m., so I enter the Pasture for a late night snack. The counterman approaches me with a glass of water and a napkin.

"What can I get for you?"

"I'll have a chocolate milkshake."

The milkshake arrives within minutes. It is not thick enough. In fact, it is barely thicker than a glass of chocolate milk. Usually the milkshakes here at the Pasture are quite thick with a lot of ice cream. I've never before seen this counterman. He might be a new employee. I drink the milkshake without complaint, despite its thinness. Perhaps I should complain so that the counterman makes thicker, and therefore better, milkshakes in the future for me and other future customers. If I don't complain he will think I am satisfied with this thin milkshake. However, I tell the counterman nothing. The relative thickness, or thinness of this milkshake does not seem important as I think about Claire's hurt feelings. Looking at the milkshake I see those hurt feelings. The moments I don't see Claire's hurt feelings in the milkshake I see Bench Woman's look of disgust and bewilderment at my declaration of love for her.

Once at home I get into bed but sleep uneasily. I am extremely tired when I awake Sunday morning. I spend this Sunday doing nothing but watching television. I do, though, go outside and buy potato chips and chocolate chip cookies from the supermarket. One part of my brain tells me to call Claire and tell her that I am sorry, but a second part of my brain tells me not to call her, that it will be better to just speak with her at work tomorrow. That second part of my brain prevails. I am haunted by my actions. Something real was developing between Claire and me. Why did I throw it away on Bench Woman, whom I do not know, who was nothing more than a pipedream? I sleep poorly on this Sunday night. I worry about seeing Claire at work tomorrow. Is there anything that I can say to her that will make it better? I really do care for Claire. She is everything I've been looking for. The night and morning we spent together were wonderful. I will tell her that. Tossing and turning all night, I get out of bed at 6:15 a.m. I take a long shower. Because it is still early, I go to the Pasture for a full breakfast instead of my usual bagel and coffee from a street vendor.

"I'll have a waffle, orange juice, and coffee."

The food arrives, but my thoughts are far from the slightly burnt waffle and sweet imitation maple syrup. Rather, I think of Claire. How different would this morning have been if Bench Woman had not been singing at the wedding? Claire and I might have been a real couple.

I get to the office early. Claire is not in the office yet. I read the sports section of the newspaper at my desk when I see Claire enter. She sits at her desk. I go to her.

"Claire. Can I talk to you?"

"Matthew, after the Friday evening and Saturday morning we spent together I thought you were someone I could trust, and maybe fall in love with. But I heard you tell the singer that I was not someone you could love the way you could love her. There is nothing you can say to me. Do not try."

Claire is right. What I said to Bench Woman at the wedding must have sounded clear to Claire. I need to explain to Claire that my infatuation with Bench Woman is nothing real, but an immature fantasy. However, Claire will not hear any explanations from me today. I will try to talk with her tomorrow. If she does not let me talk with her tomorrow, I will try every day until she hears me out. Why did I ruin everything?

It is a beautiful day, so I go to the park at lunch after buying a roast beef sandwich. Pigeons hover menacingly overhead. I sit far from the bench from where I first saw Bench Woman.

I stay at work a little later than usual. Claire is gone by the time I leave. Instead of going directly home, I stop in at the Pasture for dinner and sit down at a booth.

"Hello Matthew sweetie. How have you been?"

"I've been ok. How have you been Ellen?"

"Not bad. What will you have tonight honey?"

"I'll have the roast chicken dinner special, with mashed potatoes and an iced tea."

The food arrives. It is good, not great. I recall, fondly, the fantastic breakfast of fluffy pancakes that Claire cooked for the two of us on Saturday morning.

"Anything else?" Ellen asks.

"No thanks. Just the check."

I wish Ellen a good evening as I leave the Pasture.

"Have a good night, honey," Ellen says.

# Check out these other great
# Neshuipress titles

Made in United States
North Haven, CT
07 January 2024

47155036R00189